FINDING FOREVER

THE ROSE CITY SERIES
BOOK THREE

VALENTINA BURNS

Editing by: Jacqui Nelson

Proofreading by: Erin Delude

Cover design by: Books and Moods Graphic Design

ISBN electronic book: 978-1-7389724-5-6

ISBN print book: 978-1-7389724-4-9

For Alessandra, my sweet angel baby.

In a lot of ways, *The Rose City Series* is like my diary, an opportunity for me to write through the things that have hurt me in my life and turn them into love stories. These books have helped me take the worst that has happened to me and turned them into something beautiful. *Finding Forever* is no different.

Finding Forever contains a pregnancy loss, and I'll be honest, I was nervous about adding this part into what could have just been a super-hot, billionaire romance story. But I did it, because this book is my ode to the daughter I'll never know, and this is my way of giving her a small place in this world through something I love, writing.

Between my oldest and youngest child, I had a cervical ectopic pregnancy that ended in miscarriage during my second trimester. I remember what would have been her due date with vivid clarity. I should have had a baby in my arms but didn't, and the grief hurt so badly I knew I had to do something. So, I threw an impromptu living room dance party with my husband and toddler son. We rocked out to the current pop hits like nobody's business. It was important to me that we danced. That we found joy. That I didn't let the sadness drown me that day. You will notice a few references to dancing throughout this book.

In terms of the plot, the pregnancy loss is something that has occurred in the past, and there is no graphic representation of the miscarriage. The main characters do talk about it as they embark on their healing journey, but it is always referenced in the past. It was also important for me to represent how difficult pregnancy loss can be on the father, not just the mother, so there is a lot of attention to the matter given from Joel's point of view.

I understand this is a highly sensitive subject, and I have written Finding Forever based on my experience of having a singular, second trimester miscarriage, like the one depicted in this book. I am sending my biggest, deepest love and empathy to all of you who have been hurt by pregnancy loss.

All my love, Valentina Burns

This might not be a book everyone is ready to read. Please consider the following notes:

- Graphic sexual content (18+)
- Accidental pregnancy, ending in loss (past, off page)
- Discussion of second trimester pregnancy loss (past, off page)
- Grief after pregnancy loss

- Depiction of a side-character's pregnancy/gender reveal party
- Brief mention of the SA of a side character from a previous book in the series

Finding Forever is a standalone novel, but for continuity, I suggest reading *The Rose City Series* books in order.

CHAPTER ONE

When in doubt, hide behind the dessert buffet. That nugget of advice had saved Luciana Barone at family gatherings more than once, and it served her well now. The fact that her cream-colored dress—chosen for its subtlety—camouflaged nicely with the mascarpone trifle was a happy coincidence. The mountain of cream puffs, trays of tiramisu, and the seven-tiered cake that tilted like the Leaning Tower of Pisa provided a distracting cover, allowing her to be inconspicuous in the three hundred plus Italian wedding reception happening before her.

Safe. For now.

After spending the last several hours being interrogated by everyone from her aunts to her godmother's neighbor's daughter about her relationship status, when she might settle down, or when they could introduce her to the friend of a friend of her cousin twice removed, Lucy was desperate for a time out. Reaching for the nearest cream puff, she shoved the whole thing into her mouth and sagged behind the mound of puff pastry.

Honestly, there wasn't much difference between the

matchmaking schemes in the historical romance novels she favored and the average Italian family at any point in history. If you were past a certain age and single, then there was something wrong with you, and at least a dozen mamas were out to find you a husband. They weren't discreet about it, either. And an enormous wedding like this one was their preferred place to strike. It was for the best her own mother wasn't there.

With her parents both bedridden by a nasty flu, and her glamorous sister working on a movie set up in Canada, Lucy had been the lucky one who got to board a flight from San Francisco to Portland and represent her family at her cousin Mariana's big day.

One more hour and it would be midnight, an acceptable time to slip out of the wedding without being questioned as to why she wasn't having fun, or if she had someplace better to be. Until then, she'd remain in her current location and attempt to disregard the growing pressure in her bladder. She would have hidden in the bathroom, but that was dangerous territory. There she'd run into someone who wouldn't hesitate to give her the third degree about why, at the ripe age of twenty-nine, she'd attend the most upscale wedding of the decade without a date. It didn't help that the newlywed Mariana was four years younger than her.

Lucy sighed as she reached for another cream puff. What the hell, the skirt of her satin dress was pleated, understated, and elegant but, more importantly, it provided plenty of room for bloating...or whatever name you gave it.

"Aren't those addicting?" Nico Barone asked as he sauntered up to the buffet. He was in his mid-thirties, good looking in that typical Italian way. Olive skin, sharp features, dark hair slicked to the side. He wore a navy suit and smelled of fresh cigarettes and expensive cologne. It didn't overpower, nothing like her Zio Gambo, whose fragrance rivaled the perfume counter at Milan airport's Duty-Free shop, but it wasn't subtle either. "I've already had at least three, but I can't resist one more. I hear Mariana had them flown in from New York. We can't let them go to waste."

As he leaned over to grab a cream puff, his arm grazed Lucy's boobs. Instinctively, she almost slapped his arm away, but his impassive face left her unsure whether he even noticed or if invading her personal space came naturally to him. So, she settled for a small side-step in the opposite direction.

Good Lord, just when she thought she'd survived the worst of the night.

He shot her a cocky grin before taking a slow bite of his cream puff, and it took everything in Lucy not to gag. Nico. Her father's cousin's son. Which made him *her* second cousin. A man who existed solely to ruin her life. Not that he saw it that way. No, Nico thought he was God's gift to the Barone family. The personal Messiah come to save her father's cabinet-making company from extinction.

"You know," he said, chewing thoughtfully. "This could be our wedding someday."

Lucy tried to stifle her choke, but the damn pastry got caught in her airway and there was no hiding the retching sound she made. After a few seconds of hacking and Nico awkwardly patting her back, she cleared her throat and caught her breath.

"Are you okay, *cara mia*?" he asked, sounding more embarrassed than concerned, his gaze darting around to check for witnesses. "You shouldn't take that big of a bite next time."

Clutching her aching throat, she gaped at the sheer nerve of this man.

"It wasn't the bite, Nico," she croaked. "It was your suggestion that we'd ever get married." It was impossible. For so many reasons.

"Ah, *bella*. Don't get too excited. There's much that needs to happen between now and then." And just when she thought he couldn't get any more delusional, he held his hand out to her. "Dance with me."

Situations like this were tricky; she had to tread carefully. Nico was part of the family. Her father loved him, intended to entrust his entire business to him. A business she'd wanted and lived for her entire life. She had to keep her eye on her goal. If she ever had any hope of taking over Barone & Sons, being nasty to Nico wouldn't help her cause a single iota. But Nico, like her father, enjoyed a good negotiation. Maybe she could reason with him. So she went against her instinct to punch him in the nose and put her hand in his.

With a victorious smile, he led her to the dance floor filled with glittering dresses and tailor-made suits, then looped his arm around her waist, drawing her closer to his chest than she needed to be. She angled her nose away from the waft of cologne that stung her already sensitive throat.

Focus on your goal.

"So, um, Nico," she started as she swayed side to side with him. The live band was playing a more upbeat song, but Nico had set a slow pace, leaving Lucy to rock along awkwardly. "Don't you miss Udine?" She referenced the province in Italy her family was from.

He'd been here for the last year insisting her father needed help easing into semiretirement. A fact that irked her daily.

His shoulder shrugged under her hand. "More opportunity in America."

Yeah, like taking over my father's company. She shoved away the bitterness that crept around the edges of her mind. No point.

"I don't want you to have unrealistic expectations, *cara mia*, but when we marry, it will benefit both of us. The family will be stronger, more unified. We can merge my father's business in Italy with the one your father built in San Francisco." His grip on her waist shifted as he moved them deeper into the crowd of dancers. "Once you've helped me settle in as head of the company, you can take time for yourself, have a couple of our children, raise the family."

Lucy rolled her eyes. Who was getting ahead of themselves now?

"Look, Nico, I understand you came here intending to demonstrate your interest in our families' businesses, but you should know"—she twisted in his arms so she could catch his eye— "we're never getting married."

The poor fool looked truly shocked.

"And," she continued, keeping her voice neutral. "I have no intention of letting my father hand his company over to you, not when I've worked for it my entire life."

To her surprise, Nico smiled and pulled her closer. "Of course you'll marry me. It makes the most sense for the family, especially because you are so familiar with the business. *Cara*, you know your father doesn't wish for you to take over his company without a man by your side. He named it Barone & Sons after all, did he not?"

Thank you for rubbing that one fact into my face, cuz. The one burn she'd never soothe. After immigrating to America, her father had built a successful cabinet-making business. Luciano Barone had achieved the immigrant fairytale using nothing but hard work and long hours. For her entire childhood, he'd been at the shop seven days a week, only lately allowed himself Sundays off as he eased toward *semire-tirement.*

In retrospect, she, her younger sister, and their mother lacked nothing. She and Vanessa had enjoyed a childhood filled with activities like swim and dance lessons and movies with friends. In Lucy's case there were frequent trips to bookshops, and in her sister's, endless visits to the mall—all while her father was at his cabinet-making shop. And she didn't have a single memory of him complaining. She didn't even remember him taking a sick day. She admired him more than anyone. He'd been her hero her entire life.

And she'd been nothing but a disappointment to him from the moment she'd entered the world. Because no matter how hard she worked, studied, and shadowed him at the office and workshop, picking up the trade as she went, she'd never be what he truly wanted. A son.

Nico was the closest thing her father had to a son. His favorite cousin's son, eager and willing to immigrate to America and take over her father's company. Barone & Sons...run by her second cousin. Despite her being right here, ready and dying to do the same thing.

A familiar temper slid through her, filling her with anger and frustration, and Lucy twisted in Nico's arms, needing the space to cool her rapidly heating mood.

Annoyingly, he just tugged her closer. "Luciana, listen to me. Being married will be as good as having the company yourself. You will have title and none of the work. You can enjoy the exact life you have now. But as my wife."

Ya, no. Lucy pushed back with as much effort as she could without causing a scene. He allowed some space between them but didn't let her go.

"Nico, listen to me. I will never stop working at Barone & Sons. I love my job overseeing the finances and coordinating the bigger projects. You do know I got us the last three big contracts, right? I'll get more too." A lot more, she was just getting started putting their name on the map. "But more importantly, you and I will never be married. We can't be married."

"Nonsense. Second cousins can be married in America. I checked. An estimated 0.2 percent of marriages in America are between second cousins." He sounded like he'd memorized the first statistic that had popped up on Google. "It's not as uncommon as you think."

Right. Because that was the statistic she wanted to be part of. "That's not what I mean," she clarified, and a different pain lanced her chest, tearing an old wound. Memories flashed, but she shook her head clear of them. *Don't go there. There's enough shit happening right now.*

"*Bella*, you don't need to worry about what people will think. No one will even have to know about our family connection."

"Nico, please." This was ridiculous. His audacity had become intolerable. She struggled away once more.

"May I cut in?"

Lucy froze. *The voice had to be a hallucination.* She was in Portland at her cousin Mariana's wedding. Far, far away from San Francisco and the ghosts that haunted her there. This must be because she'd almost thought about him. Her over-active imagination had conjured his disembodied voice. Nothing more.

"Excuse me?" Nico said to the phantom voice.

If he heard it too, then there was no denying reality. A chill swept through her, followed immediately by a hot sweat. Her body recognized him before her eyes saw him, his energy consuming the surrounding space, his scent— an addictive blend of bergamot, fresh wood, and him—

filled her, soothing her raw throat, and warming her lungs.

Nonononono. What was he doing here?

"We aren't finished dancing," Nico said in a clipped tone.

"Yes. You are." Joel Morgan's rich baritone wrapped around her like her favorite memory...and her worst one, before he moved into her peripheral vision.

And then there he was. Every gorgeous, masculine inch of him, dressed in a black tuxedo befitting the occasion. His gray eyes sharp and piercing, though they had not yet moved to her. They were fixed, cold and hard, on Nico.

Four years had passed since Joel had been this close to her. She'd gone to great lengths to make sure of that.

What was he doing here now? In a different city? At her cousin's wedding?

Nico tensed, his position threatened, and his grip tightened around her waist. Lucy twisted out of his hold, but he yanked her back, his fingers digging into her hips as he secured her against him. She pressed her palms against his chest, intending to shove him away, when she caught a muscle jump in Joel's jaw.

Uh oh.

Some men yelled when they became furious, some punched walls or slammed doors, others got sullen or grumpy. But when Joel Morgan got angry, his jaw ticked.

And he hadn't even looked at her yet.

"You are interrupting our dance," Nico bit out, his Italian accent clipped and sharp.

"Let. Her. Go."

Nico scoffed. "Why would I do such a thing?" His gaze flicked to her. "*Cara mia*, let me take you away from this mad man." He shifted to leave.

Lucy's feet decided now was a good time to remain stuck

in place, as if she wore cement shoes. And the way her insides churned, she may as well have been.

"*Cara*?" Nico looked at her, confusion marring his bravado.

"I—I'm not going with you," she managed, wishing the ground would open and swallow her whole. Put her out of this misery and humiliation.

"Don't be ridiculous." Nico grabbed her arm roughly, tugging her in his direction, and Joel's hand shot out in a blur, gripping Nico's wrist with so much force he released her in an instant.

"Last warning," Joel growled, his natural authority infusing each word. "Get your hands off my wife."

CHAPTER TWO

O *migodomigodomigod.*

Lucy's mind reeled as Nico's head swiveled from Joel to her. "You're married?" Slack jawed and wide eyed, his complete shock left her feeling insulted.

"Of course not. Well, not exactly—"

"That's—absurd!" Nico sputtered. "Who even is this?" He fluttered his hand in Joel's direction.

This could not be happening. How was this happening? And why did Nico not know who Joel was? She thought everyone in her family knew the Morgan Construction successor.

"He's..." Her gaze darted toward Joel, then back to Nico. Nope, she wasn't ready to look at Joel. But she sensed his gaze on her now, and her heart responded by thumping wildly behind her breastbone. "He's a business associate of my father's." Out of the corner of her eye, she saw the jaw twitch again.

"A business associate? How is it possible that I'm unaware of this business associate who you are married to?" Nico's accent thickened the more upset he got.

"He's not my husband."

Jaw tick.

She shut her eyes to block her peripheral vision. "It's complicated," she added lamely.

"Complicated. Complicated!?" Nico laughed. "Well, *cara*, maybe you should uncomplicate it," he huffed out before he spun on his heel and walked away.

Super. God knew where Nico would go to lick his wounds, or what he would say to whom. If he called her father…

"Luciana." Her name came off Joel's lips as it always had. Like a prayer. Like she was his salvation. But she wasn't his to worship anymore. "Are you alright?"

She hated the way the smooth sound of his voice still hit her everywhere. The hairs on her neck rose in his direction. A shiver of pleasure swirled up her spine to her brain, triggering memories she'd worked years to forget. Memories of his deep timbre breathing her name into her ear as he moved inside her…

"What the hell are you doing here?" Anger had always been easier than confronting uncomfortable feelings, so she whirled on him with hers and glared at him head on.

God, why did he have to be so gorgeous? Entrancing eyes, strong, angular features, light-brown hair, and his long, lean body, built in that athletic way he'd earned from years of cross-training. He looked more fantastic in a suit than ever.

"What am *I* doing here? What are *you* doing here?" Joel demanded in return.

"This is *my* cousin's wedding," she exclaimed in a whisper-yell, tossing her hands in the air. She wasn't sure how much attention the altercation with Nico had drawn, but she didn't want to risk any more.

Italians made gossip an Olympic sport.

"Well," Joel said casually, before lifting a shoulder. "I live here now."

"No, you don't." Lucy couldn't imagine Joel living anywhere other than in his ocean-view penthouse in downtown San Francisco.

He was the new CEO of Morgan Construction, having officially taken over the business after his father had finally retired not long ago. Never in a million years would she have imagined he'd move away from the family empire.

"Yes, I do. Temporarily, at least. There's a property here I'm developing. I'm expanding the business, and Portland seemed like the natural place to start, seeing as I have family living here now."

It took a moment for her to catch up, but the lightbulb went off. "Hope."

Joel's younger sister now resided in Portland. Lucy hadn't thought about the possibility of him being here as well, or she sure as heck wouldn't have come to her cousin's wedding.

Joel nodded. "Gambo invited my family. Unfortunately, I was the only one able to attend. My sister and parents weren't able to be here."

Her Zio Gambo, whose real name was Ricardo (she didn't know where the Gambo nickname came from, only that no one ever called him Ricardo), had been a contracted employee of Morgan Construction for decades. When he'd lived in California, his company had done the flooring for Morgan builds. He'd raised his family on Morgan wages, same as her own father. But five years ago, at aged 55, Gambo suffered a heart attack that nearly killed him. So he sold his flooring business, packed up his wife and daughter and moved them to Portland, where he thought life might be less stressful. Given that he lost 25 pounds, gave up smoking, and started baking, he hadn't been wrong.

Now his only child had gotten married. Of course he'd invited the Morgans. They were *famiglia* to him and all the Barones. Between Gambo's flooring and Luciano's cabinetry, they were basically one big family business. And that's how they'd been raised. Family.

Joel's sharp eyes zeroed in on hers, telling her what she needed to know. He'd come to the wedding, hoping he'd see her. He reached out his hand. "Dance with me."

Lucy stared at his palm, then his face, then his palm again. "I don't think that is a good idea."

"Why not? I remember days when you let me dance with you in our kitchen."

Lucy remembered that, too. And that was part of the problem. The memories.

"That was long ago. We aren't—that's not us anymore." She didn't want to reflect back to when, for a brief moment in time, her life had been amazing. Perfect. The four months she'd spent with Joel, under the radar of everyone else's knowledge, had been bliss.

He brushed his fingers against hers, tangling them together, and an old, dormant burner flared to life inside her.

"You're still my wife," he said quietly, stepping closer. His body heat rolled over her, sealing them together in a bubble of warmth she only ever experienced with him.

"I haven't been your wife for four years," she whispered, her voice catching on a breath as he lifted her other hand to his shoulder, positioning them in a dancer's embrace. Her gaze clung to his movements.

His presence was mesmerizing, his rich, spicy scent

enveloping. His voice was an echo of her heart. Everything about him drew her in.

"Our marriage license says differently."

"That doesn't count anymore."

"Did you sign the divorce papers?" he murmured.

Lucy's gaze snapped up to meet his. "What divorce papers?" She'd never filed for a divorce, and as far as she knew, he hadn't either. Had he? Her heart started hammering in her chest.

"Exactly." His eyes burned into hers. Intense, triumphant. Heart breaking. "Which means you're still my wife, Mrs. Morgan."

Joel's movements mimicked Nico's from a few moments ago, but Lucy's response couldn't have been more different. Her heart pounded, and her stomach tingled. Her skin came alive under his touch. When he wrapped his arm more securely around her lower back, her breath caught. He drew her closer until their chests touched. The hard planes of his were noticeable under his suit.

She vividly remembered running her fingertips over that smooth muscle, the way his warm skin slid against her own. In the past, they fit together so seamlessly that it felt destined, like it was written in the stars. And Lucy truly believed they'd be together forever.

And then...

Planting her palms on his chest, she pushed away from him. Joel resisted momentarily, then let her go. As he'd done so many years before.

She stepped away. "I can't." To her frustration and embarrassment, tears pricked her vision. Memories tugged the edges of her mind. The embers of old wounds caught a breath of oxygen and flamed until the ache came alive inside her. Time to get as far away from Joel as she could. "I have to go."

She didn't wait for a response. Pushing past him, she wove through the crowded dance floor and headed for the main banquet doors, trying not to knock over any of the white-covered chairs as she went. Behind her, Joel called her name. The rough tone matched the agony coursing through her. Good, let him feel the pain too. Why should she be the only one to suffer all they'd lost together?

Lucy fled to the washroom, where she knew he couldn't follow. She'd hide there until tomorrow if need be.

Escaping into an empty stall, she lowered the seat and sat heavily on top of it. Burrowing her face in her hands, she struggled to process everything that had happened in the last fifteen minutes.

Joel was here. She hadn't seen him in four years. Okay, not entirely true. With her father working so closely with Morgan Construction, there were times she could not avoid his presence. But those few meetings always took place in a professional group setting, so neither of them had ever breeched the lines of corporate decorum. She'd avoided unnecessary eye contact and left at the first opportunity. The few times he'd attempted to draw her aside, she'd evaded him.

Until tonight. To say this was unexpected was the understatement of the century. She was supposed to be camouflaged between the cream puffs and tiramisu until enough time passed that she could inconspicuously leave—not confronting her husband in a ballroom full of Italians, where all of her world could witness her pain and report back to her parents.

"Luciana Barone, you have some explaining to do!" As if on cue, her aunt's high-pitched voice echoed through the bathroom, piercing the sanctuary of her toilet stall. Graziella Barone, who everyone in the family called Zia Ella, banged on the door, rattling it. "Natalie is saying your *husband* is here. And Matilde said you were getting cozy with Nico and then Joel Morgan dragged you into his arms like a man possessed. People are *whispering* Luciana, and I have no idea about what." She pummeled the door again. "What in God's name is going on? Open the door."

"Zia," Lucy grumbled, knowing the futility of resisting. "It's not a good time. Can we talk about this later?"

"We will not talk about this later. Maria put me in charge of you when she sent you here to represent your side of the family. She would be horrified if anything happened to you and I did not offer support."

Right. More like Maria—Lucy's flu-ridden mother— would be horrified to know that her eldest daughter was the center of family gossip, and Ella hadn't done her utmost to find out every single detail in her absence.

Lucy sighed. Another pair of fancy stilettos appeared under the stall door, signaling the arrival of another relation. She mentally kicked herself. This was why the bathroom was never a safe place to hide out. Joel might not be able to follow her in here, but every other female member of her family certainly could.

The toilet seat slammed down in the stall beside her before someone climbed on top of it.

Hot-pink manicured nails appeared over the top of the stall rim, followed by her youngest cousin's cherub-like face. "She's not taking a leak," Natalie confirmed from her bird's eye view. "No excuse not to come out, Lu."

"Ugh, fine." Lucy groaned, getting up and unlocking the stall door.

It swung open to reveal her aunt and five other relatives.

Her Zia Ella placed her fists on her ample hips. "Now, what is this about you being married?"

Lucy's mind raced. No way could she tell them the truth.

First, they wouldn't believe it. Second, she'd never hear the end of the insult she'd brought to the family by not inviting a single soul to what should have been the real wedding of the century. It wasn't every day a Morgan married a Barone. Especially not *that* Morgan, to *this* Barone.

"Of course I'm not married," Lucy lied, deliberately not following up the statement. Let them draw their own conclusions. They would anyway.

The moment of silence that followed was loaded with nosy expectation, but Lucy stood her ground.

"So why would people say you are then?" her aunt finally demanded.

"And why is Joel prowling the hall outside this washroom like a caged lion?" Her cousin Matilde jerked her thumb behind her toward the door.

"The way he was looking at you, all possessive and Christian Grey-like. So hot. I didn't think you had it in you, Lu. I mean a guy like Joel Morgan. How'd you do it?" Natalie asked.

"Agreed. The way he was acting, if you aren't married yet, you will be," Matilde said with a self-satisfied smirk.

"I bet you're secretly engaged!" a woman in a green dress, who she'd never seen before, exclaimed.

A collective gasp filled the room.

Zia Ella's eyes widened like saucers. "Luciana," she whispered-shouted. "Is it true? Are you engaged?"

Crap. This wasn't going how she hoped it would go. Then again, she hadn't a clue how it would go, because she hadn't expected—well, Joel.

"It's complicated," she said for the second time that night. They were beyond the point of believing her if she said it was nothing. Besides, it wasn't nothing. It was something. *She and Joel* were something, and she'd had years to do something about it. She just hadn't.

And neither had he. Until tonight.

Zia Ella gathered Lucy's hands and gently guided her to a velvet-covered chair in the corner of the bathroom. The tribe of women followed, the satin of their gowns crinkling as they moved in unison.

"Luciana, how complicated can it be? We're family. Just spit it out. You are either engaged to the man or you're not." Her aunt's glare homed in on hers with the accuracy of a lie detector.

She couldn't tell the truth; she couldn't lie. She was trapped. Trapped in this bathroom, trapped by her ginormous traditional family, trapped by the wallflower reputation she's created for herself. Just trapped. And the only time she hadn't felt that way was when she'd been with Joel.

Then, like she'd conjured him, his voice echoed through the bathroom.

"We're engaged."

CHAPTER THREE

Every perfectly coifed head in the room turned to face Joel. If he looked ridiculous taking up the doorway of the women's washroom, he didn't care. He was here for one reason and one reason only. His gaze cut through the pageant-style glamour sparkling around him, right to the quiet, subtle beauty sitting in the corner. Lucy was the only woman who'd ever claimed his whole heart.

Seeing her, just breathing the same air as her, took a thousand-pound weight off his soul. And so it had always been. Whenever Lucy was around, he felt peace.

"We're engaged," he said again, and this time he noticed her hands twitch in her lap, as if she struggled not to get up and slap him.

What are you doing? she mouthed at him, her dark-brown eyes flashing, and Joel couldn't help it.

He smiled. God, he'd missed her.

He shoved off the doorframe and entered the room, letting the door swing shut behind him. As comical as walking into a ladies' bathroom full of Italian women dressed to the nines in every color of the rainbow was, he only had tunnel vision for one—and there was nothing funny about the way his heart raced as he approached Luciana Barone.

He knew she likely chose the neutral-toned dress because she wanted to blend in, be inconspicuous. Muted. He'd seen her do this a lot when it wasn't just the two of them. But in this case, it had backfired, because the creamy tones shone like gold against her tanned skin, the silk fabric sliding tantalizingly over her legs as she squirmed on her seat. She made the understated outfit look so exquisite she'd taken his breath away. And he was fairly certain she didn't even realize it.

"I wanted to announce it tonight, but Lucy didn't want to steal Mariana's thunder." His eye contact never wavered as the lie slid from his lips. "I agreed to keep it quiet, but when I saw her dancing with another man, I lost control and my jealousy took over." Not entirely a fabrication. When he'd seen her with Nico, something snapped inside him, and the curtain fell on the four-year charade he'd been playing. "I'm not sorry, Lucy," he said as the sea of relatives parted to let him stand in front of her. "I'm tired of the secrets. You're mine, and I want the world to know."

A loud sigh rose from somewhere in the room.

He knew his words would ignite her rage. He watched, resigned, as her face transformed into a mask of anger, color infusing her cheeks and darkening her iris'. Four years clearly hadn't been long enough to stem the flow of raw and volatile emotion in her. Why would it be? It hadn't been enough for him either. Years couldn't cool his tension, but there was only minimal satisfaction in knowing she'd suffered the same.

No, she's suffered more. Much more, he reminded himself.

And because he understood that, he made no attempt to stop her when she surged to her feet.

"Maybe *I* didn't want the world to know, Joel. Did you ever think of that?" she demanded, raising her voice.

"Luciana..." her aunt, Graziella Barone, hissed from beside her.

Furious blinking, gaping mouths, and indistinct whispering surrounded Lucy like a hive.

Joel didn't blame her family's reaction. Lucy didn't often have outbursts, preferring to assume a more reserved demeanor in public. She'd told him that every member of the Barone family had inherited so much of the drama gene there'd been none left for her. She said she was an afterthought in her family, overlooked or ignored.

That had never been true for him.

He'd noticed Lucy from—the moment he could remember noticing women. It had been that defiance, the not giving into the deafening theatrics that her family was known for, that had made her stand out to him. In a world where everyone wanted to be loud and seen, Lucy had built a life in the quiet, and that made her *interesting*.

"I didn't want a scene!" She swept her arm around her, indicating the women who'd crammed themselves into the bathroom.

Okay, so maybe there was some temper left in her. He kind of liked it, too because it mostly came out just for him.

"But you never listen, Joel, because you're The Fixer. The one who knows what's best for everyone. You blow into people's lives and try to make everything better. But sometimes it can't be made better." She wasn't talking about his engagement stunt now, and they both knew it. "There's a time and a place for something to happen, and this isn't our time or our place." She dragged in a desperate breath before continuing. "And maybe you and I need to accept that we'll never have one."

Beside her, Ella gasped loudly. "*Luciana, basta*, you don't know what you're saying." She whirled to Joel. "She's upset." Then she addressed the women in the room. "Why don't we all leave and give them space to talk, no?" She waved her hands, herding the women toward the door.

"No." Lucy lifted her hand. "I need *my own* space. I'm leaving." She jabbed her finger at Joel. "Do not follow me."

Without looking back, she strode out of the washroom. Leaving him with a pack of overdressed, overly perfumed, and overly interested women who all stared at him like he was the latest person on the cover of *People Magazine*. Which he hadn't been. This edition.

That didn't go as he'd planned. Not that he really had a plan. With Lucy, he never seemed to have a plan. Life with her just happened, and he went where it called him.

He jerked his thumb over his shoulder. A wave of lash extensions blinked at him expectantly.

"I should go after her."

Everyone nodded enthusiastically.

"Yes! Yes, you should go!" Ella flapped her hands again, shooing him out the door. "Go now, before you change your mind."

Joel opened his mouth to tell her he'd never change his mind when it came to Lucy. She lived in him, day and night, hurt him in the way no other person had ever hurt him, and still, he'd never change his mind about being with her.

But Ella slapped her handbag across his thighs in a sweeping motion, and before he knew it, he was out in the hall, the bathroom door hissing shut behind him.

Not having a clue where she'd gone, Joel followed his instinct, and exited the hotel's side entrance, which led to a little garden patio with a fountain. He'd seen it on his way in, before he'd realized Lucy was inside the reception. The sound of the fountain triggered a memory of her. She used to love fountains, and apparently, she still did because he found her standing with her back to him, watching the water.

Her arms wrapped protectively around herself, as if she was trying to hold herself together. He could relate to the feeling. Seeing her was like an old wound that had reopened after healing poorly in the first place. It fucking hurt.

There'd been no way of knowing if Lucy would travel from San Francisco to Portland for her cousin's wedding. He'd taken a chance coming here.

In the back of his mind, he'd hoped to see her, as he did anytime he went to an event where there'd be Barones. He'd mentally prepared himself for the possibility every time. What he hadn't banked on was seeing her with someone else. Or how he would react. He prided himself on never losing control, but one glimpse of Lucy in the arms of another man and he'd forgotten himself. Now here he was, staring at her gorgeous silhouette in the shimmer of moonlight and water, and he thought maybe losing control every once in a while wasn't so bad.

Taking a deep breath, he stepped forward.

"I wish you weren't here," she stated, not turning around to look at him.

"Ouch. I wasn't expecting you to jump into my arms, but considering you're still my wife, I was hoping for a little more enthusiasm."

She whirled around and pointed her finger in his face. Her cheeks were flushed with anger, her wavy, chocolate-colored hair a halo. Her dark-brown eyes flared.

"This isn't funny," she seethed. "And don't call me that!"

A smart man would have retreated. But Joel had never been smart when it came to Lucy, and like a moth to a flame, he stepped closer until her finger jabbed his chest. "Wife?" he asked innocently, provoking her. He knew it was unfair to stir her temper, but damn, he had one of his own, and it had been dormant for too long. Seeing her with Nico sparked it to life.

"Yes, that," she insisted again. "I'm not."

"You are."

"No!" She flattened her hand against his chest and shoved. When he didn't budge, she stalked off to the other side of the fountain. "If I were your wife, we wouldn't have spent the last four years avoiding each other. We wouldn't have moved on with our lives like the whole world hadn't just crashed around us. Like we hadn't just spent months playing house and spending every spare minute we had together. Like we hadn't made a—" Her voice broke, and the choked sound gutted him.

He'd been there too. He remembered it all in vivid detail.

"Like we hadn't made a baby together?" He finished for her, even though the words stuck thick in his throat. It had been the single most important thing that had ever been gifted to him, and he'd lost it. They'd lost it. There weren't words to describe the pain. "Is that what you did, Lucy? Move on?"

She huffed out a breath and plopped down on a bench by some rose bushes, folding her arms across her chest. Her telltale sign that she was feeling vulnerable and didn't want to show it.

Too bad. Four years of not talking about his deepest regret, likely hers too, and he was done hiding feelings. His or hers. He needed to know.

"Did you move on?"

She turned her face away.

"Did you?" He controlled his voice. There would be no losing his cool tonight. "That man in there." He pointed back to the hotel. "Did you move on with him?"

The answer was none of his damn business, he knew that. But it had been four long years, and they were still legally married, so the time for answers had come.

If her answer was yes, he'd find a way to live with it, but he needed to know. He'd been living half a life, burying himself in work to avoid feeling the pain that coursed through him now. He'd denied himself every opportunity to be happy in atonement for the way he'd betrayed her. If she chose to move on, it would be her right.

"No," she whispered toward the rose bushes.

He sighed. "I'm sorry I wasn't—"

She cut him off by jumping to her feet and taking several steps away from him. "Joel, don't. Please, please don't." She pressed her fingers against her temples before raking them through her hair. "I didn't move on with anyone else, but that doesn't mean I want to move on with you."

"I figured that one out by the way you've been avoiding me for four years," he murmured.

"You told them we're engaged," she shouted incredulously. "What were you thinking?"

"I wasn't," he answered honestly. "I saw you dancing with that guy, and I didn't like it."

"Nico is my gross second cousin. It meant nothing."

Joel shrugged. "I didn't like it."

Lucy sighed. "So you told Nico we were married? Then, when you could have let that go, laughed it off, you tell my aunt and cousins we're engaged? What did you think was going to happen? That they'd just congratulate you, give you a big ole slap on the back, and never wonder what left field that came out of? What am I supposed to do now, go in there and tell them it was a joke? I'd never live that down: *Lucy's fake engagement, the closest she'll ever get to escaping a life of spinsterhood.*"

"Stop." He held up his hand and watched her inhale a deep breath. "Of course that's not what I want, Luciana."

"Don't call me that," she spat out.

"What now? Your name? I'm running out of things to call you."

"I mean like *that*. All slow and commanding. You're 'business Joel' when you say my name like that. *Luciana.*" She dropped her voice a few octaves, mimicking him. "I don't like business Joel."

A smile lifted the corner of his lips as he shoved his hands in his pockets and walked closer to her. He couldn't risk touching her. She wouldn't accept it right now, but God, he loved her like this. Riled up and alive with temper. He'd only ever seen her like this with him. Like she saved the most fiery parts of herself for him and him alone.

When she was angry or frustrated with him, the truth rolled off her tongue with no inhibition. The good girl was tucked away, and the real Lucy came out to play.

"Lucy," he offered in a hushed tone, using his voice to touch her instead of his hands.

Her mouth opened on a slight intake of breath. Desire clouded the temper in her eyes. "Shit," she whispered. "I think that's worse."

Joel let his smile pull fully across his mouth, but it wasn't enough to relieve the weight on his chest. "I'm sorry for telling everyone we're engaged," he said, using his tone to soothe the tension that had built around them. "It was inconsiderate, among other things. And I'll go back right now and make it right." He owed her that much, at the very least, so he started making his way back down the path to the hotel.

"And say what? That you were joking?" Her words stopped him. "Don't bother. They'll never let me hear the end of it if you tell them that. Or anything else. I'll deal with it tomorrow when I've thought of something to say that will minimize their third degree."

"Lucy—"

"Yep, definitely worse," she whispered, more to herself than him. Then, after one last lingering moment, she stepped around him to leave.

He didn't move, just stood where he was, paralyzed by his inability to manipulate the situation in his favor. He thought she was already gone, but then she said, "Tell your sister I said hi."

By the time he'd turned around to watch her leave, she was gone.

CHAPTER FOUR

At 3 a.m. in Zia Ella's house in Portland, Lucy called it. She'd lost enough hours tossing in fitful spurts of sleep filled with raw, emotional dreams. Her mind was on the Joel Morgan hamster wheel and there was no getting off anytime soon. Which was why she'd gone to such great lengths to avoid him and stay off the wheel. The only problem was that when the wheel stopped, she missed the hamster.

She let out a long-suffering sigh, kicked off her covers, got out of bed, and started rummaging around the guest room for a sheet of paper. She'd read in a self-help book that the best way to cure the restless brain at night was to write down everything you were thinking, put it in a box, store the box somewhere else in the house, and surrender yourself to sleep knowing that your thoughts were tucked away to be dealt with at another, more appropriate time.

There might never be an appropriate time for her and Joel, but it sure as heck wasn't at 3:24 a.m. in her aunt's home.

Coming up empty in the guest room, she padded down

the hallway and descended the curved staircase, trying not to creak the hardwood with her footfall as she moved throughout the house in search of a notepad. If her aunt and uncle were anything like her parents, they kept every free promotional notepad they got in the mail.

Her mother was partial to the real-estate related ones because she liked the headshots of the local agents that were front and center on every sheet. She'd told Lucy that she felt like she was on a date with Devon Wiltshire every time she took her grocery list to the store. Knowing her aunt, she'd think the same. They were sisters-in-law through marriage, but Maria and Ella Barone were two peas in a pod.

Lucy stopped short when she entered the kitchen on the ground floor. "Holy sh—" She clamped her hand over her mouth.

The marble countertops overflowed with leftovers. Stacks of cream puffs on serving plates, casserole dishes filed with rows of cannolis, and trays of traditional Italian cookies and biscotti were covered in plastic wrap or paper towels.

Her aunts and cousins spent days cooking for the family events. Even though Mariana's wedding meal itself had been catered, they'd made enough to feed the village they came from in the old country—where Nico lived before he recently invaded her life.

Lucy went to the fridge and gasped in delight when she found it filled to the brim with charcuterie plates, meatballs, risotto balls, pasta dishes, prosciutto wrapped asparagus spears, and more. It had been a few years since her last family wedding. She'd forgotten the sheer volume of food that these multi day events involved. And since she'd only arrived in Portland this morning, she'd missed most of Mariana's pre-matrimonial parties.

Better make up for lost time. She filled a plate with finger foods and headed to the dining room, snagging a real-estate notepad off the fridge on her way. Colton Rodrigues was almost as good looking as Devon Wiltshire.

She was digging into her second meatball and writing down her first problem for another time, when her aunt shuffled in carrying her own plate of goodies from the kitchen. Zia Ella wore a red silk robe and matching fuzzy slippers and had her hair in curlers.

"Couldn't sleep," Ella said before Lucy could ask, then sat down next to her. "Too much excitement. It has my blood pressure up." She ate while looking straight ahead into the sunken living room.

"You can't sleep when your blood pressure's up?" Lucy queried. There was nothing wrong with Ella's blood pressure, and they both knew it.

"All the stress of the wedding wreaked havoc on my nerves. Thanks be to God I only have one daughter."

"Thanks be to God indeed," Lucy murmured, hiding her smirk by shoving a prosciutto wrapped melon cube into her mouth.

Her immediate branch of the Barone family tree consisted of her father Luciano, his brother Gambo, and their sister Marta. After Luciano had two daughters and Marta had three, Gambo and Ella had Mariana—and decided to be one and done. Because clearly the Y chromosome would not make it into this generation of Barones. For the Italian mamas, life then became all about marrying the six girls efficiently and prestigiously. Like regency England, but in cobbler aprons.

So far, they'd had success with only two. Her cousin

Sofia had bagged herself an Italian human rights lawyer who worked for the United Nations. They were currently living in Geneva. And Mariana was now married to the son of the CEO of a famous athletic footwear and apparel company based in Portland.

Which meant four Barone girls remained. Unless you counted Lucy secretly being married to Joel. Which she did not. Because the marriage was a farce and not the least bit legitimate beyond a sheet of paper with a State of Nevada seal on it.

"Luciana, I understand why you did it," her aunt said as she nibbled on an Italian pastry.

"Did what?" she asked, dragging herself out of her thoughts.

"Kept your engagement a secret." Zia Ella ate slowly while studying Lucy meaningfully. "You wanted to let your cousin shine on her special day, because you're a good girl and you know your place." With a pat on Lucy's hand, her aunt got up and took both of their plates to the kitchen.

"Right," Lucy murmured. A good girl who knew her place pretty much summed up what everyone in her family thought about her. Even though she didn't feel the same way at all. Her ambition was a fireball burning inside her. Her determination gained strength with every day that passed. At Barone & Sons, she oversaw the financials, but she kept her eye on every aspect of business, watching and learning as she plotted and strategized for the best possible future of the company. She was constantly working.

But that's what no one saw. No one but Joel. The only person who'd ever acknowledged how invested she was, how badly she wanted to keep her father's legacy alive, and how much she deserved it. He'd been her champion, the one she could talk to about anything. Until he'd left. And now it was just her.

Her aunt returned to the table with two narrow crystal glasses and a bottle filled with clear liquid.

"Zia, it's four in the morning."

Her aunt shrugged, filled the glasses, and handed one to Lucy. "Grappa helps with my indigestion." She took a sip and sighed in relief, as if to prove her point.

Lucy took her glass but didn't sip. Instead she twirled the glass, letting the floral aroma fill her nostrils.

"That was thoughtful of you, what you did for your cousin," her aunt said, continuing the previous conversation thread, much to Lucy's dismay. "But the wedding is over now, and it seems silly to keep such big news to yourself."

"Is it?" Something about Ella's tone put her on edge.

"I think we should have a big engagement party while the family is all still in town."

And there it was.

"Absolutely not."

"Oh Luciana, don't be selfish. Do you know how much a plane ticket costs these days? Or how exhausting airports are? Do you expect your Zia Marta to fly all the way back from Colorado for another party with her bad knee? What about Nico?"

"What about Nico? He thinks we're getting married so he can have Barone & Sons while I sit at home with our babies!"

"Pfft." Ella wiped away the words with a dismissive hand. "That one is a dreamer, like his father. He thinks too little and talks too much. Luciano will never give him Barone & Sons."

"Are you sure about that?" Lucy muttered. "Nico is the son my father never had."

"Wrong. Your father is feeling old and desperate. He is worried about the future of his company, but Nico is not the answer."

"Have you told either of them that?"

Ella tossed out a laugh. "Barone men are all the same. Pig-headed from the womb. But they always come to the right conclusion. It just takes longer sometimes."

"You sound sure about that, Zia?"

Her aunt shrugged and took another sip of grappa, nodding to encourage Lucy to do the same. Lucy glanced at the round plastic clock on the wall, 4:28 a.m. What the hell? It was happy hour somewhere, right? The liquid burned a path down her throat.

"You know, Lucy, your *bisnonna* on your father's side was a savvy businesswoman." Ella settled back in her chair as she randomly brought up Lucy's great-grandmother. "Noemi was ahead of her time by light-years. After the First World War, Italy was a mess. The poor had less than ever, and even the wealthy struggled. Everyone had to start over. Noemi was the oldest child of four. She was just eighteen when the war ended. Her family were farmers, but the land was poor and most of the animals had been killed to feed soldiers. Everyone in the village shared the same fate. Noemi was smart and knew that if they were to thrive again or even just survive, they had to work together."

Lucy wasn't sure where this early-morning storytelling was going, but she sat in silence while Ella finished her first drink and then poured another.

"Back then, marriages were not viewed in the romantic way they are these days. Love was a luxury no one could afford. So one day, Noemi asked her father to offer her hand in marriage to the neighboring farmer's son, who was twelve years older than her. The next day, after she finished her work in the fields, she went to the village and was married. She wore her work clothes, and the church was half rubble from war damage, but she married, and the two families became one. The farms combined, and the land doubled." Ella gesticulated as if the point had been made.

Lucy sipped her grappa, the warmth of alcohol heating her lips as she listened.

"Your *bisnonna* had five children. Your nonno was one of them. Your father's father." Ella finished her second grappa and sat back with a satisfied smile. "That land is still Barone land. When the families merged, they tore down the farmhouses and built one big one. The villagers were impressed with what the Barones had built and asked for help rebuilding their own damaged and fallen structures. The Barones built barns and houses for many villagers. They even rebuilt the church. Construction is a Barone legacy, brought on by your great-grandmother. It started with her choice."

The words and grappa swirled around Lucy's brain. She'd heard the story before. But this retelling...hit different. Or maybe it was the grappa.

"Noemi died three months before you were born. Your father said you inherited her spirit." Ella patted Lucy's hand again. "You understand what I'm telling you, Luciana?"

"I think so?" Lucy wasn't sure she understood anything anymore.

"See, you're a bright girl. You'll always find the solution. Now, I'm going back to bed." Ella rose and cleared their glasses from the table. "Tomorrow I'll call your mama. Flu or no, she will come to Portland for her daughter's engagement party. I'm sure of it." She kissed Lucy on top of her head. "Don't stay up too much longer, *bella*. There will be much to do tomorrow."

Lucy sat at the table, thinking about her eighteen-year-old great-grandmother and the grit it must have taken to get through that time in history as a young woman with few opportunities. What lessons could she pull from Noemi's story? Lucy was the opposite in almost every way. Older, college educated, living a life filled with privilege.

You're a bright girl, her aunt had said.

In the dimly lit room, Lucy looked down at her real-estate notepad and the words she'd written next to Colton Rodrigues' beaming face.

Problems for another time:
#1—Joel Morgan

This is a very bad, horrible, no-good idea, Lucy thought as she walked up to the brick building on the corner of a busy street in the Pearl District. The stylish neon sign above the big double doors read *Bowie's*.

This was the place? She checked her phone's maps app. Earlier, she DM'd Hope and asked where she might find Joel. Since he didn't have much of a social media presence—and she'd deleted his number from her phone during a particularly lonely night with too many glasses of Chianti a year ago—his sister seemed like the most logical starting point.

Hope had immediately DM'd her the address of the apartment Joel rented in Portland, which was how she now found herself standing at the corner of Hipster and Trendy looking up at a building that was the farthest thing from what she'd ever imagine a man like Joel, heir and CEO of Morgan Construction, would live in.

The structure was gorgeous, no doubt about that, but it lacked the sleek, ultra-modern look of the properties Joel built and lived in. Not to mention height. There would be no posh penthouse suite here.

Nevertheless, this was the address Hope had sent her, and she was on a mission, so she marched down the side of the block to the entrance to the apartments.

Her finger hovered over buzzer #2, her heart picking up speed. This morning, everything had been so clear. Her plan had seemed perfect. Now her feet tingled and her fingers trembled. Could she do this? Was this the right path? Would Joel Morgan agree to help her become the head of Barone & Sons?

Only one way to find out. The strip next to the number read, *Occupied*. Time to find out if Joel had really left his San Francisco penthouse for an apartment above a bar in Portland. Taking a deep breath, she punched buzzer #2 with her index finger. A loud buzz filled the air in a jarring sound.

Enough seconds passed that she was about to double check the address, then a promising *click* and a gravely "Hello?" came through the speaker.

God, did he have to sound sexy even through an intercom? Her palms broke out into a sweat and her voice stalled in her throat when she opened her mouth to talk.

"Anyone there?" Joel demanded through the intercom.

Oh shit, oh shit, oh shit. Here went nothing. *Or everything,* her brain taunted. "Um, hi, Joel. It's—" *Shit.* What was she doing? "It's Lucy."

"Lucy?" He sounded so utterly dumbfounded that a blush inflamed her cheeks.

She was such an idiot. "Never mind, this was stupid. I'm going. Sorry to bother you."

"No wait—" There was static and a bang, then a curse. "Lucy—"

A long buzz sounded behind her, but humiliation had her hoofing it down the street.

There had to be other ways to get through to her father. Maybe she could land a bigger client outside of San Francisco and convince him the company had what it took to grow. Or she could try talking to him again—although the last time she'd done that, Nico had showed up three weeks later and crushed the progress she'd made. Not that she'd made much. Her father had all but laughed off the idea of her as the boss.

Still, there had to be an option she hadn't thought of yet. Faking an engagement with her estranged husband was preposterous.

She was halfway down the block when Joel called out, "Lucy!"

Please, ground, crack open and swallow me whole. She blamed no one but herself. She'd come here on a grappa induced hair-brained idea that held zero weight and even less potential.

"Lucy, stop!" Joel called again, but this time from much closer—like right behind her closer. Strong fingers curled around her hand. Together, they slowed. "Please."

Resigned, she turned to face him. He wore a white t-shirt, well-worn jeans, and...no socks.

She stared at his bare feet. "Joel—" The man was crazy. She had a newfound foot fetish, but he was crazy.

"You came to me," he said, sounding slightly winded, but she suspected it had nothing to do with his sprint. "Why?"

"Um." She fidgeted with the strap of her bag, wondering if she should lie or tell the truth. She settled for somewhere in the middle. "I wanted to talk about last night, when you, well, told everyone we were engaged."

Joel's gaze didn't waver. "Sorry about that." He didn't look sorry at all. He appeared hyper focused and intense, his sharp eyes tuned deeply to hers, like he was trying to figure out what she really wanted.

Funny, she was starting to wonder about that herself.

"You said you wanted to talk to your family yourself, but if you want me to, I can."

"No." Drawing a deep breath, she blurted, "I'm here because I was kind of hoping that maybe you'd be okay if we —" Crap, this was mortifying. She was never drinking grappa with her aunt ever again.

She cleared her throat and started from the top. "I was hoping we could continue with the engagement story a bit longer."

Joel didn't move, didn't blink. This was probably what he was like in the boardroom while he brokered deals and negotiated with city planners. Focused and unyielding. Solid poker face. He'd never been like this with her. He'd always been so...open, trusting her with his rawest emotions and letting her see the pieces no one else got to see. And that was why, that night in Vegas, between highballs and five-dollar shafts, it had been so easy for them to say yes to each other.

But that part of him wasn't for her anymore.

"Why?" His eyebrows drew together, but other than that, nothing.

Excellent question. And since she was here, she might as well lay it all on the line. It's not like Joel didn't know her dream.

"I'm hoping that if my family thinks I'm engaged to you, my father will talk seriously about me taking over Barone & Sons one day."

There, she'd said it. And saying it out loud sounded

ridiculous. *She* sounded ridiculous. Because the idea was ridiculous. What daughter had to get engaged for her father to take her seriously?

She did. That's who.

When Joel stood there for several seconds, head inclined, sexy lips pressed together, expression immobile and unreadable, she tugged her hand out of his and started walking backward. "You know what? Forget it."

He jerked forward, like he wanted to grab for her but tempered himself in the last second.

"Wait, Lucy."

Their gazes collided. A big mistake.

His eyes, knowing and steady, held her captive. "Come up to the apartment and we can talk."

A hysterical laugh bubbled from her throat. Up to his apartment? She'd come here to talk, so she wasn't sure what she'd been expecting, but hearing his invitation out loud made the reality of being alone in a room with him laughable.

There was enough history between them to make a Netflix documentary. If you looked unfinished business up in a dictionary, you'd see their faces. The tension between them sizzled even now, on a public street, with people walking around them and gawking like they were a circus sideshow. Going upstairs, alone, into his apartment spelled...disaster?

Joel didn't appear to think so. His focus remained razor-sharp and centered on her. He'd moved closer, or maybe it was her who'd moved closer to him, she hadn't been paying attention, but his proximity caused goosebumps to pop up along her arms, little electrical currents of awareness sizzled under her skin. All of which made her feel even more certain they shouldn't be alone together inside four walls.

"It's okay, really. This was silly. I'm just going to, uh, go." She spun again to walk away.

Warm fingers found her wrist this time, looping gently around her pulse and stopping her, and those little currents combusted into full blown sparks. "Luciana."

Oh fuck. The way he used her full name, like other men used the term "good girl" or "sweetheart." Like it was a term of endearment, a little dirty and special at the same time. Like she was both sexy *and* sacred to him. And when those syllables fell off his lips, she almost believed she still was.

He came up behind her. His chest to her back. His breath against her ear. So familiar, so comforting. "Come upstairs with me. I want you to."

The rich, husky sound of his voice flooded her lower abdomen with heat. As if he was inviting her up to do more than just talk. As if a broken marriage, a lost pregnancy, and four years of next to no communication weren't sitting between them like a creepy second cousin at a family wedding. How could her body so quickly forget the pain they'd inflicted on each other? How could it ignore the torment in her heart?

"Please." He didn't sound like he thought she was crazy, and he didn't sound like he was laughing at her. His tone held no pity, just the subtle strength and confidence that allowed him to bend any audience to his will.

This man exuded a power unlike any she'd ever encountered. But he made no one feel less than. He respected everyone and listened to every idea brought to his table. That was the reason he succeeded in all things, the reason she'd come to him, and the reason she gave a brief nod before she let his fingers weave through hers as he led her back toward his apartment.

CHAPTER SIX

Lucy coming to find him because she wanted to discuss staying married was like Christmas, his birthday, and their honeymoon all rolled into one. He just couldn't show it.

With Lucy, he'd made so many mistakes. A mountain of complicated history stood between them. So many kinks needed to be worked out. He wanted to address the issues so they could move forward, at the very least.

Filled with resolve, he held out his arm, inviting her up the steep staircase to his apartment.

At the top of the stairs, he motioned her right. "This one is mine."

Her brow furrowed slightly as she scanned the sparse hallway with only one other door across from his. He understood her confusion. It wasn't like any of the places he owned in San Francisco.

He swung the door open and stood aside, letting her precede him into the apartment.

As she did, a whiff of her perfume brought an onslaught of memories. Waking up with her back pressed against his chest, her mass of hair sticking to his cheek where he'd slept on it. The sound of her laugh, loud and joyous as she stirred a delicious smelling sauce in a pot on the stove. The way she pretended to be annoyed when he pulled her away from the sauce to dance with her in the kitchen. How she'd come home from work smelling of sawdust and talking excitedly about the latest Barone & Sons project. The habit she'd formed of walking around with her hand resting on her still flat belly, humming quietly, before everything changed.

Their life together came back on one whiff of vanilla spice. So much for being careful with his heart. He was fucked, and he knew it.

Leaning against the wall, he shoved his hands into his pockets and watched her take in his space. It was night and day from what she'd experienced with him in San Francisco where his décor was sleek and modern. Grays and whites, cool accents, and marble countertops.

Here, Hope had mostly done the decorating. A long L-shaped couch, filled with throw pillows he would have never bought. An oak table large enough to fit his whole family in the dining room. She'd hung some family photos, too. It came across as very domestic.

Lucy would recognize the woman's touch, and he didn't want her to get the wrong idea.

"My sister decorated."

"Hmm." Lucy nodded. "Makes sense. It's very homely, permanent." She tilted her head. "Are you putting down roots in Portland, Joel?"

"I have no roots to put down." She should know that better than anyone. "But I'll be here long enough that Hope told me staying at The Heathman would be pretentious, even for a Morgan. So she set me up here."

Lucy continued to walk around, taking in the surroundings.

In the silence, he felt compelled to go on. "Her husband, Gabe, used to live here. And Hope lived across the hall with her friend, Ivy." He jerked his thumb over his shoulder to the door, even though Lucy wasn't looking at him. "Hope and Gabe moved out when they married."

"Does Ivy still live there?"

"Yes. She lives with her fiancé, Sean. Who moved in here after Gabe moved out."

Lucy finally stopped and stared at him, eyebrows knit together. "So Gabe lived here and then got together with Hope, who lived across the hall. Then Sean lived here and got together with the girl who lives across the hall? Am I getting it right?"

He chuckled, running his hand through his hair. "That's exactly right."

"Matchmaking apartments," Lucy murmured as she crossed to a wall of photos.

"Yeah." He huffed out a laugh. "Never thought of it like that."

Lucy pointed to a photo and glanced at him with a raised eyebrow.

"That, uh, that's Ruby. My niece," he explained, hesitant to bring up children around Lucy, not knowing where she stood in her grief. "Hope and Gabe's daughter. Hope's in the process of officially adopting her. She just turned seven."

"She's adorable."

Her smile was genuine and filled him with relief because there was no hiding his pride when he spoke about his niece. "She's the best." Almost instantly, Ruby felt like family. Her joyful light was a balm to his bruised soul. He'd do anything for the little girl, no questions asked. "She has a keen business sense already. You'd be impressed."

Lucy finished her perusal of the apartment with a slow spin. "You look settled here. Are you happy?"

Happy was a distant memory. Although it was starting to feel closer with every passing minute in Lucy's presence. "I work too hard to be anything but busy."

She nodded, like she knew exactly what he was talking about, and something about her understanding bothered him. They'd both lost so much four years ago. He'd hoped that the sacrifice would have at least resulted in one of them finding contentment.

"Let's sit down." He headed for the couch, with her following him. "Can I get you something to drink? Coffee or water? Wine?"

Lucy laughed. "It's not even ten. I haven't become dependent on a morning drink since you left me, Joel."

Her words pierced like a knife to the gut. He stopped abruptly, turning as she stumbled into his back. He caught her arms to keep her balanced and held her against his chest. She was so close her breath fanned against his lips.

"Leaving you isn't how I remember it, Luciana."

Her eyes widened. Two dark moons. She inhaled a stuttering breath, and he released her. Here was the hurt that stretched between them. She thought he left her, but he remembered she'd given him no choice.

He sat down on the couch, nodding at her to do the same. She chose the farthest opposite corner.

"So." This is what it had come to. The most important person in his life, sitting across from him like a stranger. "Luciano is still dead set on selling his business to a third party when he retires?"

Lucy threw her hands in the air, then let them drop in her lap. "Either that or he'll leave it to my cousin, Nico. The one you met at the wedding."

"That was your cousin?" The bastard had his hands all over her. No cousin he'd ever known cozied up like that on a dance floor.

"Second cousin," she clarified, as if it made a difference. "Nico is here from Italy to show his interest in Barone & Sons and convince my father he's the best one to take over."

"No way in hell that's happening. You have my word on that." If that was what she was worried about, he could take care of it before nightfall. Second cousin or not, he'd have this Nico character back on a plane to the motherland before dinner.

She stared at him with an odd expression. One he couldn't place until she said, "Nico thinks he's going to marry me."

"Fuck. No." His curse slipped out before he could stop it. He'd made it good practice never to swear in her presence... unless they were in bed. His legendary control wavered like a string being plucked. "You're married to me."

"Yes. But no one knows that." She fiddled this time with the hem of her shirt. "But they *do* think we're engaged." She peeked up at him. "Because of you."

She was trying to get at something, but he couldn't think past the horror of Lucy married to another man. No matter what had passed between them, she was his, and he had the paperwork to prove it.

She doesn't belong to anyone, you idiot. That's why you let her go, remember? His one still functioning brain cell reminded him.

"So, what do you want me to do?" he asked, trying to keep the maelstrom of emotion out of his voice.

Lose control of your emotions, and you lose control of the situation. His father taught him that. The motto had served him well in life and business. But with Lucy, he notoriously lost his grip on his control and emotions.

Seconds, that felt like minutes, passed before she spoke again. "I want us to pretend to be engaged long enough to get Nico off my back and convince my father that I'm the right person for Barone & Sons." She blew out a breath.

While he tried his damnedest not to show a single reaction.

"I know it sounds stupid. My hard work and dedication alone should make him proud. I thought it would! But he's old school and in the weirdest ways. I can't figure out why he'd rather I be a CEO of literally any other company than his. But there it is. He's stubborn." Lucy turned to him, edging closer up the couch, until their knees almost touched. "But so am I, Joel."

And didn't he know it?

"Will you please say something." She looked at him with big, guarded eyes, her brows pinching above them.

His mind reeled with all the things he wanted to say. The questions in his heart were too raw, too scattered to be coherent, so he started with the most logical. "Have you talked to your father about this?"

"Of course I have! So many times, in so many different ways. He brushes it off, deflects, or changes the subject. A couple of times he flat out said no, but never with any concrete reasons. Just things like 'oh you don't want that', or 'we'll see Luciana, we'll see.'"

The way she mimicked her father's voice was spot-on and Joel would have chuckled if it weren't so heartbreaking. Her humiliation rolled off her, hitting him like a rogue wave. He couldn't imagine what it would be like to ask someone you loved for something so important, and not be taken seriously.

"So I gave up asking and started doing," she went on. "I took on more than just the books. I got us more clients, worked on rebranding and upgrading our marketing." Her defeated sigh was heart-wrenching. "I don't think he even noticed."

If Luciano didn't notice all of that, then he didn't deserve his daughter working for him.

Although he knew the answer to his next question, he asked it anyway. "Have you thought about starting your own company?"

As he expected, she shook her head vigorously. "I don't want some other company, some other career. I want Barone & Sons. It's in my blood. It's my legacy. Please." Her eyes took on a shine he didn't like. "Will you help me?"

This was his wife. Boldly determined, stubborn as hell. She wanted something, she got it. He'd been caught on both sides of her will before. The best and worst moments of his life had been with her.

"Why don't we just tell everyone the truth?" Secrets had almost torn his family apart two years ago. Even with the best intentions, he knew hiding the truth hurt more than it helped.

"The truth?" Her brow furrowed with astonishment that he'd suggest such a thing. "Like the we-got-drunk-in-Vegas-then-hitched-then-made-a-wedding-night-baby-then-lived-together-for-almost-four-months-without-telling-anyone-until-we-lost-the-baby-and-broke-up truth?"

When she said it all in one breath like that... "Yes."

Their marriage was never meant to be a secret. The plan was to tell everyone at a special dinner with both their families. But the rug had been pulled out from under them before they could, and they'd lost the plot. Nothing had mattered after that.

"You're kidding, right? They'd never forgive us. Me. I can't tell my mother, or any relative, that I secretly married into the Morgan family. She'd kill me."

"That's a bit of an overdramatization, don't you think? I'm sure she'd understand if we explained we had every intention to tell her."

Lucy cocked her head to one side, still frowning at him. She blinked twice, as if she was waiting for him to come to his senses. "You've met Maria Barone, right?"

He blew out a breath. "All I'm trying to say is that if we get caught in another web of lies, we'll complicate things more than they already are."

Lucy took great interest in her lap, then started nodding to herself in a way he didn't like the look of. Then she scooted back to her end of the couch. "You're right."

"We'll tell them?"

"No. Never. They won't understand. Besides, the truth would hurt them, and there's no reason to do that at this point. It's over between us."

He ground his teeth at that statement. *Over* was such a final word. Like a movie coming to an end, or curtains closing on a show. Even though years of silence had passed between them, nothing about what had played out felt finished to him.

She sighed. "But you're right. This is complicated. It's not fair to put you in the middle of what's between me and my father." She met his gaze. "Maybe it's best if we get the divorce and put the past behind us."

She continued looking him dead in the eye. Like she had when she'd told him that their marriage had been a mistake and she needed space. Back then, he'd understood her unwavering eye contact to mean that she was being fully honest with him, so he'd given her what she asked for because he never wanted be the one who held her back.

But four miserable years later, he wasn't sure he could count on anything other than how fucking perfect it was to be this close to her again.

When she moved to get up, his hand flew out to take hers. "Wait."

It came down to one thing: Lucy had a problem, and he could make it better for her. What he was about to agree to might crush his heart, but he'd consider it his penance. Punishment for the time he hadn't been there for her before. "We'll do this your way. Barone & Sons belongs to you, and I'll do whatever it takes to make sure that after Luciano retires, no one runs it but you."

She raised a single, perfectly shaped, eyebrow. "There'd be nothing in it for you. That's not fair."

Redemption was in it for him. His chance to atone for his sin against her. "This is a business deal, and good business benefits me. Being closer to Barone & Sons will give me an opportunity to network and make new connections in the industry." His words were bullshit, but her hand relaxed in his.

The truth was, he didn't need more connections. If she'd considered him wealthy and well connected before, she'd be shocked at his status now. Turned out, he responded to heartbreak by submerging into the black hole of sixty-hour work weeks. And while he was under, he'd grown his father's empire into a galaxy. He'd incorporated Morgan Construction into Morgan Enterprises, which he'd created to accommodate the investment side of the business he'd grown. He'd been smart and relentless, and the payoff had been massive. The Morgan millions had become billions. He didn't rent private jets anymore—he owned them.

Squeezing her hand, he made her a promise. "Barone & Sons will be yours, Lucy. Whatever it takes. Okay?"

He would keep that promise or die trying. He owed her that much.

CHAPTER SEVEN

Lucy couldn't tear her eyes away from Joel's piercing gray ones, and she couldn't think of a single thing that would make her want to. They were like magnets locking into hers and holding. A connection that was decades old, since they were in elementary school and growing up around each other's businesses.

Morgan Construction had been contracting out Barone & Sons for their interior cabinetry since Lucy was in kindergarten. Joel's father, Walter, had been one of the first to give Luciano steady work after he immigrated to America, and the two men had grown their businesses alongside each other, their families intertwining.

Lucy grew up on invitations to the Morgan Christmas parties and Fourth of July barbeques. She and Joel had shared a keen interest in their fathers' companies for as long as she could remember, so it wasn't uncommon for them to meet at construction sites, wearing oversized hard hats and steel-toed boots, following their fathers around the perimeter as the older men discussed business. Little mini-mes, wide-eyed day dreamers.

Now Joel sat on his father's throne, while she sat on the sidelines.

Joel was offering her a chance at her dream. Nerves exploded in her stomach like a million butterflies.

"Okay," she breathed.

A small smile lifted Joel's lips, and Lucy couldn't help but mirror it. For a moment, they were thrown back in time, when things between them had been perfect.

Without breaking eye contact, Joel grazed his knuckles up her cheek, pushing her hair back as he went. The light touch felt both tantalizing and dangerous, awareness reaching every part of her body. Was her heart ready to play a game like this?

Something passed in Joel's eyes as if he thought the same thing, and he dropped his hand. "So, do you have any guidelines?"

"Guidelines?" Lucy parroted, summoning 100 percent of her impulse control to not touch where his hand had just been.

"Yes, you know, like rules. Specifics. Dos and don'ts," he clarified. "Or will we be behaving like any other engaged couple would."

She resented how deeply a single movement of his could affect her entire being. "I wouldn't know how engaged couples behave. I've never experienced it."

His smile faltered. They'd gotten engaged and married in the span of an hour. What did either of them know about the process?

"But if you're referring to us sharing a bed, that's not going to happen. We don't have to live together."

"If memory serves me correctly, you loved every second you spent in my bed, Luciana. I made sure of it," he rasped.

That's it. Putting her game face on, she raised her index

finger as she prepared to tick off the rules. "Guideline number one: No bed sharing, this isn't a one bed romance, it's a business plan. Two, we'll have to make public appearances. That's unavoidable, and some light PDA may be required, but no kissing on the mouth, groping, or anything that could lead to my panties being removed."

Joel smirked. "What about my panties?"

"Shut up." She smacked his knee as he chuckled, then pressed his lips together in mock silence.

Sometimes Joel Morgan was king of the construction and property development scene, and sometimes he was a child.

"Three," she said, flicking up another finger, her ring finger, the most important. "We need to be careful. I want my family to buy this, but I don't want them to be heart-broken when it ends. I need to buy myself enough time so my father doesn't hand his legacy over to my clueless second cousin, who'll run it into the ground."

"Will it be enough?"

An excellent question, but she hoped the answer was yes. She dropped her hand and sighed. "If my father sees you by my side, he'll feel reassured his company will be in good hands. He'll forget about Nico, God willing. Then, I can use that momentum to get my father to see my work in a new light. That I'm just as capable of running Barone & Sons alone as I am running it with you."

"What could possibly go wrong?" Joel quipped, his dimple making the briefest appearance as the side of his mouth quirked.

Lucy sighed. A lot could go wrong, the worst of which would be bad blood. Which meant rule number three was the most important. "My father loves you, and he considers your dad one of his closest friends and associates. Whatever happens between us can't affect any of that. When we end this"—she motioned between the two of them— "arrangement, it must be amicable. Our breakup has to appear mutual and in both of our best interests. We part happily and with no baggage between us."

"Historically, we haven't been very good at that.".

"No. We haven't." She lifted her chin. "We must do better this time. See it all the way through."

"Since you brought it up," Joel said, his jaw flexing as his expression grew serious. "Are we going to talk about our...baggage?"

Lucy swallowed. She'd thought about this. How long could they avoid talking about the things that caused their demise? The conversation was unavoidable. Long overdue, in fact. If they were ever going to move on with their lives, they'd have to talk about the past. But—

"We will. Eventually. Just not right now." But if not now, then when? How could she explain to him her years of silent avoiding? What words were there to describe the hole in her heart that she couldn't face? "I'm not ready," she said simply.

Joel nodded and went to a small bar by the window. He clutched the neck of a decanter holding an amber liquid, hesitated, then reached for a taller vessel with a clear liquid. "Do you want some water?" he asked as he poured a glass.

"No thanks. I'm okay."

"I agree that we have to protect our families. My sister, if we can even convince her on any of this, will be..." He seemed to consider his next words carefully. "Very excited to see me engaged to anyone, but especially you, I think. She always liked you."

Lucy didn't know Hope as well as she would've liked. Hope was two years younger and had hung around Vanessa more. It had been impossible not to adore Hope's charm and relentless optimism. The Morgans held a special place in Lucy's heart.

"We'll convince her, and we won't hurt her. Or anyone. We'll be careful."

Joel took a sip while he looked out the window, not saying anything more about their families and the fine line they'd have to walk. "What about location logistics?" His back was to her as he spoke. "You're in San Francisco, and I mostly live here for now."

"Right." That thought hadn't occurred to her until she'd stepped into his apartment and seen it set up like a cozy home. She'd had no idea about his life in Portland. "Well, I'm here for a week."

He faced her with a raised eyebrow.

She shrugged. "I decided to take my holiday time around Mariana's wedding. Tag on a little road trip up to Canada and visit Vanessa in Vancouver for another week. But I don't have to go up for that long. I could extend my time here, so we can take advantage of my family being in town and do something together with everyone. If that works with your schedule."

"I have meetings and during these early days of construction, I like to stay close to the site to make sure things get off to a good start, but otherwise I can make time where needed. I travel back to San Francisco at least twice a month. So it shouldn't be a problem when—after your two weeks of vacation—you go home. We can continue making enough public appearances together."

Funny how her plan was suddenly under his control. Just like Joel though, taking a plan and making it work, asking questions, thinking it through, and strategizing while she tended to let an idea lead her. For this reason, conversation had never been a problem between them. They could talk for hours, their different mindsets fueling each other's creative energy. She missed that.

"I have one condition." He'd returned to the couch and stood in front of her. No, towered over her, forcing her to bend her neck to look up at him.

She should have been annoyed by the power imbalance this position created, but instead, she took the moment to admire him. He was so tall, so perfectly built. She could make out the firm lines of his torso beneath the fitted cotton t-shirt. His forearm was flexed as he held his glass, and her height at sitting brought her in the direct line of sight with his crotch, the denim covering it no match for her memory. And he was still barefoot...from when he'd chased after her down the street.

Slowly lifting her gaze to meet his, she wondered what his condition would be and if she could meet it. "What is your condition?"

"I'll tell you over dinner tomorrow night." Joel moved to the door and opened it, signaling the end of their conversation.

Alright then, meeting adjourned. Rising on surprisingly unsteady legs, she joined him on the threshold of his door. "What if I don't agree to...dinner?"

"You will." The statement rolled off his lips with his signature confidence. It was infuriating when it wasn't so damned impressive, the way this man's sheer presence compelled you to obey him.

"I might not," she affirmed, determined to maintain her façade of control over the situation.

With the crook of his forefinger, he raised her chin until their eyes met and held. "You will."

And then she found herself on the other side of Joel's closed apartment door, alone in the hallway, wondering how she'd ended up at *his* mercy when this was *her* plan.

CHAPTER EIGHT

As expected, news of her fake engagement had spread faster than gossip among the Barones, and Lucy had spent the next twenty-four hours fielding more messages than she had in a very long time. Or ever.

Surprisingly, most messages were congratulatory rather than inquisitive. Everyone appeared…relieved as opposed to curious, which Lucy would have found more insulting if she wasn't rejoicing because her relatives had chosen this opportunity to mind their own business.

Her mother had never honed that particular art, but their phone conversation last night had gone better than expected.

"Luciana, this is an answer to my prayers," Maria Barone had cried when Lucy had called her. "I prayed for a good husband for you. A nice boy who needed a good steady girl to settle down with. I said a novena every night the week leading up to Mariana's wedding in hopes that you would find someone there. And it happened. Not only that, but it's Joel! Only a miracle could have made this occur. God is good, *patatina*."

Lucy cringed at the term of endearment her parents had used for her since childhood. Why her sister had scored a nickname *principessa* while Lucy had been the "little potato" she had no idea. She figured it might have been her very potato like form before she'd grown into her curves. Or maybe a reference to the hours she'd spent with her nonna in the kitchen making potato gnocchi. But wherever the name had come from, it had stuck, and now she was forever their "little potato." No wonder her father couldn't envision her at the head of Barone & Sons.

"When will you marry? I think it's best to make it a brief engagement. At your age, why wait?"

Lucy would have reminded her mother that twenty-nine was not old, if she could have gotten a word in edgewise.

"We should take advantage of the summer weather. I'll see if I can book St. Mary's. Usually, they book a year in advance for the summer weddings, but Fr. Alfonso owes us a favor for the time Luciano fixed the damaged pews for free, so maybe he can squeeze you in by late August."

"Mom—"

"By next week I can get invitations made by your god-sister's cousin's girlfriend. What's her name? Diana? Daisy? Anyway, she's in the stationery business, and I'm sure she'll be happy to do this rush order considering the circumstance. They could be in the mail by the end of next week! The Italian relatives might not all come back, since they were just here for Mari's wedding, but *patatina*, this is a gift from God. We shouldn't waste it by worrying about the small things. It's about the marriage in the eyes of God, not the wedding."

"Mom, please," Lucy insisted, trying not to be insulted by how desperate her mother must have been feeling to not mind not having every last relative present at her daughter's wedding. "I haven't even talked to Joel about a date. Besides, he lives in Portland right now. He's only just broken ground on the new construction here. He can't have a rushed wedding at St. Mary's. A wedding is at least two years off." Hopefully, she'd need less time than that to convince her father.

There had been a loaded pause on the other end of the line. Then, "You're right. We should have the wedding in Portland to make it easier for Joel. And if we move the wedding there, we can use the centerpieces and decorations from Mari's wedding."

Once her mother had finished verbally planning out the entire affair, she'd handed the phone over to Luciano.

"*Patatina*," her father had exclaimed before she could even say hello. "Congratulations! Joel is a lucky man."

Her father's joy had guilt tugging at her heart, reminding her there was a lot at stake if this all went south.

"It would have been nice if he'd talked to me about it first, but when a man is in love he doesn't always wait for the formalities. Then again, who am I to criticize? I didn't ask your mother's father for permission either. I was too love-struck to think clearly." He laughed raucously. "Does Walter know?"

"I don't think so," she replied honestly. She wasn't sure if Joel had told his family yet or not. "And can you and Mom please not tell Walter or Audrey. It's a surprise for everyone, and Joel wants to tell them in person." She wouldn't put it past her parents to be speed dialing the Morgans the moment they had a chance. Shit, maybe they already had. "You didn't already tell them, did you?"

"Of course not!" her father exclaimed, sounding affronted. "This is your news to share. Besides, I heard they're on vacation. That's why they couldn't attend Mariana's wedding. They should be due back soon though."

Right, so the only reason her parents hadn't called the Morgans was because Walter and Audrey were on holiday, and not because Luciano and Maria were staying in their lanes. Perfect.

"Will you just promise not to say anything to any of the Morgans until I give you the go-ahead?"

"*Ma*—" he started, sounding perplexed.

"No *buts*, dad. Joel has the right to tell his family first, and he wants to do it in person." She really needed to drive this home or it could get out of hand fast. "Promise you and mom won't say anything until I tell you it's okay to."

Silence stretched across the phone line.

"Dad?" she exclaimed. "Promise?"

"Alright, alright. I will wait for you to tell me when it's safe to call my best business associate to congratulate him on the union of our children. I'll wait. I'm a patient man."

Lucy rolled her eyes, but only because she knew her father couldn't see her.

"But you are wrong, *patatina*," her father went on. "I wasn't surprised at all when I heard about your engagement," her father said in a serious tone. "You and Joel have always been like-minded. Good things will come from this match, including the future you deserve. I am happy for you."

Here went nothing. "Speaking of the future I deserve..." She chewed her lower lip as she considered her phrasing. "I'd like to talk to you again about the future of Barone & Sons."

"Luciana, *basta*. This is no time to talk shop. There's plenty of time for work later. The future of Barone & Sons is long enough. This is a time to celebrate."

Or to scream into a pillow.

"Wait, your mother wants to talk to you about the wedding reception and—" Her father was cut off as her mother took over again.

And so it had gone with the rest of her relatives. Each offered first their stunned congratulations, in one way or another likened her engagement to a miracle, then nose-dived into planning a wedding that everyone seemed to think had to happen within the next six weeks at the latest.

By six o'clock on Monday evening, Lucy was looking forward to leaving Zia Ella's house and spending time with someone who wasn't a blood relative, even if that someone was Joel.

She was applying her last stroke of mascara when Ella barged into the guest room.

"Your parents will be here Thursday afternoon."

Lucy lost focus and almost stabbed herself with the mascara wand. "But they have the flu. Mom still sounded sniffly on the phone."

Behind her in the mirror, Ella shrugged. "It's a cold. And she's not contagious anymore." Her hands fluttered. "Anyway, by Thursday she'll be fine. You expect her to stay put when her daughter is getting married?"

"I'm only engaged! We haven't set a date." With luck, she'd never get to her fake wedding. "There's no reason for her to come to Portland."

"We're hosting your engagement party here in less than two weeks. Your mother needs to plan."

"What?!" This time she put down her mascara before she hurt herself.

"Your mother and I agreed that since our relatives are here, we should use the opportunity to have the party. It makes sense, Lucy."

"It makes no sense. At all." Before she could argue further, the doorbell rang.

Ella's face lit up like a freaking Christmas tree. "I'll get it!" she sang as she bounded back into the hall before Lucy could blink.

This was a very bad, horrible, no-good idea. So why didn't she put an end to it now? Because of her father. And Nico. And the fact that this was her best—and maybe last—shot at running her father's company.

"Lucy, your fiancé is here!" Ella hollered from down the hall.

Showtime. Lucy stood up, assessing herself in the full-length mirror. Vanessa would be proud of her fashion choices this evening. She'd gone for a long flowy *Anthropologie* dress. Casual but summery, pretty and flirty. Slipping her feet into a pair of sandals and grabbing a jean jacket, she made her way to the front door.

Seeing Joel tower in her aunt's doorway in Portland was simultaneously bizarre and exhilarating. He stood there, talking to Ella like he did this all the time, looking positively delicious with his hands in the pockets of chambray-colored shorts that matched his iris'.

When she drew closer, he glanced her way, did a double take, then smiled. "Lucy."

A thrill shivered up her spine as his heated appraisal scanned the length of her body. "Joel," she replied, making her way to him.

"Well, you two have fun tonight," Ella exclaimed in a shrill voice, then chattered on. "You should set a date. Maria and I think sooner is better. Before the weather turns. You agree, no?"

Joel hadn't taken his eyes off Lucy's. "I agree that making Lucy my wife can't come soon enough." He glanced at Ella.

"Enjoy your evening. Don't wait up." He winked, then guided Lucy out the door.

"Can't come soon enough?" She made sure he heard the eyeroll in her voice as she headed down the front steps.

Joel grabbed her hand and shot her a smile. "You want people to buy this or not?"

She tried to tug free, but he held fast.

"Your aunt's looking out the window." He squeezed her hand tighter. "And for the record, if this were real, I'd have already made you my wife. Oh, wait." He offered her an inscrutable side-eye that made her squeeze his palm as hard as she could in protest, but he merely chuckled under his breath.

The beep of a car unlocking drew her attention to the Porsche parked on the street.

"A Taycan? Subtle," she quipped.

"I know it's not a cherry-red Ferrari, but this is Portland, so I went with low-key."

Lucy halted mid-step, tilting her head up to him as an old memory began to resurface. "What?"

"A Ferrari." He smiled down at her, a faint dimple appearing in his right cheek. "Cherry-red. One that will hug the curves of the Mediterranean roads like a man curls into his love," he recited, his tone forlorn and over-the-top.

She jabbed him in the ribs. "I did not say it like that!" Had she? She did have a flair for dramatic expression at times.

"You said it exactly like that." Joel laughed. "Word for word."

"Oh please!" A cherry-red Ferrari was her dream car, and she'd once described how an item on her bucket list was to race along one of Italy's famous winding coastline roads in one. She'd probably used those exact words, though she couldn't remember. It had been years since she'd said it, and if she couldn't remember, how could he? "How would you even remember that?"

"Luciana," he rasped, his gaze serious. "I remember everything about you and our time together." After a beat, wherein Lucy swore she heard the thundering of her own heart, Joel released her hand and continued to the passenger side of the sleek black car. "Also, win gold and wear it, Barone. Your father taught me that."

Giving herself a mental shake, she ignored the panicked giddiness surging through her and caught up with him. He'd shaken her—best cover that with a snarky comment. "Funny, he always told me not to show off."

"Yes, he taught me that too." Joel opened the Porsche's door, and she inhaled him as he stepped aside.

The best smell in the universe was his bergamot and cedar soap mixed with the warm scent of his skin. Her hormones went nuts for it. Like the combination had been designed with the sole purpose of attracting her.

"But he always reminds me to enjoy my success. Wearing your accomplishments with confidence is good for business. Wearing them with arrogance is a disaster."

Lucy laughed. "Now that sounds more like him."

Blunt and unsubtle. That was Luciano Barone. But she would play it to her advantage. Her marriage to Joel was an accomplishment in her father's eyes, and she'd leverage that advantage however she could. Including using it to have him see her in a different light when it came to the business.

She slid into the seat and waited until Joel shut the door before she let out an indulgent sigh. The leather was like butter against her skin, soft and luxurious, and the new-car scent told her this must have been a recent purchase.

Seconds later, Joel was buckling into the driver's side.

"Comfortable?" he asked as he pressed a button to start the car.

The electric vehicle was so silent that she jolted when he pulled away from the curb. He looked over at her with a raised eyebrow.

"Oh, yeah. I'm fine. This is fine."

Now he laughed because the way the seat molded around her body wasn't just fine. It was magical, and he knew it.

They had left her aunt's suburb and were flying down the highway when she asked, "So, where are we going?"

"There's this pizza place across the bridge that I discovered a while back. Best thin crust I've ever had. I thought we could go there." He glanced over at her. "You okay with that?"

Her stomach grumbled at the thought. "If I could only eat one thing for the rest of my life, it would be pizza."

"Because you could change the topping every day, so you'd never get sick of it." This time he stared straight ahead before he murmured, "I remember."

That had been a Vegas conversation. They'd been on their third round of shots, halfway to get-married-on-a-whim drunk and had been talking about what they would choose if they could only eat one thing for the rest of their lives. She'd said pizza. He'd gone with his mother's Christmas dinner, complete with prime rib and Yorkshire puddings. Lucy had commented that she'd never had Yorkshire puddings, and weeks later, she'd come home to Joel in his penthouse kitchen with an apron on making her some, his mother's recipe handwritten on a notepad beside him. She remembered that.

Deciding it was safest if she spent the rest of the drive in silence, Lucy dedicated the next fifteen minutes to watching the scenery out the tinted window.

The city flew past her, then slowed when they entered downtown, passing a stadium, then weaving through Portland State University, before driving over one of the many bridges. The town was beautiful, and she saw the appeal. There was enough big city flare to feel exciting, but it stopped short of having the overpopulated and busy vibe that San Francisco gave off.

Portland had the perfect small town, big city balance.

They pulled into a parking lot, and Joel climbed out, rounding the Porsche to open her door. Lucy took the hand he offered, but once she got out of the car, he didn't let go. Instead, he held fast as they walked to the front of the restaurant.

When he caught her looking at their joined hands, he lifted them, brushing his lips across the back of her palm. "Win gold and wear it," he murmured, before he opened the restaurant door for her.

CHAPTER NINE

They were two slices into their arugula and prosciutto pizza when Lucy set down her wineglass, looked him dead in the eye and asked, "So, moneybags, what's your condition?"

Joel had been preparing for her to ask him this since he'd told her yesterday that he had a condition to her terms. But now that they were here, enjoying good food and wine, chatting comfortably for the last hour, he didn't want it to end. Even though they'd kept to safe topics like business, family, the differences between San Francisco and Portland, there was a hint of what had been between them, the effortless ease that he savored like the wine he was drinking.

But alas, he'd learned that all good things came to an end. Unless you threw millions of dollars at them. Or negotiated yourself into a position that provided a second chance, which he'd done almost by accident with Lucy.

"My condition is...I want us to see this engagement through to a public wedding." He took a breath before he delivered the kill shot. "And then I want us to stay married for at least a year."

Watching Lucy absorb the information with a montage of minute facial expressions would have been amusing if he weren't so nervous. At first, her brows knit together, then her eyes narrowed, followed by her lips tipping down at the corners. Then it all briefly smoothed out before her eyebrow raised, and she glanced around the restaurant as if a candid camera might jump out at her. Finally, her lips pursed and her gaze snapped back to his. This was why she was a terrible liar. Every thought and emotion lived on her face at any given moment.

"Those are two conditions," she informed him.

"Correct." He did his best to match her businesslike tone, already missing their previous interaction. "But the second one follows naturally from the first, so I categorized them as one. We can't get married only to divorce twenty-four hours later."

"Well, it would be four years later, theoretically," she volleyed.

"True, but as you said, nobody knows that."

Lucy exhaled loudly through her nose, stared at her wineglass with great concentration before lifting it to take a long sip.

"Why?" she asked as she set her drink back down.

"Because I thought a lot about what you said regarding protecting good relations between our families, and this needs to be a priority. It might not take long for your father to see reason and for your useless cousin to be removed from the equation." He was already in the process of eliminating Nico, but no one needed to know that.

"Second cousin."

"Whatever. He's irrelevant." And he truly was. Joel couldn't wait until Nico was back on a plane to Italy. "And a brief engagement followed by a breakup shortly after your father sees reason won't only be obvious, it will be disrespectful to our families."

Lucy's lips pursed again, relieving some of the pressure in his chest because he saw her concede to his point.

"If we have a wedding, stay together for a while, and then separate, it will make everything smoother and more believable. Besides, a quick, half-hearted engagement and marriage doesn't suit either of our personalities and would be bad for our reputations. Drawing everything out just makes more sense."

Lucy seemed to consider this as she lifted another slice of pizza off the tray and took a bite, dragging her tongue along her full bottom lip to catch the crumbs. He could watch her for hours and never get bored. There was never a dull moment in her expressive eyes, and her long silky hair glided over her shoulder like melted chocolate as she moved. Stunning, all around. And being this close to her was torture on his restraint. She'd lived in his bed for sixteen weeks, then in his fantasies for years. He knew every detail of what he was missing, and his body and soul longed for no one else.

Even watching her chew turned him on, so he distracted himself by reflecting on what he didn't tell her, that his timeline had an ulterior motive. A year would buy them time to work out the things between them that had been the cause of their demise, one painful tragedy at a time.

She'd said she wasn't ready to talk about certain things yet, and he couldn't entirely blame her. But a short fake engagement and marriage made time his enemy and, as a practice, he crushed his enemies.

"A year is a long time, Joel," she whispered, and he barely heard her over the hum of the busy restaurant. "But I guess you'll be in Portland a lot of the time, and I'll be in

San Francisco. So we won't necessarily see each other frequently."

He fully planned on seeing her as much as he possibly could.

"In fact, it might even work in our favor. People will see how hard the long distance is, and it will help excuse our inevitable break up." She was rationalizing, working it out so that what he was presenting made sense, because deep down she wanted that time too. He knew it.

"Okay. We'll have a wedding. A small one," she emphasized. "And we'll stay married a year. But then we divorce. For real this time."

Nodding, Joel kept a neutral face, always essential in huge, life-changing business deals, but his heart pumped at his victory. She'd given him a second chance. And he'd just bought himself some time to convince Lucy they deserved a forever.

CHAPTER TEN

A week had passed since Mariana's wedding. A week since Joel had blown back into her life like no time had passed between them. A week since she'd gotten engaged, and it had gone like this:

Saturday had been Mariana's wedding. Sunday Lucy had gone to visit Joel with her proposition. Monday had been their pizza date, and the best night of her week so far. Tuesday and Wednesday had been dedicated to eating leftovers at Zia Ella's, cleaning out one batch of Barone wedding prep to make room for the next, and catching up on work emails so she didn't fall too far behind while on holiday. Thursday her parents had descended like Taylor Swift finally making it onto the stage after a very mediocre opening act. The crowd had gone wild, and life had reached a new level of crazy. There was hardly enough room in her aunt's house for them all, and the sheer volume of the talking had nearly driven Lucy to insanity. If Joel had been there, he would have brought a level of calm to the scenario, but unfortunately, he'd been working most of the day.

That night, when he'd called and she'd filled him in on

her parents' grand arrival, he'd calmed her rising anxiety right down. Even after all these years, it was easy to let the steady thrum of his voice and his calm reasoning lull her into a sense of peace. She'd had her most peaceful sleep that night until she'd woken on Friday morning to the sound of her mother and Ella shouting in the kitchen about which coffee to serve at the bridal shower. Even her father and Zio Gambo had escaped to the hardware store to catch a break from the constant chatter of the maternals.

She'd been seconds away from calling Joel when he'd magically appeared at Ella's doorstep with an enormous bouquet for her mother, a box of fresh pastries for everyone else, and informed Maria and Ella that he was stealing Lucy away for the morning.

Then he'd taken her for a walk along the river, and she filled him in on how her mother and aunt had hijacked the wedding planning, which was to be expected really, but it did squash any hope of them having a small, understated exchanging of vows.

But it was the worries over her sister that she really needed to get off her chest. After her calls went unanswered, she'd texted Vanessa to inform that she might not make it up to Vancouver after all, given the turn of events. She hadn't heard back, but since her sister treated her phone like it was another limb, this sudden silence was unnerving, especially since something like the engagement would have made her easily excitable sister's day. What was worse, no one other than Lucy seemed to notice because everyone else was too busy picking napkin colors and making calls to reception halls for a last-minute booking.

At some point during their walk, Joel had started holding her hand, and she took comfort in the warm, weight of his palm against hers. He absorbed all her worries, with calm reassurance, validating affirmations, and logical explanations, but mostly, he'd simply listened. And that was something Lucy hadn't experienced much of in her life.

When he'd pulled the Porsche back up in front of her aunt's house, he turned off the ignition and stared straight ahead, not making any move to unbuckle his seatbelt or get out of the car. In the silence, it became glaringly obvious that Lucy had monopolized most of their talking time.

"Everything okay?" she ventured.

This new relationship they'd founded was unchartered territory. She wasn't sure how much of him she was privy to. He hadn't been much of a sharer at the best of times, but he'd always been forthcoming with her.

"My parents are in town," he stated as he continued to stare straight ahead.

"Okay." Unsure of what to make of his blank tone, she proceeded with caution. "Do they know about us? Because if you want to back out, you totally can." Panic gripped her at the thought, but she didn't let it show. This was never meant to be a prison sentence for him. "I have a prospect for a big job down in Santa Monica that I think I can get my father excited about. It would be our first job out of San Francisco, but it might get him to see that Barone & Sons is ready to grow, and that I can help us grow—"

He turned to face her. "I don't want to call it off, Lucy. They've been away and I haven't told them about the engagement yet." He tapped his long fingers against the steering wheel.

"Yeah, you might want to get on that, I'm not sure how much longer I can hold my side of the family off. I've told everyone that they need to let you tell your parents the news yourself, but—" she let the insinuation hang there. Her family's penchant for spreading the buzz was well known.

"I appreciate that. I think they'll be surprised in a good way, but it does need to come from me." He sighed heavily. "Honestly, I think my family was getting a little worried about me."

Yeah, she could relate. "So, what is it, then?"

"They want to get together while they're here." His tone was hesitant.

Right. *'Man of few words'* was an under exaggeration when it came to describing Joel.

"I'm going to need more clarity. Do you want us to get together with your parents? Dinner at your place? Picnic in the park? Barbecue at Gambo's?"

"My sister's baby shower is tomorrow. I'm expected to be there."

Oh. Everything clicked together then, and sympathy flooded her. "Joel." She covered his hand with hers as she spoke. "If it's me you're worried about, don't. I'm used to this kind of thing. It's par for the course in a big family like mine. If we aren't going to a wedding or a funeral, we're going to a baby shower or baptism. Hatched, matched, and dispatched on rinse and repeat. I've been to more than one since—"

His eyes flicked to hers, and the uncertainty in them encouraged her share what she'd come to accept over the last few years. "It's possible to be happy for someone and unhappy for yourself at the same time, and that's okay, but I believe it's important to support the people we love, even when it's hard." Especially when no one else knew what they'd gone through.

He held her gaze for a beat, then nodded. "It would mean a lot to Hope."

"Of course it would. Tell them we'll be there. I'll grab a present this evening."

"Already taken care of." His fingers twitched under hers like he wanted to do something with them, but didn't.

"Okay then." Lucy forced a bright tone. "I'll see you tomorrow."

Joel offered that famous half-smile of his, before he got out of the car, rounded the hood, and opened her door. He took her hand as she rose from her seat. Neither of them spoke as they walked up to her aunt's house.

When they got to the front stoop, he brushed his lips against her cheek. "I've missed you, Lucy," he whispered. Or maybe he didn't.

With her brain short circuiting from his kiss, it was hard to tell. Then he left her there and headed back to his car before she could say another word.

She watched until he drove out of sight, wondering how she'd ever keep things fake between them when he kept making everything feel so real.

CHAPTER ELEVEN

"If you want to leave at any time, just say the word," Joel repeated for the fifth time as he led Lucy up the sidewalk to Hope and Gabe's house, guiding her with his hand resting low on her back. His hand itched to get closer to her skin, closer to her, but he held his distance.

"I won't," she told him. "I already told you, I'm used to this kind of thing."

He stopped before they got to the door, shifting her gently so they were face to face. He didn't want to come across as pushy, but he did want to make sure. This was the day he introduced Lucy as his fiancée to his family—at a freaking baby shower. So, he leveled her with what he hoped came across as a meaningful yet empathetic look. "But if at any point you're not, you'll tell me, right?"

Her soft lips curved into a smile. "I promise."

Maybe she was right, and this was normal to her. He reminded himself they'd spent the last four years leading separate lives. Maybe she'd gone to dozens of parties similar to this. But he hadn't. He couldn't remember the last time he'd been to a *baby anything*.

As Lucy studied him, a crease appeared between her eyebrows. "Are *you* okay?"

Grief struck his gut like a sucker punch, something that hadn't happened in a while. Just as his chest started to tighten, her gentle touch trailed down his arm, and he snapped out of the moment, locking eyes with Lucy. Hers were luminous with concern. As she interlocked their fingers, a sad sort of knowing smile touched her lips. Whatever he was feeling, she'd felt tenfold.

"We're in this together, right?" Her tone was reassuring, and after another few seconds, she drew her shoulders back and inhaled deeply. "Okay, now let's go make everyone believe we're madly in love." She tugged him toward the door.

This was crazy. So fucking crazy he couldn't believe it was happening. But it was. Lucy was holding his hand like it had always been there, so they could tell everyone they were happily engaged.

Four years ago, he'd imagined this scenario a thousand times. He'd memorized a heartfelt speech. He and Lucy had practiced over and over how they'd tell their families that they'd married on a wild whim in Vegas and hadn't regretted it for a second. At the time, he'd settled on making a declaration of love and devotion so profound that neither family nor Lucy would ever question the depth of his sincerity.

Then reality had hit in the form of his empty apartment and a heart so shattered he hadn't glimpsed a speck of light for months. The void had left him cold and bereft, and he'd promised himself to never feel any emotion that could lead to a similar scenario. Shit like that just ended up hurting too much, and he wasn't going to let his heart ripped out a second time. Especially not by Lucy Barone.

Until he'd finally gone looking for her at her cousin's wedding, and it was like the other half of him had locked back into place. He couldn't resent her or hate her or deny her anything. Even if it cost him his heart.

He took a bracing inhale and knocked on his sister's door. Three loud raps. Almost immediately, the tap of high heels made their way to the hall, along with a dog barking and a little girl squealing, and despite the chill in his heart, a smile tugged his mouth. He loved his family, now more than ever before.

There had been a time when he wasn't sure they'd ever get to where they were. Two years ago, they'd almost been torn apart by his parents' secret. He and Hope's world had shattered the moment they'd found out, by accident, that Hope was adopted. When she's run away to Portland, he'd become the glue that held everyone together. Not easy to do with an angry sister, a mother who did not do well with confrontation, and a father who, for the first time in his life, found himself in a situation he couldn't control.

Keeping his family together had become his responsibility. Months of mediating between his sister and their parents had ensued. Endless negotiating for peaceful visits, and navigating awkward family get togethers. All because he couldn't stomach losing more family, especially not after he'd lost the fragile one he'd built with Lucy.

When the door flew open, his niece and her dog exploded onto the porch, and Joel's heart clenched. Those months of hell, anxiety, and drama had been worth it for this. One family saved.

"Hey cutie," he said, laughing as he scooped Ruby up for a hug.

"Uncle Joel," Ruby squealed, wrapping her arms and

legs around him in a full body embrace. "It's about time you're here. We had to wait for you to eat cupcakes!"

He hugged her back, absorbing her shock wave of joy. She bounced off him as quickly as she'd bounced on and grabbed his hand, tugging him. "Come on, come on."

"Ruby!" Hope chided lovingly, as she waddled down the hallway. "Let them come in the door first."

Hope was massively pregnant, which might have been the cause of her glow, but there was more. Gabe and Ruby had changed his sister. And in a few months, Hope would officially be adopting Ruby.

This adoption process seemed to bring her closure and allowed her to experience what she'd doubted when she'd been blindsided by her own adoption. That the bond of family wasn't blood, it was love. Ruby was family. She was Hope's daughter, down to the soul, and it had nothing to do with genetics. Same as Hope was Walter and Audrey Morgan's daughter.

She was five weeks from giving birth and wearing a fancy dress, her hair perfectly done, and a pair of high heels on her feet.

"You look amazing," he said, leaning in to give his sister a peck on the cheek.

"I feel like a bloated hippopotamus with heartburn, but thanks." Hope looked over Joel's shoulder and smiled brightly. "Oh my God, Lucy! Joel said he was bringing you, but I didn't believe it. It's been forever." She moved toward Lucy with open arms.

The barking dog intercepted, jumping paws up onto Lucy.

"Get off of her, you silly pup," Hope scolded, shooing the beagle away. "Come in. Everyone's in the backyard. I'll give you a proper hug out there, if you can get your arms around me."

Joel glanced at Lucy, trying to assess her first impressions. Her happiness and comfort around his family was crucial to him, so when her gaze met his as she moved past him to follow his sister down the hall, the smile she gave him went straight to his heart and tattooed itself there. Because there wasn't a damn fake thing about it.

CHAPTER TWELVE

S tepping onto Hope's back deck was like stepping into a photoshoot for some high-end parenting magazine. An impressive archway made entirely out of blue and pink balloons held a big sign in the middle that read "Boy or Girl?" In the garden, round tables were decorated with blue or pink centerpieces. A long table off to the side had themed snacks and a massive tower of cupcakes topped with either pink or blue icing.

"Oh, it's a gender-reveal party," Lucy breathed as Joel came up beside her.

He glanced down at her and registered the delight on her face. And it was hard not to be caught up in everyone's joy. He was genuinely happy for his sister and Gabe and knew there had been a journey to get to this moment. But his concern for Lucy's mental well-being was his priority. So there was some relief in seeing her okay being here. At a baby shower that was also a gender-reveal party.

Without thinking, he reached for Lucy's hand. She immediately linked her fingers with his, leaned against his shoulder, and looked up at him with a reassuring smile. A swell of pride lifted the dread that had weighed on his chest. This was his woman, and her smile was the center of his universe. There would be hell to pay if this ended, but at the moment, he couldn't muster a single fuck about that.

"Um, okay, so this is new," Hope said, interrupting his thoughts. Her gaze was locked on his and Lucy's joined hands.

Right, here went nothing...or everything.

"Hope, there's something you should—"

"Joel!" His mother's trill shot through the air and a second later, she appeared beside his sister. "Darling, I'm so glad to see you. I miss having you in San Francisco, not that I ever saw much of you there, but at least I knew where to find you if I wanted to." Audrey Morgan opened her arms for a hug.

Joel leaned into them, letting his mother's arms settle around his shoulders.

When she pulled back, she regarded Lucy. "The last time I saw you must have been at a Christmas party five or more years ago. You look lovelier than ever, Lucy. How are you doing?" she asked as she reached for Lucy next. "I'm so happy that you're here to join us for this."

Lucy nodded. "I'm so glad to be here. Hope, you must be excited to add the newest member to your family."

Hope smiled, rubbing her enormous belly. "Yes, I'm 100 percent ready to have this little guy...or girl. I swear, it feels like this baby is trying to push every single one of my organs out through my esophagus."

They chatted and mingled in the garden with friends and relatives who'd come to share in his sister and brother-in-law's special day. Finally, he led Lucy to a table.

She tugged his hand, and he leaned closer. "When are

you planning on telling your family about our engagement? Before or after cupcakes?"

Excellent question. As a man who meticulously planned most things in life, he was finding himself in more situations than ever where he was making shit up on the fly.

He pulled out a chair for Lucy to take a seat. "Definitely after. As they say, first gender reveal, then engagement reveal."

A soft gasp drew his attention from Lucy's unamused eye roll, and behind his shoulder, where Ivy had halted dead in her tracks.

Shit.

"Ivy," his sister called from across the garden by the punch bowl, summoning her best friend with a wave.

With one last wide-eyed gawk, Ivy turned from Joel and hustled straight to Hope.

Double shit. Those two had a bond thicker than cement. If Ivy thought she uncovered the news of the century, no way would she withhold it from Hope for even one second.

Sure enough, Ivy immediately launched into an excited monologue as Hope poured lemonade into a glass.

"Who is that?" Lucy asked, as she followed Joel's gaze to Ivy and Hope.

"Ivy. She and Sean are my neighbors across the hall. She's also Hope's best friend." He watched as Hope's eyes widened to saucers and her mouth formed a small *o.* Yep, the tea had definitely just been spilled.

Great, now Hope was waddling toward them. He straightened in his chair and reached under the table to grasp Lucy's knee in a protective gesture.

"What is it?" she asked, placing her hand over his under the table, and the touch nearly distracted him enough to forget his sister was approaching with a look of determination.

"She's coming," he whispered.

"Who's coming?" Lucy whispered back, moving her hand to his upper thigh, leveraging herself to look behind her shoulder.

Christ. *Jesus.* Her hand was an inch away from his dick, but she might as well have been stroking it by the way he was reacting.

Bloody hell. Now he was going to have to face down his sister about his no longer secret engagement with a raging hard-on. Perfect.

Somewhere from heaven, an angel rang a bell, and his sister halted in mid-waddle.

The bell rang again, and Ruby shouted, "Time to eat the cupcakes!"

When Gabe came up and took Hope's hand and lead her to the cupcake table, Joel released the breath he'd been holding in a low whoosh. Lucy rubbed her hand up and down his thigh, as if to get his attention. His pants were so tight now, he'd have to remain sitting for at least a half an hour.

"Who's coming?" Lucy asked again. "What are you talking about?"

He was about to come if she didn't stop touching him, that's who. He gripped the innocent fingers under the table and moved their joined hands to her lap. *See how you like it, honey,* he thought as he ran his fingertips along her upper leg, skimming the thin fabric of her dress. When she sucked in a sharp breath, a surge of victory hit him.

"Nothing," he murmured into her ear. "False alarm."

When Lucy swallowed and nodded, he smirked, satisfied that he wasn't the only one turned on at a gender-reveal garden party.

Gabe and Hope took the top two cupcakes off the tower, which were both covered with white frosting, and made a production of counting down to taking a bite.

Joel marveled at his brother-in-law. Gabe's curmudgeonliness was his brand, and while Joel was sure he'd softened somewhat since getting together with Hope, he still had a reserved, vaguely pissed off way about him. Given all he'd gone through, Joel couldn't blame him. And yet, here Gabe stood under a bright balloon archway, holding a white cupcake, posing for an invasive amount of photographs, and grinning from ear to ear like he couldn't wait to post this on the family Instagram account that Hope had mentioned she'd started.

Hope was an enchantress, and Gabe was head over heels in love with his new life. Ruby ran up to her father, and he swung her into his arms. At the final countdown, he held his cupcake so they could take a bite from either side together. Hope simultaneously took a bite of her own.

When pink icing oozed from the center, Ruby's fists pumped the air as she whooped with joy, cupcake flying out of her mouth. Hope threw her arms around Gabe and Ruby in a group hug as the crowd cheered and clapped. Gabe's rumbling laugh sounded stunned and elated at the same time. He looked a little shell-shocked but happier than Joel had ever seen him.

The unbidden memory of Lucy telling him four years ago that she was pregnant hit him like a Mac truck out of nowhere.

In that moment, he too had felt the most terrified and happiest he'd ever been in his life. He too had choked out an astonished laugh, half shock, half overwhelming emotion, when Lucy had softly uttered the words.

With pink icing sticking to their lips, the expectant parents kissed, and something coiled in Joel's gut, snaking its way up his chest and lodging in his throat. The sensation was unfamiliar and awful. Not quite resentment, he'd never begrudge his sister this happiness, but it was ugly, and it left a bitter taste at the back of his throat. He drank deeply from his glass, but the cool champagne did little to ease the sourness.

Beside him, he heard a sniff.

"A girl," Lucy whispered.

Her eyes were blurred and lost, but so beautiful Joel caved into the longing that had been pounding inside him, into his need to comfort her and be comforted by her. He cradled her against his chest and pressed a kiss to her temple.

"It's beautiful, right?" Lucy said, her voice muffled by his shirt. She hid her face on his shoulder. "I'm sorry, I just need a second."

"Take as many as you want." Christ, was that his voice? It sounded raw and foreign. He hugged her closer, willing himself to regain his usual control. He needed to be strong for her. "I'm right here," he murmured hoarsely as she buried her face in the fabric of his shirt. He stroked her arm, shielding her from the surrounding guests.

Their mutual pain was a private bubble, bonding them together for one singular moment, despite the people that surrounded them. The sounds of joy and congratulations were everywhere. And for the first time, he resented that not one of them knew about the son they'd lost.

"It's okay. I'm okay. It's—just—" Her words stuttered to a halt.

"I know," he murmured. He could finish her sentence for her—It's just that their gender reveal had taken place in a hospital, and their baby had already been gone when they'd found out a little boy had almost been theirs.

Slowly, she pulled away, looking up at him with wet lashes that sliced another year off his life. "I'm okay," she said again. "And it really is beautiful, Joel. Some of these are happy tears. Believe it or not." She choked on a laugh and dabbed her eyes with a napkin.

Anger flooded him. How had he been such an idiot? *I'm fine,* she'd said. *I've gone to baby showers before*, she'd said. Why hadn't he listened to his gut? He knew better. Four years ago, Lucy had grieved in private. No one had known what she'd been through. She'd only had him. They'd only had each other. And then not even that.

He shouldn't have brought her here. "Come on." He pushed his chair back. "Let's go."

"But—"

"But nothing." He was getting her out of here, away from the reminders of what they didn't have, away from the happy family that should have been them. Jumping to his feet, he reached down for Lucy's hand when his sister's voice rose above the crowd, delaying their escape. He'd have to get Lucy out of here discreetly. Causing a scene would only make it worse for her.

"I want to thank everyone for coming today to share this with us. We are so unbelievably excited to be meeting Baby Girl Walsh *very* soon." Hope gave her husband another lingering kiss.

Gabe cupped the back of her neck to keep her locked in, and someone in the crowd, probably Sean, let out a loud whistle.

Taking the distraction as an opportunity, Joel tried again,

clasping his hand around Lucy's but she shook her head marginally.

We can't, she mouthed.

He furrowed his brow in confusion. Of course, the fuck, they could. This had been his fear, he didn't want to subject Lucy to this.

Hope's laughter filled the garden as she pushed playfully at her husband's chest. "Okay, clearly we have a lot of celebrating left to do, but first, I wanted to hand the floor over to my big brother, Joel, because we are celebrating more than just our little baby girl today. Joel, why don't you come up here and tell everyone your news?"

What the fuuuuck?

Swiveling his head, Joel leveled his sister with a glare, and her answering sugar-sweet smile screamed, *This is what you get for not telling me first.*

He shot a look at Ivy, who shrugged innocently while Sean sat beside her, shaking his head warily.

"Oh shit," Lucy whispered below him where she still sat.

He glanced at her, his hand still tightly clenched in hers. Her eyes were wide, tear stained, and anxious. He couldn't blame her, but he wasn't letting her down again, either.

He gave her hand a reassuring squeeze before lifting his champagne glass and seeking his parents in the crowd. His mother watched him, with a curious smile. His father appeared confused.

Joel cleared his throat. He was going to have to break the news of his fake engagement in front of everyone at a fucking gender-reveal garden party.

"Thank you for that, Hope," he said through the smile he saved for his boardroom. "Let me start by asking you to join me in raising our glasses and toasting my beautiful sister, her husband, and my perfect little niece Ruby. You deserve every happiness, and I'm so glad that you are building on perfection by adding another little future CEO into the mix for me to dote on and spoil. Cheers to all four of you." He raised his glass and a sea of hands followed.

Hope's eyes got misty as she took a sip of her sparkling apple juice, and Joel knew he was forgiven for not telling her about Lucy first.

When everyone had had a sip from their glasses, he turned to Lucy. Her hand was still tightly clasped in his, mostly because he couldn't let go. He'd forgotten how much strength he drew from her.

"As most of you know, I have spent the better half of this last year in Portland working on expanding Morgan Construction out of state. During that time, I have spent what free time I had with Hope, Gabe, and Ruby. Seeing them together has made me realize what I've been missing in my life."

Someone in the group sniffled, but he didn't check to see who it was.

"I have my work, and it's brought me great success, but other than that, I realized that I lacked any real purpose." Spending a night at the office was not uncommon for him. "I wanted a reason to come home every night. A reason to take a vacation. A reason to walk around grinning like my brother-in-law over there." He tipped his drink toward Gabe, and his audience chuckled.

Lucy stared at him blankly, with her gorgeous mouth open a crack, like she didn't know what to make of the speech he was giving.

"What most of you don't know is that this woman right here, Lucy Barone, she's been my friend since we met as kids at one of my father's Christmas parties. After that, we used to chase each other around construction sites while our fathers talked shop, which"—he waggled his finger at his sister and Gabe—"was completely illegal and not a pro-tip on parenting, but hell, it was the 90s."

Another chuckle rippled through the guests.

"I've been chasing Lucy ever since, and somewhere along the way, she became my reason."

A chorus of "*awwws*" wrapped around them, but he couldn't have moved his eyes away from hers if the whole world was burning down. He was trying to gauge her reaction, every flicker in her pupils, every quiver of her lip, the way her hand went boneless in his. He needed to know that she was absorbing what he was saying, because even though she'd hurt him more than any living person ever had, she had been his reason, dammit. All along, she'd been his reason.

And even if this wasn't exactly as he wanted it to be between them, he needed her to know that one truth. "So, I asked her to marry me, and by some miracle, she said yes."

He forced himself to look away from her and at the crowd. His mother was crying. His father's jaw was on the floor.

"So I want to offer a toast to my new fiancée, Lucy. For making me the happiest man on earth." He lifted his glass, and a roar of cheers erupted.

Lucy rose to stand beside him. "That was—" She took a long sip from her champagne glass. "Better than expected."

Joel grinned at her. "Get used to it, baby." Before he could think better of it, he pulled her close and kissed her.

CHAPTER THIRTEEN

The first time Lucy had been kissed by Joel, she'd been drunk. They both had been. And not just the tipsy, one-too-many-kinds-of-cocktails drunk, but the zero inhibitions, shit-faced drunk that she'd never been before and hadn't been since.

One moment they'd been celebrating a win at a blackjack table in Vegas, and the next they'd woken up, spooned in a hotel bed, the mother of all hangovers pounding in her head and a gift shop wedding ring on her finger. Her biggest regret was having very few detailed memories of that night, but she did remember the first instant his lips had touched hers.

They'd met by chance at a *Builders of the Future* conference in Vegas. Joel had taken her to dinner, and they'd spent a perfect evening talking over decadent food and expensive wine. When dinner ended, Joel had asked what she wanted to do, and already tipsy on the cabernet, she'd said dancing. They'd strolled the strip until they stumbled upon a club blaring music and a dance floor with strobe lights inside.

They danced and drank for another couple of hours until Lucy told Joel it was his turn to pick an activity.

He'd taken her to the Bellagio, where he'd been staying. They'd found themselves in a private room, at a blackjack table, a Scotch in his hand and a martini in hers. Every time he rolled, Joel asked her to blow on his dice for luck. They'd laughed and joked, and before she knew it, he'd swooped her up in his arms because he'd won. She didn't remember how much money or how much he'd bet before he'd won it, because as soon as his lips landed on hers, everything else fell away.

At first, they'd yanked apart, shocked apologies falling from their lips. They'd stood wide-eyed with chests heaving. Out of nowhere he'd said, "Fuck, I should've done that years ago" at the same time as she'd said, "Do it again." And then they were kissing ferociously.

The kiss now, in front of thirty people, in his sister's backyard garden gender-reveal party was much the same. Joel devoured her like he was starving. Another inappropriate kiss at an inappropriate time, but she couldn't bring herself to push him away. Not after everything he'd just said. Not when her emotions were scattered all over the place, and the only thing anchoring her to sanity was him. It didn't even matter that the engagement wasn't real. It didn't matter that he'd likely exaggerated most of what he'd said. All that mattered was that he was here, holding her, his pulse thrumming frantically against hers, like they were having a conversation in heartbeats.

Somewhere in the crowd, came a deep clearing of a throat. A hum of murmurs followed, buzzing into her consciousness.

"Mom?" A little girl's voice cut through everything,

jolting her back to reality. "Uncle Joel had his tongue in her mouth. He didn't even use any hand sanitizer."

Lucy tore her mouth away from Joel's, setting her palms firmly against his pecs as a barrier between them. His chest rose and fell as he caught his breath. His gaze was lit with a flammable kind of desire, and she recalled how that look had her flat on her back within seconds, once upon a time.

"Well then." Hope's voice cut through the garden. "Congratulations to the happy couple. Can't wait to hear all the details, big brother."

For a moment so brief that Lucy wasn't sure it even happened, she caught the shock of truth in his eyes. Those steely grays were wild and chaotic, a maelstrom of emotions so very unlike Joel. With a slow blink, his familiar mask of restraint fell over his features, shuttering anything she thought she might have seen. The composed businessman was back in control.

He gave his sister a curt nod, signaling the end of this portion of the party. The guests immediately went back to chattering amongst themselves, happily moving on from the display they'd just witnessed. Lucy marveled again at his ability to control a room with one look alone. He held such power, and most of the time, he didn't even realize it. His presence demanded obedience, but he lacked the arrogance of a bully, maintaining respect by staying humble. So much like his father, Lucy thought as she turned her gaze to Walter Morgan.

The older man stood by his wife near the back of the garden, watching her and Joel with an unreadable expression on his face.

Walter Morgan had always treated her well. He'd treated her entire family like an extension of his, inviting them to important events, remembering birthdays, sending her flowers when she graduated college. Over the years, she'd acquired a deep respect for him and felt she earned his in return with her work ethic and dedication to family.

Knowing that she was deceiving him this way sat uneasily in her chest. He'd never cheated his way to anything. That sense of integrity he shared with her father was too deeply engrained. Guilt nudged her.

"I have to say, Joel, I never thought I'd see the day." Ivy appeared beside them. Petite and fine featured, her pale skin looked extra translucent against her raven-colored hair cut short to brush her neckline. "I mean, I won't say I wasn't surprised. I was, but..." Her pale-blue eyes scanned Lucy from head to toe, as if trying to size her up. "I'll withhold my judgment until after the party."

"Party?" Lucy echoed.

Ivy smiled devilishly. "Oh hell yes, a party. No engagement is truly official until it's been posted online or there's been a party. Since I know Joel doesn't have any social media accounts, we'll have to settle for a party. How long are you in town, Lucy? We should throw it before you leave, and more importantly, before Hope pops out the latest Walsh descendant."

Lucy cocked her head toward Joel, who was shooting an exasperated look at Ivy. "You don't have a single account?" She should have known, since she'd run his name through every social media search available in the Webiverse, and yet for a man of his level of achievement, she was surprised. When she'd come up empty-handed, she'd figured he'd blocked her. She never considered that he had no online presence. That just seemed absurd.

He shrugged. "The Morgan Construction PR team runs our social media accounts, I think. What would I need one for?"

"I don't know," Lucy said, still incredulous. "To promote your business using your personal platform, show off your latest vacay destinations, get followers by sharing pictures of your ripped abs as you lounge on your couch in your Morgan Construction penthouse? Tons of reasons."

Joel snorted. "You don't get followers because of your abs."

"Yes, you do," Sean said in his raspy baritone as he came up beside Ivy.

All eyes swiveled his way, and it was his turn to shrug.

"My regular *Monday Muscles* posts bring in new followers each week, and some of those buy memberships for my gym or my online fitness programs. I've even received requests for collaborations with different companies in the fitness industry that way—protein shakes, athletic gear, that kind of thing." He shrugged the boulder of his shoulders again. "Lucy's right. People love that kind of shit."

Everyone continued staring at Sean. Lucy couldn't speak for the others, but she was going to cyberstalk him when she got home. She wanted to see the abs in question, for the sake of curiosity, of course.

"My abs won't bring in customers in the same way," Joel commented.

"Why wouldn't they? They certainly measure up." The second the words left her mouth, Lucy kicked herself for speaking without thinking. But she couldn't help herself, she remembered Joel's abs all too well.

"I mean..." What did she mean? She meant what she said. Crap. She hated putting her foot in her mouth. "You have nice abs, that's all," she muttered, staring at her toes.

"Okay, now that I have that uninvited image in my brain, let's lock down the engagement party next Saturday at Bowie's, 7 p.m. I'll confirm with Gabe that the space can be cleared, and then I'll send an email." Ivy spoke like she'd been Lucy's bosom buddy for years, and not like they'd just met.

Lucy considered the circle of friends. They'd come here for Gabe and Hope's family, but were now celebrating Joel and her without blinking an eye.

She could get used to this kind of immediate love and acceptance. Deep inside her another kernel of understanding grew as to why Joel now spent more time in Portland than San Francisco.

Back home, his life was all business and work. Here, he was surrounded by friends who loved him for who he was and were genuinely excited for his news, no matter how shocking it might have been. That was a very special thing.

"What's your number?" Ivy regarded her expectantly, phone in hand. "I'll need to reach you since it's partially your party. You probably have relatives who'll want to attend, so I'll need contacts. You can stay until next Saturday, right?"

Things were shifting so quickly, her mind whirled. Her long overdue, two-week vacation had turned into a two-week wedding planning, fake engagement, party-hardy extravaganza. How had her life gotten so out of control?

All she wanted was to run her family's company when her father retired in six months, and keep the business thriving. Now she was involved in—and distracted by— planning a party for her fake engagement.

Numbly, she rattled off her number, and Ivy typed it into her phone.

"Great." Ivy shoved her phone back in her bag. "I'll be in touch. We'll need to meet to go over details, which is easy since you're staying across the hall from me while you're here."

"Uh." Lucy shot a glance at Joel, who was watching her with that odd glint in his eye that she'd caught earlier. A swirl of unidentifiable emotion. Quickly averting her gaze, she went with the truth, lest the lies pile up so high she lost track of them. "I'm staying with my aunt."

Unfortunately, at the same moment she spoke, Joel said, "She's staying with me."

Ivy blinked, and Lucy felt her face warm. Crap, crap, crap. They'd forgotten to discuss this. Served her right for not devising a strategic plan on this Hail Mary of an idea.

"Well, while you guys figure it out, I'll be in touch by text."

Ten minutes later, and after several awkward congratulations by well-meaning strangers, Lucy was finally back in Joel's car. She slumped against her seat and let out a long breath.

As soon as Joel rounded to the driver's side and got in she said, "I don't know if we can pull this off."

He started his Porsche with the push of his finger. "Pull what off?"

She glared at him. "*This*, Joel. A fake engagement, a fake wedding. A fake party. A fake marriage."

"Our marriage is real, Lucy, and has been since that neon chapel in Vegas." Smoothly, he pulled away from the curb and onto the quiet residential street.

Frustration bubbled in her throat, tasting bitter. "Is it, Joel? Is living separate lives, in different cities, without a soul knowing the truth, considered an actual marriage these days? Because if so, then we're killing it."

He glanced at her, then back at the road. When they were together, they hadn't fought often. But when they did, this was how it went. She lost her temper and her voice elevated, loudly. Joel replied calmly or more often remained silent. Which only riled her more. Infuriating man!

"I don't understand you sometimes. To the rest of the world, you're the perfect person everyone depends on. You have your shit together at all times. You're not supposed to have a secret wife no one knows about that you're too loyal to divorce. Is this what you envisioned when you thought of yourself as married? Not talking to each other and keeping secrets from the people we love."

Joel's gaze remained fixed on the road. Not even the damn muscle in his jaw ticked this time.

It only amped her up. If her hurt and frustration over being in this situation was fueled by her anger, his silence was the match. "Faking an engagement to the secret wife so she can get her father to take her seriously for once? I'm sure that was right up there on your list of things you were looking for in a partner."

Why couldn't her father see her differently? Why did he have to be so stubbornly stuck in his beliefs? Why had she gotten drunker than she ever had, been married by a two-bit Elvis, then proceeded to have unprotected sex with her childhood friend? Why did she want to run a company? Why couldn't she be content to work at a job she loved, surrounded by family she loved for the rest of her life?

The thing that made her angriest was that she couldn't bring herself to regret any of what she was lamenting. It would make everything easier to deal with if she could. Regrets gave a nice cushion for those pesky emotions like anger, bitterness, and resentment. If she regretted her choices, needs, and desires, it would make them easier to walk away from.

Easier to get the divorce she should have asked for long ago, easier to stay in a job that she was good at, easier to maintain a smooth relationship with a father she loved. Just easier. But she didn't regret any of it, dammit—and so here she was, married to a man who she felt bonded to on an almost spiritual level, and deceiving her father on her climb to the top of a company that was her heart and soul.

"Do you even know what you want?" she asked, suddenly deflated.

He said nothing. Damn silent, cerebral man.

"Because I do. I want to run my father's company and I want to have that chance without having to lie to him. I want to be free from the assumption that I'm a mouse who does as she's told and is too insecure to stand up for herself. I want to feel happiness and not have to hide it." Why were her cheeks wet? Was she crying? Great, her humiliation was complete, and Joel still hadn't said a word.

The lurch of the Porsche stopping and its door slamming jolted her out of her pit of self-pity. Blinking away her tears, she realized they were parked in front of her Zia Ella's house. Had she really been venting for the entire car ride?

Her passenger side door ripped open, and Joel offered her his hand to help her out of the car. Happy to unload her, she bet. Guilt swamped her. She shouldn't have dumped on him when he'd only been trying to help.

When she was out of the car, he frowned at her, scrutinizing her face until she averted her gaze. When the pad of his thumb swiped tears off her cheekbone her gaze bounced back to his, and she couldn't stop the gasp of shock for the ache she saw in them.

Then he slammed the vehicle door shut and stomped down the path to her aunt's house, leaving her in the wake of his anger. The force of it was almost visible, like heat waves on scorching asphalt. Half intrigued, half terrified,

Lucy followed him slowly, unsure of what flame she'd ignited inside him.

When she made it to the stoop, he glared at her again, his look hard but still magnetizing. She was locked in by the power of that stare.

"Do you know what I want, Lucy?" The authoritative rumble in his tone sent a shiver up her back; goosebumps broke over her arms. "I want you to go inside and pack your bags."

The door swung open, revealing her aunt on the other side. Ella's toothy grin froze when Joel announced, "Lucy's moving in with me."

CHAPTER FOURTEEN

So what if he'd basically ordered her to move in with him? Or if it was too soon, and too emotionally volatile a decision to make following her outburst yesterday. After a restless night thinking about it, she decided she didn't care about any of that, because the thought of being able to leave the noisy, crowded, wedding obsessed house she was currently residing in was too tempting to walk away from. Or so she was telling herself. And that was why, the morning after Joel had demanded she move in with him, her suitcase was packed and ready to go.

As she zipped her luggage closed, a high-pitched laugh —that sounded something like a hyena riding a firetruck— echoed down the hallway. She would have been able to pick out that laugh if she were standing in the middle of Milan train station. Abandoning her bag in her aunt's guest room, she bolted to the kitchen where the joyous sound was coming from.

"Nat!" Lucy greeted her cousin, who launched herself into Lucy's open arms. "Thank God you're here! The mothers have been driving me crazy."

"I heard that!" Maria shouted from the other room.

Natalie giggled as she took a seat at the kitchen island. "She was just in here showing me the napkins she's picked out for the engagement party. They're so hideous it's hilarious. Now she's gone to pout because I said she'd embarrass the family if she put those out at your party. Sorry not sorry."

"Well, thank you for saving me from a napkin disaster." Lucy pulled out a plate of espresso bean biscotti and set it on the island. She glanced at the kitchen clock, which read II a.m. "It's a bit early for you, isn't it?"

"I know, right?" Natalie snagged a biscotti and took a bite. "It's ridiculous that any human should be up this early, but I have a client who needed an emergency blow out for a blind brunch date, so I had to go into the salon earlier than usual."

Natalie had the Barone entrepreneurship spirit. Just over a year ago, at the tender age of twenty-five, she'd opened her own salon. One of the many reasons Lucy admired her cousin so much.

"Wow, it is so quiet in here without Mar around, I can hear myself chew. We should have married her off years ago."

Lucy laughed out loud at Natalie's quip. Of the cousins, Mariana and Natalie were the closest, not only because they were the same age, but because Mariana had been an only child and Natalie the youngest of three, so Natalie had spent more time in Zia Ella's house than at her own. It had worked out well, and their similar boisterous personalities and complimentary looks had everyone in the family calling them The Twins.

"Do you miss her?" Lucy asked, filling the kettle in the sink.

"Not as much as I used to." Natalie shrugged. "I'm kind of used to her not being around as much since she got busier with Jeff. I mostly notice it when I'm here and she's not. It will be weird visiting her at the mansion. I can't believe she waited to move in with him until after they were married. I mean, who does that?"

Lucy grinned. The thing about growing up with only girl cousins in a close-knit family was that she often felt like she had five sisters instead of one. And she'd loved every second of that. "How long is Mariana honeymooning?"

Natalie snorted. "I dunno, forever? Jeff's family has gazillions. She's going to live the perma-vacation."

Lucy couldn't imagine living the trophy wife's life, not having to lift a finger for anything she got, not working. If boredom didn't kill her, a sense of worthlessness would.

"Speaking of gazillionaire," Natalie said around another bite of cookie. "I didn't think it got richer than Jeff's family, but then you come in with the Morgan bomb, and I was like 'mic drop! Someone in the family snagged a Forbes billionaire!' I love you, Lu, but I never would have guessed it would be you."

The kettle whistled, so Lucy took it off the burner and poured the hot water into the French press. "Don't be ridiculous. The Morgans do well, but not Forbes well. Besides, that's not why I married Joel." Oops. Shit, she was going to have to get better at this, and fast. Luckily, Natalie didn't seem to notice her slip up, as she was laser focused on thumbing through her phone.

Lucy brought the coffee pot and two cups to the island where Natalie sat. "Also, I'm insulted. Why wouldn't I be able to snag a Forbes billionaire? Rude."

"No offense, but you don't get out enough to meet the upper echelon," her cousin muttered as she focused on her phone. "Vanessa? Maybe. But you—see here!" Natalie thrust her device into Lucy's hand. "Joel Morgan is on the list. Told you so," she said smugly and proceeded to pour them both a coffee. "Honestly, Lu. How could you not know your fiancé was richer than God?"

"Everyone is richer than God. He's a deity, not a businessman," Lucy mumbled as she stared at the screen, and Joel's handsome face staring back at her. Holy shit. When did this happen? She always knew Joel was wealthy. Morgan Construction built and owned half of San Francisco. But Forbes wealthy...there was no way anyone made it that big building apartment towers. Jesus. What had she missed?

"Well, some might argue." Natalie stirred sugar into her coffee. "Anyway, see, you don't get out enough to know your fiancé is a billionaire. I swear, if I hadn't seen the lovesick look in his eyes, I would have bet my salon that the two of you were making the whole thing up."

Lucy nearly choked on a sliver of guilt. Setting the phone on the marble countertop, she said, "He didn't have a lovesick look."

"Please, he looked so pathetic, I thought Zia Ella was going to adopt him and put a collar on him. Which she still might, you know? She and your mom have gone nuts this week. With those two behind the wheel, it's going to be the biggest wedding ever planned in less than six weeks."

"Yes, and I've been here living every high-strung moment of it." Not for much longer, though. She'd find some reprieve from the chaos at Joel's apartment, at least.

"So I hear your engagement party is going to be at Bowie's?"

"What?"

"Yeah, Ivy and Hope arranged it with the Zias."

Too much information was coming at her at once. "How do you know Ivy?"

Natalie raised her eyebrow. "Have you seen that girl's bangs? Perfection like that only comes when you book with me every four weeks."

Her face must have been giving away her shock because Natalie laughed. "It's all in the family, cuz! Portland is an incestuous little place. Everyone knows everyone. Sometimes I swear I'm living in small town America. But hey, look, this is a good thing, right? Everyone is happy for you."

"Natalie! You're making a mess," Maria scolded as she came into the kitchen. "There are enough crumbs on the table to make another biscotti." She walked straight over to Lucy and kissed her cheek. "Where have you been, *patatina*? I haven't seen you all morning?" She shoved a package of napkins under Lucy's nose before she could answer. "These are pretty, right? They'll look so nice on a white tablecloth."

Lucy stared at the package of napkins. They were floral, which wouldn't have been bad, but the roses on the napkin were an orangey red, and not the sunset-colored kind of orange red, but more of a rusted metal kind. The green stems were a vomit green. "Um."

"They're hideous, Zia. I told you already."

"Quiet," Maria grumbled at Natalie in Italian. "You are so negative all the time. Be happy for your cousin."

Natalie threw her hands in the air. "I am happy for her! I'm trying to save her from barf-colored napkins on one of the most important days of her life."

"What time are you leaving to move in with your fiancé?" Zia Ella asked, coming into the kitchen carrying a stack of fabric.

"Say what?" Natalie's head swiveled toward Lucy. "You're moving in with Forbes?"

"Who's Forbes?" Maria asked.

"Nobody," Lucy said to her mother before turning to her cousin. "It's only until I go home to San Francisco."

"You don't think it's too soon to live together?" Her mother asked, as if she hadn't been the one championing for a rushed wedding since she'd found out about the engagement.

"Mom, it's just while I'm in Portland. I'm heading back to San Francisco as soon as the engagement party is over," Lucy reminded her mother. And herself.

"Maybe you should stay here. It might look better. You know, appearances—" Maria said.

"Zia, look on the bright side, you can use the spare room Lu has been sleeping in as the sewing room now, to—" Natalie fluttered her hand to the fabric on the counter. "To make handmade napkins. We can let people take them home as party favors." She turned back to Lucy. "I think it's perfect. You can get out of this zoo and don't have to hold back while he's drilling you." She wagged her eyebrows suggestively.

Lucy gasped, horrified, checking to make sure no one over the age of thirty had heard her raunchy cousin. To her relief, Maria and Ella were fussing over fabric swatches, deep in their own conversation.

"Nobody is going to be *drilling* anybody," Lucy hissed to her cousin, who responded with a snorting laugh.

"Why? Because you're not officially married yet?" Natalie raised an eyebrow. "Come on, Lu, we're all cafeteria Catholics around here, you know that. Take what you want, leave what you don't want." Her hands flapped as she spoke. "You can screw the billionaire against the wall tonight, but you'll still be married in the Cathedral in your virgin white." She shrugged extravagantly. "It is what it is. Embrace it."

It was official. Her family was insufferable.

As if to prove the point, her mother glanced up at her from a rose-colored swatch. "Oh, and *patatina*, you should change. You look like you can't afford real clothes."

Lucy glanced down at her high-rise jeans and off the shoulder Tragically Hip t-shirt.

"He's invited you to stay in his home. He didn't have to. The least you can do is look nice. And don't forget to bring him the gnocchi that I made yesterday. He likes my gnocchi. There is Tupperware in the refrigerator. Take the big one." Gathering the fabric and vomit-colored, store-bought napkins, her mother and aunt made their way into the living room. "We'll make napkins out of the rose-colored fabric, so find a dress to match."

Lucy stared after the matriarchs, then at her cousin, who wore a crumb-dusted smirk and said, "You're welcome."

CHAPTER FIFTEEN

This was happening. Joel was about to pick up Lucy and bring her home with him. Where she belonged.

Standing in front of Graziella and Gambo Barone's home, he tried to summon the signature composure he prided himself on. But he hadn't slept a wink last night, replaying his kiss with Lucy in his mind until his whole body was hot with need.

The effects of the freezing shower he'd forced himself to take at 2 a.m. to tame the mad lust coursing through him had long since faded. Not for the first time, he wished he could flip a switch on how his body tuned into her without much provocation at all. Lust had ruled a huge part of the time he and Lucy had lived together, and he recognized now how that had been a mistake. He wouldn't let their physical attraction overrule him and compromise either of them again.

Which shouldn't be this hard. They had a lifetime of effortless companionship between them. What had started in childhood had maintained after they'd gone to different parts of the country for college. Even though he was three years older, they'd continued to exchange emails and text messages. On visits home, they'd make a point to catch up in person. Things between them had always remained casual and platonic, and he'd never thought of her as more than just...Lucy. Nor had he gotten the feeling that she thought more of him, either.

Until Vegas, where everything snapped together, like fate had been waiting for her chance to jump into action.

And then he'd fucked it up and left her that night four years ago.

Now he was picking her up and moving her in with him, and this new bridge between them was so fragile, every step was like walking on cracked glass. But, maybe, with time, they could build something sturdy. And he had a plan to do so. If someone ever opened this goddamn door and let him in.

He lifted his finger to poke the doorbell again, when it flew open, and Luciano Barone appeared in the doorway.

Surprised to be face to face with Lucy's father, Joel straightened and raised his chin. Ultimately, he had so much respect for the man in front of him, he'd looked up to him almost as much as he had his own father. He admired the grit and tenacity it must have taken to come to a new country with next to nothing and build a company to the level of success that Luciano had.

The cabinetry that came out of Barone & Sons was some of the most sought after, elite woodworking this side of the country. Luciano was the best. And Morgan Construction always hired the best.

But the man before him had also hurt Lucy, by not seeing her for the fucking brilliant woman she was, and by denying her the one thing she'd earned by hard work. After his recent conversations with Lucy, he was having trouble reconciling his respect for her father with his bitter disappointment in him.

Still, none of that changed the fact that this man was the father of his wife and also a traditional, old-school Italian patriarch, who expected respect when he felt it was due.

"Sir," he said with a deferential nod as he extended his hand.

Luciano nodded curtly before gripping Joel's hand in a firm, calloused handshake.

He stood about a head shorter than Joel, but he had a solidly powerful stance, his body thick and hard from years of physical labor. He took up the entire doorway, making no move to let Joel in.

"Joel," he replied in his thick Italian accent.

Understanding his place, Joel didn't hesitate to say what needed to be said to the father of his bride. "Sir, I know that everything with your daughter seems fast and unplanned, but I want you to trust that I have admired and cared for Luciana from the start. And I promise you I will take care of her in every way possible. I'll spend my last breath making sure she's happy." Or he'd die trying. "And I apologize for not coming to you before I asked Lucy to marry me, but with all due respect, I think we both can acknowledge she has the right to do whatever she likes with or without our permission."

For a tense few seconds Luciano said nothing, and Joel had a flash where he thought he might see the back side of the door before he saw Lucy. He'd never challenged the man before, but when Luciano's face broke out in the biggest grin Joel had ever seen on the man, he breathed a sigh of relief. Luciano was fucking beaming as he stepped out of the doorway and lifted his hand to give Joel's cheek three light claps.

Gripping his shoulder, Luciano gave it a firm squeeze. "Son, I couldn't be happier. When I heard the news, I told Maria that it was the fourth happiest day of my life. First was, of course, when I married my own beautiful wife, the second and third when my daughters were born, and fourth was the day I heard that you were to marry my Luciana."

Fuck, were those tears in Luciano's eyes?

"You're right. Lucy can do whatever she likes, but she always does the right thing. She's a good girl."

Joel clenched his teeth at the term, trying to hold back his rebuttal, but it didn't work. "She's so much more than that."

After an awkward beat of stunned silence, the older man threw back his head, a laugh bellowing throughout the entryway. Before Joel could say another word, Luciano enveloped him in a massive hug. "Welcome to the family. You were always like a son to me, but now I can tell everyone that you are family. It is a proud day for me."

Joel embraced Luciano, already used to it. The Barones were huggers and had never made a secret of it.

Lucy's father released him and turned to walk into the house. "Now I hear you've come to take my daughter." He gave Joel a stern look over his shoulder. "But first, you'll eat."

And with that rule declared, Joel followed his father-in-law inside.

"**Z**ia, we're going to a place that has a kitchen, a refrigerator, and food. We don't need six Tupperware of leftovers and cheese," Lucy lamented as her aunt put another container in a reusable shopping bag.

When she tried to remove one, Ella slapped her hand away, and Joel hid his grin. He was staying out of this one.

"Don't exaggerate. I'm just putting together some simple things in case Joel hasn't had a chance to go grocery shopping." Ella glanced in his direction, as if merely noting his presence in the room confirmed her suspicions. "Your fiancé is a very busy man. He has no time to shop. Right?"

Joel accepted the stuffed bag, while ignoring Lucy's scowl. "Thank you, Ella. This is a welcomed contribution." He didn't have time to shop, but he also didn't need any food because he paid someone to keep his fridge stocked with groceries and pre-made meals. Still, there was no way in hell he'd disrespect Lucy's family by not accepting what they offered.

Luciano entered the kitchen, carrying two bottles of wine. "Take these. They aren't as good as mine, but Gambo had them in his cellar. If you like it, we can serve it at your engagement party."

"Dad, are you kidding? You've tasted Zio's wine. It's vinegar, on a good day." Lucy grimaced but still accepted the bottles.

"Then we can use it in the salad," Maria piped up. "It would mean a lot to your uncle. You never know when it's his last batch."

"And we're leaving," Lucy said as she stuffed the bottles in the grocery bag of leftovers. "When they start talking about how they aren't going to be here much longer, it's time to go." She straightened and met Joel with a forced smile. "Ready?"

He lifted the bag with one hand and took Lucy's hand with his other. "Always."

"You'll come for dinner in a couple of days. We must

discuss the wedding," Ella shouted after them as Lucy hustled Joel down the hallway and out the door.

"Ciao everyone, love you. Thanks for everything. I'll touch base soon," she called over her shoulder, then shut the door behind them and groaned. "I'm sorry. They've been a lot. Thank you for rescuing me."

"My pleasure." And it was. The sensory overload that were the Barones was worth it and then some, because now he had Lucy to himself. "You look beautiful, by the way." He'd wanted to tell her earlier, but they'd been swallowed by a sea of meddling relatives almost the moment he'd arrived. Looking at her now, he admired the way her long silky hair fell down her back, and the smooth hint of shoulder that peeked out of her scooped neck shirt. He'd wanted to put his mouth there the moment he'd walked into the house and seen her.

"Thanks," Lucy said with a laugh. "My mother thinks I look like an ungrateful peasant, but I'm glad you don't agree."

"I definitely don't agree." He held her hand all the way to the car. Now that he had her, he was afraid to let go, which left him wondering who was rescuing who.

"You don't have to do this," Lucy said, once they were buckled into the car. "I know there isn't as much in it for you as there is for me, so I want you to know it's not too late to back out. I totally get it if you want to. With them." She jerked her thumb in the direction of her aunt's house. "My family, it's just going to be more of the same. Overbearing, invasive questions, and forced feedings. It's not exactly a win-win situation here, Joel."

It wasn't. This arrangement hadn't been a bargain, a tit for tat, a soul for a soul. It was more her dream for his soul, but he knew what was in it for him—her happiness. Which was all he'd ever wanted.

"We do this, and we close the circle, like we agreed. This time, when we walk away, we walk away clean. No more hiding the truth, no more secrets. When this is over, it's over and we won't have to drag this marriage around like a dirty secret anymore." He stared ahead as he said the words, feeling her gaze on the side of his face like the sun burning his cheek. "That's the win, Lucy. Closure."

Closure for her, at least.

CHAPTER SIXTEEN

"Welcome home," Joel said as he opened his Pearl District apartment's door and stepped aside so Lucy could precede him inside.

Home. When she'd come to him with this proposition several days ago, she'd never imagined she'd be moving in a few days later. But now that she was here, away from the noise of her aunt's house, it felt...nice.

"The second bedroom is made up for you," Joel said as he brought her bags in. "Come on, I'll show you."

Lucy followed him to a door at the end of the hall. "Wow," she said as she took in the spacious room. "It's big for a second bedroom."

"Yeah, they don't build them like they used to." Joel smirked when he said this, and she understood the quip.

He was putting up buildings every day. Most new buildings focused on more units with less space. Housing demands required it, but also, prioritizing units over space was profitable. And Morgan Construction excelled both in profiting and creating well laid out spaces, so the square footage was utilized to its highest potential, even if modern builds were smaller than these older apartments.

"This place was built in the sixties," he told her. "But I still can't get over them building only two units up here. I keep telling Gabe he could reno and make at least four."

Lucy fully entered the room and did a little spin. "But then you'd lose all this." The hardwood floors creaked under her feet, sending a thrill up her spine. She loved older spaces like this.

Old wood, exposed beams, all that history bleeding through the walls. How many lives had been lived in this room?

"I love the old feel of the wood under my feet, the character of the arches, and the solid framed doors. And you're wrong," she went on. "Barone & Sons builds it like they used to. Just like this, sturdy and refined. Timeless and built to last."

Joel regarded her with a raised eyebrow and a quirk on his lips.

"What?" she demanded, propping her fists on her hips. "It's true. We've increased our business a lot in the last few years doing work on furniture and doors for those big old heritage homes in San Francisco. People want the nostalgia and coziness in their hundred-year-old houses, but they don't want to compromise on quality. So they call us."

"As they should," Joel agreed.

She couldn't tell if he was teasing her or agreeing with her, but his stupidly handsome face was firing her up, so she went on. "We're the best, Joel. No contest. You should know. *Morgan Construction only hires the best*," she shot back at him with Walter Morgan's famous quote.

Joel's good-natured expression faltered. A flame lit his eyes to a metallic silver, and a serious air thickened the room as he watched her. For a few tense moments, they simply stared at each other across the room.

"Fuck, you deserve it." His rumbling tone matched the inferno of his gaze.

"Deserve what?" Her own voice wavered as his intensity consumed the room.

"Everything, Lucy. You deserve everything. But especially your father's company."

When he came closer, her heart slammed against her rib cage. The thrill of having him within touching distance sent shock waves of electricity up and down her body.

Unsure of what she wanted, she took the smallest shuffle backward. Either he didn't notice or didn't care because he took another step in her direction. The kiss they'd shared at Hope's gender-reveal party shoved its way to the forefront of her memory, and her gaze homed in on his firm lips as he pressed nearer. He was so close now she could smell every unique spicy scent of him, and her hormones went wild for it.

But for every heart-melting memory between them, there was a heart-breaking one to replace it. There'd been heat and adoration, followed by betrayal and communication breakdown. When they'd lost the one thing holding them together, everything had fallen apart. This time, she'd be careful not to get lost in his animal magnetism again.

This was bad, very, *very* bad. Her attraction to him was a storm. It always had been, and she needed to find a way to calm it if she was going to keep her sanity over the next year.

A year. She'd agreed to stay married to him for a year. And she'd been sober when she'd done it. Shit, she was screwed.

In an effort to re-establish control over the situation, she stepped away and took in the rest of the room. This time, he didn't follow her.

"Well, it's a lovely space. Gabe is right not to change it."

Joel remained silent, and she felt stripped bare as he assessed her.

When he finally spoke, she was a mess of nerves. "Gabe's done some upgrades, mostly things that help with insulation, and sound proofing with the bar downstairs. But he's not interested in adding more units. Says he has no time to manage anymore overbearing tenants."

"Hmm, overbearing. Sounds like you, Mr. Morgan."

"Mr. Morgan," Joel murmured with a laugh. "That's my father. And I haven't quite earned that honor yet."

"I'd say you've more than earned it."

How could he not think so? Apparently, he was a Forbes billionaire! But the odd insecurity in his gaze reminded her of what she'd often felt herself.

When your father was a man like Walter Morgan or Luciano Barone, well respected in the community, loved by all, a powerhouse in business—you ended up spending a lifetime trying to live up to their potential, and never quite feeling like you've made it.

She didn't have the answer for Joel. If she did, she wouldn't even be in the position she was in. So Lucy opted to lighten the mood with a joke. "Maybe you'd prefer something more suitable to your personality then, like, *Sir.*"

The designation seemed fitting, he was so damn authoritative and austere, but she realized her mistake almost instantly. The electricity in the room climbed several volts.

"I haven't earned that one yet either." His eyes flickered, two stormy swirls of promise. This wasn't business Joel talking, it was sex god Joel. He could earn any title he wanted, and he'd do so easily.

She knew it.

She swallowed and looked away, breaking the spell once more. "Um, I should unpack and—things."

"And things?" His smile reflected the things they would have gotten up to in another lifetime, but he took a step toward the door. "Old building, no ensuite. The shower is down the hall. I installed a removable head when I moved in, which you might find enjoyable." With a cheeky wink, he left the room.

CHAPTER SEVENTEEN

Lucy hadn't needed a shower but took one anyway just to give her a little breathing room from Joel and all his...Joel-ness. Purposefully, she left the removable shower head in place. The last thing she needed was for him to overhear her from down the hall.

When she emerged from the bathroom, relaxed and refreshed, a spicy scent hit her nostrils and her stomach rumbled in a reminder that it must have been dinnertime.

Sure enough, when she rounded the corner from the hallway, Joel was carrying two steaming plates to the dining room table.

An annoyingly shrewd smirk broke out on his face. "Nice shower?"

"As a matter of fact, yes." It could have been fan-fucking-tastic, but her PG version wasn't bad either.

Joel did nothing other than throw a presumptuous smile in the direction of her rosy cheeks while he set a plate on either side of the table.

"I'm glad to hear it. Hope you're hungry."

"I'm Italian. Food is life. I'll eat on demand."

He pulled out a chair for her.

She took her place in it. "Aside from homemade York-shire puddings, I don't remember you being a chef."

He smiled. "I'm not. Sarah comes once a week, stocks the fridge with groceries and simple meals. This chicken curry is one of my favorites." He poured them each a glass of wine, then sat down across from her.

"Sarah?"

"She's my housekeeper."

"Right." The Morgans had housekeepers. The Barones had Maria.

When Lucy had been growing up, her family had a cleaning lady scheduled to come once. Her mother had spent the entire day before scrubbing the house from top to bottom because she didn't want the cleaner to think the Barones were untidy. Then she'd been grossly dissatisfied with what the cleaner had done, claiming she could do better herself. That had been the single time her family had ever paid for any help.

"Oh wow, this is good," Lucy moaned after a bite. "Give Sarah my compliments."

Joel chuckled around his own bite. "You can tell her yourself. Now that you live here, you're bound to run into her. I think you'd like her." He took a sip of wine. "I sometimes wonder how much I'd have to pay her to come back to San Francisco with us, when it's time."

With us? When it's time? There was too much to unpack in that sentence, so she changed the subject. "What's this about you being on the Forbes billionaire list? Since when did building high rises in San Francisco push you to the top one hundred status?"

Joel blushed, and boy, did she ever love it. "Been googling me, Luciana?"

"You wish. Natalie was all over it this morning. She showed me the fancy black-and-white photo of you on the fancy website with the fancy numbers beside it."

"Stop it." He tossed his napkin at her. "I fucking hate it. You get on a list like that and you can't live life anymore. I never know who is talking to me because they actually care or because they're after my bank account. I hate it," he repeated before taking a big gulp of wine.

The way his shoulders tightened and glare hardened told her he truly hated being labeled with the prestigious designation. Morgan Construction had always been lucrative. The Morgans were millionaires many times over, but what they'd built was not a billion-dollar company. Or so she thought.

"How did it happen?"

Across the table, he leveled her with a challenging look, as if she already knew. But she honestly didn't, so she remained silent.

After a moment, he said, "I felt lost. There was nothing left but work. So I drowned myself in it until it consumed me. I expanded my father's business, used the money I was making from Morgan Construction to do more investing. I bought land and companies across the country, and then more internationally. I created Morgan Property Development. When that took off, I started making other investments. That's when Morgan Enterprises was born." He shrugged as if it was nothing, then took another bite of food.

"So you just worked?" she asked, dumbfounded by the dedication it must have required. "Non-stop?"

"I was good at it and the ventures paid off. So I didn't stop. But I also *couldn't* stop. Because if I did, for even one second, I would think about what I didn't have anymore.

And that void was too dark. I was afraid of what would happen if I lost myself in it."

Her chest tightened around her pounding heart. She knew what he'd been talking about. The difference was, she'd fallen into that void. The darkest dark that had stolen too much of her life until she'd found a way out. Then, she'd also fixated on work, getting to know Barone & Sons inside out, until she understood the business better than her own father. It had become her new reason.

She understood, but that didn't mean she knew what to say. What was there to say? He was right. They'd lost so much. And nothing could change that.

Swallowing hard, she pushed the food around her plate. "I'm sorry," she murmured.

"Me too." It was the most meaningful thing they'd said to each other in four years.

"I'm surprised it took this long for someone in my family to mention the billionaire thing," she told him, needing to relieve the heaviness in the air between them. The time was coming where they'd have to dive deep into what had happened between them, but she wasn't ready yet. Baby steps. She could do baby steps.

Joel sighed, seeming to understand, and she appreciated him so much in that moment. The man had the patience of a saint.

"Me too, actually. I assumed your sister would have told you at her earliest convenience."

A shadow of worry for Vanessa notched itself in her heart. As far as topics of dinnertime conversations went, they were really clinching some doozies tonight.

Joel, being Joel, picked up on her tension, because he set down his fork and asked, "How is Vanessa these days?"

Great question, didn't she wish she knew. But maybe this

was something else he could help her with. "I honestly don't know. But I'm worried about her. You know Vanessa, she's usually so—" Lucy stared at her wineglass and considered how best to describe her younger sister.

"Larger than life?" Joel supplied.

"Yes." That was the perfect description for her jet-setting model/actress sibling. "She's usually so present all the time, even when she's in another country. We text daily. FaceTime at least once a week. But that's tapered off over the last little while. I assumed she was just busy filming, but the last five days she's gone even more silent. Even after the news of our engagement, which she'd normally flip over, all I got was a text line of heart emojis. Not that I need more than that, but it's just weird for her, you know?"

Joel leaned forward, resting his forearms against the table. "It would be. I remember you two were close."

She sighed and pushed her plate aside, her appetite gone. "She's in Vancouver right now. I was planning on going there while I was on my vacation, try to convince her to come back with me for a while. A mini vacation, to reset and talk or whatever she might need. But then *this* happened." She waggled her finger between them. "And I'm not sure if I'll be able to go now. I can't explain it, I just have this sisterly gut instinct telling me she's not okay, and I won't believe otherwise until I see her for myself."

Joel sat in silence, nodding between bites of food and sips of wine as she told him more details about how her sister's communication had tapered off, how difficult she was to get a hold of now even though Vanessa basically was attached to her phone.

"I'm sorry." She huffed out a half-hearted laugh. "Long answer to a very simple question."

Joel leaned back in his seat. "Obviously not that simple.

She's your sister, and you've always been close. You're worried about her, and you're allowed to be."

Tears came out of nowhere and flooded her eyes. She lowered her gaze to her lap, not wanting him to see.

"Vancouver, you said. Canada, I'm assuming? Not the one across the bridge twenty minutes away."

She knew he was trying to lighten the mood, but—now that she'd voiced her concerns about Vanessa, and her heart had sunk like a stone—she wasn't up for faking it. "Yes, she has a side role in a paranormal drama series. She's been there for just over a year. The last time we really talked, she'd been excited that her character made it to season two."

When Joel's hand touched hers across the table, she glanced back at him.

He brushed his thumb over her knuckles as he watched her. "I'm sure she's alright. But if you want, we can go there together after the engagement party."

A heavy sigh escaped Lucy's lungs. She would have much preferred to have Vanessa at the engagement party, but she didn't want to appear ungrateful. "That would be nice."

Joel continued to regard her quietly, his fingers stroking her knuckles in a steady rhythm. Then abruptly he rose and collected her plate.

"Let me clean the dishes and then I have somewhere I want to take you."

"No, no, no. Don't you know the rules? Whoever cooks gets out of kitchen cleaning duty."

"I didn't cook. Housekeeper, remember?"

Fair enough. "Well, you warmed it up and served it."

He laughed. "How about a compromise? I wash the dishes and you dry."

"No dishwasher?" This surprised her, what with the

housekeeping and the Forbes list and all. What kind of billionaire was this guy?

"Companies don't build them like they used to remember?" he said with a smirk.

"Really? What about an in suite washer and dryer for laundry?"

"Gabe had that installed out of sheer necessity when he lived here alone with a small child constantly in need of a clean change of clothes. But for some reason, a dishwasher never ranked his list, and I wasn't planning on being here long enough so I didn't bother getting one. Besides, dishes for one aren't hard."

"Alright then, I'll dry." She followed him to the kitchen carrying their glasses. "Where are you taking me after?"

He glanced over his shoulder, eyes enigmatic. "You'll see."

CHAPTER EIGHTEEN

Joel absolutely fucking hated seeing Lucy sad. It was part of the reason he'd left four years ago, because he'd become the reason that she was miserable, and everything else he'd tried to do to fix it had failed.

But she was back in his life now, and while she was, he planned on doing everything in his power to make sure she wasn't unhappy. As he parked at their destination, he knew a few diamonds wouldn't erase her anxiety over her sister's silence, but he hoped he could at least distract her.

"Where are we going?" Lucy asked as she got out of the car.

Joel opted not to answer as he guided her along the sidewalk with one hand at the small of her back. He pulled out his phone with his other hand and tapped out a quick text. When he stopped by the small boutique shop, Lucy peered through the door.

"Is this a jewelry store?" she asked, her nose pressed against the glass. She jumped back when someone came toward them from the other side.

Moments later, a well-groomed, middle-aged man

unlocked the door and greeted them with a massive smile. "Joel, welcome." He turned to Lucy and held out his hand. "And you must be Lucy. It is so nice to meet you." When she placed her hand in his, he lifted it to his lips. "More beautiful than my friend described."

Lucy laughed before blushing Joel's favorite shade of pink.

"Dino, stop flirting with my fiancée or I'll take her somewhere else to get a ring."

"Wait, what?" Lucy's face morphed from bashful to shocked.

"Lucy, this is Dino Mastore." With a neutral smile, he gestured for her to precede him into the store. "And I think it's time my fiancée got an engagement ring from me, don't you?" Even though they were still technically married, they'd missed so many steps the first time, like a proper engagement or giving her a proper engagement ring. This time, for better or for worse, he wanted to give her everything.

Dino led him and a stunned Lucy through the store toward a long counter in the center, where he pulled out a tray of sparkling diamonds.

Lucy looked around her. "Are we the only ones here?"

"We are. Take as much time as you need," Joel reassured her.

Lucy leaned toward his shoulder so only he could hear her. "Did you have him open the store just for us?" At half past nine, the store had long since closed.

"He owed me a favor." There was no reason to go into greater detail than that. Joel liked the older man, admired his work ethic, and had bought any gift he'd needed for his mother, sister, or niece from Dino since arriving in Portland.

So when things had taken a turn with Dino's business, Joel was happy to help.

Like many other independent shop owners in town, Dino had met hard times. Rising rents, customers unwilling to pay for quality made, top of the line jewelry. Earlier that year, he'd confided in Joel that he'd probably have to close his business in a few months. Joel had a soft spot for the owner and his family. And what was a drop in the hat for him was a life-changing amount for the Mastores, so Joel offered to become a silent partner, giving Dino the money he needed to continue running his shop and feeding his family. Which is how he now owned a percentage of Mastore Jewelers and was able to get the man to open the store for him after hours.

"Tell me, Miss Lucy, what do you like? Teardrop or princess? Eternity diamonds or solitaire? I promise you at Mastore we will have whatever your heart desires."

"Oh, I don't really know," Lucy murmured shyly, glancing at the tray in front of her. Her brow furrowed as she took in the brilliant jewels.

From a past life, Joel knew that she enjoyed her jewelry, and her favorites ranged from simple and elegant to big and sparkly. Her jewelry box held a necklace and earrings for every occasion, so he knew she was salivating over the tray in front of her and trying not to.

Getting a ring was a big step, one that turned their agreement into a promise.

"Perhaps the lady likes something a little more unique?" Dino withdrew another tray from the showcase. "If these are not satisfactory."

"Oh, no, it's not that. They're all so pretty, but I've never—"

Dino set down the second tray, and Lucy gawked.

"Oh, that one, I want that one." She pointed to a beautiful round-cut diamond set on a delicate rose-gold band. It almost looked like a rosebud, with a swirl of smaller diamonds surrounding it. "Jesus, that's gorgeous."

She leaned over the counter, inspecting the ring, her wild waves of hair coming loose from her ponytail.

"I couldn't agree more," Joel murmured, not taking his eyes off her.

She'd always been the most gorgeous woman he'd ever seen, but she was breathtaking like this, when her face was lit with joy, her cheeks flushed making her skin glow the color of the band she was ogling.

"We'll take it."

Dino removed the ring from its slot and held it out to Lucy, but Joel intercepted, taking the diamond and turning to her. He caught her left hand and slipped the ring onto her finger with ease—like it had always been meant for her. The diamond sparkled against her skin, and for a heartbeat everything felt...right. When he lifted his gaze to hers, they locked, the gravity that had always existed between them making it impossible to look away.

When Dino clapped his hands, Lucy jerked as if coming out of a trance. "Perfection! The perfect ring for the perfect woman." He put the trays away as if the matter was settled.

"So, that one then?" Joel asked, letting her hand drop from his.

"It's pretty big, Joel. You don't have to. It's not nec—"

"It's done, Lucy. The ring is yours." Then, for clarity's sake, he added, "And you'll wear it, so everyone knows you're mine."

The cost was irrelevant. He could buy her anything she wanted in this store. Everything if she asked for it. But the fact that she'd be wearing what he'd given her was some-thing no money could buy.

"I'll wear it," she promised. Then whispered, "For a year."

And with those words, his heart sank as quickly as it had been lifted, because at the end of the day, Lucy had no intention of staying with him.

CHAPTER NINETEEN

The moment Lucy opened her bedroom door the next morning, she felt Joel's absence. The eerie silence was one she recognized from a different time, and she knew instantly he was gone. Not just away from the apartment, but away from her. Funny how his absence had always been more noticeable than his presence.

Why did she care? This wasn't four years ago, and he wasn't bound to her anymore. The scent of coffee coaxed her down the hall and into the kitchen. A box of fresh pastries sat next to a steaming pot, a sticky note curled off the side.

Had to leave unexpectedly for business.
Hope to be back in a day or two.
I'll be in touch.
Joel.

The car fob sat beside the box with another sticky that read: *The car is yours.*

With her disappointment tasting a lot like bitterness, she reminded herself that this time was different. Different because he owed her nothing. She had no agency over his comings and goings anymore, no right to feel slighted.

So why did she? Maybe because they'd been living together less than twenty-four hours and already he was gone, damn it.

To distract herself, she poured a massive cup of coffee, and tugged the sticky note off the pastry box, staring at the neat handwritten words. In the past, she might have sent him a cheeky text reminding him of a little thing called an iPhone, which was a perfectly good option to communicate. Especially for moneybags, such as he was. But their time for cheeky banter and teasing was history. This was fake, and she'd do better to remember that.

Truthfully, she used to love the little notes. When they'd last lived together, he'd left them all over his San Francisco penthouse. What had started out as little love notes had morphed into messages for her and the baby. A note on a glass of water with her prenatal vitamin beside it reading: *for mama and Lights* (they'd nicknamed their unborn baby Lights because they conceived in Vegas, sue them.) Or on the bathroom mirror that read: *can't wait to see you naked tonight.*

They'd lived together for sixteen weeks, and he'd left a sticky note somewhere every day. Apparently, he was back at it.

Lucy drank her coffee, ate her almond croissants, and went on with her day. Then another day. She filled her days being bombarded with wedding planning family while also trying to work remotely. Even though she was technically on holiday, she told herself she didn't want to fall behind...and she hated the thought of Nico having his hands on Barone & Sons unchecked while she and her father were in Portland.

Each morning she'd woken to an empty apartment, and no new sticky notes of explanation.

She wasn't sure if his two days had turned into two weeks or if he'd be walking through the door any minute. What she did know was that caring where Joel was and when he was coming back was not a habit she wanted to get back into, so on the Wednesday morning, the third day of his absence, she ditched her laptop, grabbed the fob to the Taycan and left him a sticky note telling him she'd be home by dinner.

Refocusing her mental energy, she navigated her way through a city she didn't know very well in a vehicle that cost more than her annual income. And that was saying something, considering she earned a very healthy salary at her father's company.

The massive diamond on her hand blinked back at her as she gripped the steering wheel. When they'd made the spontaneous decision to get married four years ago, they'd stopped at a souvenir shop beside the chapel, and Joel had bought a simple silver band with hearts engraved around it. It had cost twenty dollars, but she'd treasured that ring.

The day she finally removed it, she'd cried so hard her stomach ached the next day.

Thanks to the GPS goddess, Lucy arrived at Natalie's salon fifteen minutes later. *Natalie's Hair and Beauty* was tucked between a coffee shop and a local clothing boutique. The sleek store front and trendy signage was eye catching and inviting, and Lucy felt a surge of pride for her younger cousin. While most twenty-something's were dabbling in dead-end jobs, traveling, or generally trying to figure life out, Natalie had taken her talent, combined it with her guts and created a business that had turned out to be both popular and successful.

As Lucy walked in the front door, she admired the glossy, elegant décor. Natalie had done a bit of a redesign since Lucy had last visited and there was an elite, sophisticated air to the space. All but one of the five well-lit stations were occupied. Stylists worked and chattered at each chair.

"Good morning," a young man greeted her cheerfully from behind the front desk. One side of his head was shaved, while a glossy dark-purple sheet of hair fell down the other side. He tapped on the MacBook in front of him, his nails matching the color of his hair. "Do you have an appointment or are you a walk-in?"

"Neither. I'm here to see my cousin, Natalie. I have no appointment, but she said she'd give me a trim, so I guess I'm a walk in."

The stylist gave her hair a once over, his professional eye probably picking apart everything including how she'd finger combed her hair before pulling it into a ponytail secured with a rubber band.

After a moment of blank faced scrutiny, he grinned widely. "You must be Luciana! Nat said you'd be stopping in. I see the family resemblance now." He pushed off his chair and held out his hand. "I'm Colin. Nice to meet you." He pumped Lucy's hand a couple of times. "She went to the cafe to pick up a round of treats and lattes, but she won't be long. Come, you should definitely sit in her chair. She'll die when she sees you in it."

"Well, die is a bit of an exag—" But Lucy didn't bother finishing her sentence, as Colin was already several paces ahead of her.

He patted the chair, and Lucy took his lead, plopping onto the seat. He met her gaze in the mirror. "Do you mind?" he asked, gesturing to her ponytail.

Lucy nodded. "Go for it."

Colin's grimace deepened as he gingerly tried to unwrap the rubber band. "God Lord, honey, I should have used scissors."

The tie snagged on her hair, and she winced.

"You know these things are meant to tie up bundles of mail and not your stunning mane, right?"

"Yeah." Lucy winced again as he tugged. "I grabbed it out of my—" Her what? Roommate, friend, husband? "My fiancé's junk drawer this morning. I couldn't find my scrunchy and got desperate. It's scorching today, and I wanted it off my neck."

"Scrunchy," he muttered through a chuckle. He squinted at her hair as he untangled the last of the elastic and let her locks tumble down around her shoulders. He caught her gaze in the mirror with a satisfied smile. "Promise me you'll never put a rubber band into this glorious hair ever again. It's criminal."

Lucy laughed. "Promise."

"So, you're engaged? Are you seeing Nat for an up-do consultation?"

"She's seeing me, because I'm her favorite cousin," Natalie said as she came up behind Colin holding a massive pink cardboard box. "And if she doesn't let me do her up-do for her wedding, she will be disowned." She shimmied her hips until they nudged against Colin. "Shoo. You don't get to stand in my spot."

Colin playfully stuck out his tongue at Natalie as he relieved her of the box and pried it open. "I've so been waiting for this." He presented the box to Lucy.

Inside was an array of fancy donuts. One was topped with full-sized Oreos, another was covered in thick choco-late shavings, and one appeared to have bacon bits sprinkled on the icing. Every one of them were frosted to the hilt with bright, shimmering sugar.

"Bride gets first pick," Colin said with a smile.

Another stylist approached them. Beautiful braids cascaded down her back. Some were black, and others were dyed turquoise with a stunning ombre effect where they faded to a lighter shade at the tip. They almost shimmered, like a mermaid tale.

"The gooey fudge is my favorite." She reached into the box, and Lucy's mouth fell open. The woman had the longest bright-pink fingernails she's ever seen, but she plucked out a donut with caramel icing without any difficulty, so she must have been used to them. "I'll leave it for you, bride," she said with a wink.

"Oh, I—"

All eyes were on her, the donut box looming in front of her.

"I think I'll pass. Need to fit into the wedding dress and all."

Turquoise braids threw back her head and laughed, a loud sound that reminded Lucy of a late-night lounge singer. "Oh bestie, you don't fit the dress. The dress fits you. Take the fudge, you won't regret it."

Lucy's gaze shifted to Natalie, who nodded at her.

Conceding, Lucy dug into the box. When everyone had a donut in hand, the three stylists circled behind Lucy's chair and stared at her head.

"Okay, people," Natalie said. "We have an engagement party in five days. What are we doing?"

"Keep her hair down," Colin said with a decisive nod.

"Oh no, with this volume and natural curl, it needs to be up like a crown on her beautiful head," mermaid hair insisted. "She's a queen. She should look like one."

"Really, Brit? I was thinking about an elegant, understated twist. After all, this is Lucy." Natalie took a huge bite of her sugar encrusted jelly donut.

Mermaid hair, Brit, slammed Natalie with a look that made Lucy's bite her lip. "What do you mean 'this is Lucy'? Lucy is a *bride*. *Brides* are *Queens*. Queens wear *crowns*."

"Yeah, but Lucy is understated. She's not one for the limelight. Are you, Lu?"

Three sets of eyes stared at her expectantly. Lucy knew her cousin meant it kindly and not to insult her. This refrain was familiar in their families. Lucy, the understated one, the good girl, the obedient daughter.

And she was an out of the limelight kind of girl, because that's who her family expected her to be. It was partly her own fault she'd let their perception of her eclipse her real identity and ambition, but that wasn't why she couldn't imagine being the queen Brit was describing.

She liked a little bling and glamour as much as the next Italian girl, but she couldn't afford to lose sight of the fact that her engagement to Joel was not the real thing. This wasn't some special occasion where she bought her dream dress and had her dream day with all her dream trimmings. She was nobody's queen. Sitting in this chair with three hair artists assessing her like she was a lump of clay for their molding suddenly felt ridiculously farcical.

"Natalie's right. I don't want to make a big deal out of this. It's just another day."

Brit's eyeballs practically bugged out. "Just another day? Just *another* day?!" She tipped back her head and released a loud breath. "Why do you send me the difficult ones?" she asked the ceiling. Then she straightened and lifted a single finger, her long fingernail sharp and pointy. "No."

She waggled her finger from side to side, and Lucy followed it in the mirror like she was being hypnotized.

"This is not just another day. This is your day. This is the beginning of a new era. An era where you are a queen and you look like one, talk like one, and live like one." Brit's voice rose above the other noise in the salon. She waved her hands animatedly, putting most of the Italians Lucy had ever met to shame. "Bestie, look at me."

Lucy's gaze snapped up, obeying Brit's commanding voice.

Colin murmured under his breath, "Here she goes." Then he squeezed Lucy's shoulder in a supportive gesture.

Natalie came around on her other side to hold her hand. Brit straightened to her fullest height behind the chair, filling the whole space of the mirror. Lucy felt like she was in the presence of a genie who'd been released from a thousand years trapped in a bottle.

"I'm telling you that you are going to manifest your greatest self. You will manifest queen energy, aura, *and* hair fit for royalty." Brit snapped her three-inch nails with a loud resonating *snap*.

Two women appeared beside her.

"Jess, Lynn, this is Queen Lucy. We are doing full hair and makeup today. Think big, think power, think badass bitch who makes a man the kind of Mister who wants to spend the rest of his days worshipping the ground she walks on."

Jess and Lynn started arranging trays with brushes, color palettes and hair styling supplies.

Brit raked her nails under Lucy's hair, gathering the mass and propping it on top of Lucy's head. "Think goddess who owns her fine-ass curves. Who drinks champagne and eats charcuterie. Who wears Dolce and Gabbana like it's her job. We're gonna immerse her in beauty Queen energy so thick her man and every other person in the room won't be able to look anywhere else." Brit met Lucy's gaze in the mirror. "Are you waxed or lasered?"

"Uh…" She was pretty sure that *neither* was the wrong answer.

Sure enough, Brit closed her eyes and gave a small shake of her head, then turned to the stylist on her right. "Jess, clear your afternoon, looks like we need the works."

Lucy looked helplessly at her cousin, who shrugged.

"This is why I give her a chair, hon. She works magic like no one in this city. By the time she's done with you, you'll see a version of yourself you never knew existed."

CHAPTER TWENTY

ucy spent the next four hours under Brit and Natalie's complete mercy. After Brit, who was an award-winning colorist, had her in foils for a good chunk of the afternoon, Natalie snipped Lucy's hair with precise confident clips, while chatting casually about family, weddings, and how grateful she was that at least now the limelight was deflected off her for another few months. Lucy sat in her chair, mute for the most part, as the flurry of salon activity buzzed around her.

Later, she emerged from a little room down the hall after being well and truly tortured by the aesthetician named Jess, whom Lucy was pretty sure had waxed every single hair off her body, except that on her head. Lynn handed her a thin flute of golden bubbly liquid as she walked back into the main salon, and despite herself Lucy had to admit, she could get used to being pampered this way.

Brit was right. It did feel good primping and preening, to be given the permission to look and feel your finest. For the first time, she understood why her sister invested all the time and energy into her looks. It felt *good*.

Thinking about Vanessa brought the usual pang of longing and worry. She'd wished her sister could see her now. When they were little, Vanessa always begged to do makeup on Lucy. Sometimes she'd cave, and they'd sit in Vanessa's bedroom, on the bed littered with tubes of concealer and palettes of makeup.

They'd had some of their best conversations during those times, commiserating over family dramatics and their dreams for the future. Vanessa had always supported Lucy's wish of taking over Barone & Sons, even if she hadn't understood it. Much like Lucy supported Vanessa's thirst for adventure and fame—even if she didn't always think it was what was best for her.

"Shut the front door." Vanessa's voice echoed through the salon like Lucy's nostalgia had conjured her. "Nat, who is this stunning creature who looks like my sister, walks like my sister, but has the freshly shaped eyebrows of a goddess?"

Lucy blinked in the direction of the voice. Vanessa stood by the front door, suitcase in hand, hair in a sleek high ponytail, immense black sunglasses pushed down her nose as she peered over top with wide, expressive brown eyes, rimmed with thick dark lashes. Her cherry-red lips glistened in the bright light of the salon. A twenty-first century picture of Audrey Hepburn.

"Vanessa?" Lucy shot from her chair, shock and elation catapulting her toward her younger sister, who met her halfway and jumped into her arms, nearly bowling her over. She inhaled Vanessa's expensive, signature scent and tried to absorb the shock that she was in her cousin's hair salon. "What on earth are you doing here?"

Vanessa reared back and whipped off her sunglasses to shoot Lucy a look she'd seen many times in her life. Part affronted, part pout. "What am I doing here? Where else am I supposed to be when my big sister sends me a *text message*," she said these two words in a deeply accusatory tone, "telling me she is engaged to the Western Hemisphere's most eligible bachelor, followed up by a super melodramatic call from Mom telling me there's an engagement party in Portland on Saturday for my sister, and I better not embarrass the family by missing it."

"Mom made you come here?" Lucy's gaped because, heck, that was unexpected.

"Made me? Sissy, she threatened to disown me. But I have to say she didn't have to work too hard to convince me. I wouldn't miss this for the world."

Something about that statement didn't ring right to Lucy, since Vanessa had expertly avoided her messages the last few days. But Vanessa hugged her again, wrapping her arms around Lucy like a bow—so Lucy pushed the inkling that something didn't feel right aside and hugged her sister back fiercely.

She'd missed her sister, and knowing the craziness that would be coming up this weekend for the engagement party, she felt instantly better knowing Vanessa would be by her side. Her sister lived for the limelight, knew how to work magic in it. Lucy avoided it like the plague.

When they pulled apart, Vanessa was blurry-eyed and had a big ole smile on her face. "I missed you, Lu, you have no idea how much."

They weren't hugging anymore, but Vanessa still had her arm draped over Lucy's shoulders, and from that vantage point, Lucy took a closer look at her sister. Exhaustion was etched around her eyes, even under the meticulously applied makeup, and professionally curated eyebrows and lashes. Dark shadows hollowed out her cheek bones. She stared intently, trying to piecemeal what could have her sister appearing so...bone-weary.

"How'd you get here?"

Vanessa shrugged. "Caught a flight."

"And how'd you know I was here, at the salon?"

Pulling back completely, Vanessa laughed as she moved toward Natalie who was plugging in a curling iron. "What is this? The third degree? Geez, Lu, I wanted to be here for you, okay? And to answer your question, I didn't know," she said as she busied herself rifling through the supplies at Natalie's station. "I came here to avoid going to Zia's madhouse for as long as I could, and to see Nat, of course," she added hastily when their cousin gave Vanessa the evil eye. "So, I texted to say I was on my way, and lo and behold, you're sitting in the chair looking like you belong on the cover of *Elle Magazine*. Looks like I came in time to do your makeup."

"I don't need makeup. In fact, I don't need any of this." Lucy ran her hand over her new silky hair. "The wedding date hasn't even been set, and the engagement party isn't for another couple of days."

Natalie and Vanessa exchanged a look, having a full conversation telepathically that Lucy was not privy to.

"What?" she demanded, not trusting the smug looks on either of their faces.

"Well, Brit put so much effort in, and when I realized Vanessa would be here too, I figured we shouldn't let any of this go to waste." Natalie gestured down the length of Lucy's newly primped, preened, and plucked body. "So I put the word out to get some girls together."

"Get some girls together?" Lucy parroted. She didn't know any girls to get together. What was her cousin planning?

"Let's call it a practice bachelorette party," Natalie said, guiding Lucy back into her chair.

The moment her butt hit the leather seat, Brit descended on her with a hot iron. "You cannot let my fine talent go to waste," Brit insisted, wrapping a strand of Lucy's hair around the hot wand. "Go out and make them all fall at your feet. Queen energy, right babe?"

Lucy looked helplessly at Natalie in the mirror. Natalie shrugged and Vanessa appeared in front of Lucy, holding what looked like a massive toolbox.

"Come on, Lu. The Barone sisters together again, looking like sex on a popsicle stick? We gotta go out. We'll call it a girls' night if it makes you feel better." Vanessa dabbed liquid cream on the four points of Lucy's face, then went at it with a big makeup blender. "Besides, with you there, what could possibly go wrong?"

CHAPTER TWENTY-ONE

By eight o'clock, Joel was ready to lose his ever-loving mind. He'd come home at noon to a sticky note from Lucy saying she was out visiting her cousin and would be home around dinnertime.

Now, seven hours later, he sat at the dining room table trying to concentrate on the figures on his laptop, but his eyes kept wandering to the note stuck to the table beside him. Lucy's chaotic, loopy handwriting stared back at him.

Back at dinnertime.

Even considering that people ate at different times, and Italians generally ate later, eight o'clock would still be considered past dinnertime. Right?

His unavoidable trip had taken longer than expected, and what he'd hoped would only be one night had become two. They'd only spent one full day living together in this apartment, but damn, he missed her. And it annoyed him how much he did knowing she planned to leave as soon as their year was finished.

It didn't bode well for his self-preservation, this pining and making himself totally vulnerable to her again. And now she wasn't coming home for dinnertime like her sticky note said she would. He couldn't fucking take it.

With a gruff sigh, Joel shoved his seat back and took off the glasses he only wore when he was staring at a computer screen for too long. He loosened another button on his white-collar shirt. He'd discarded his tie hours earlier. He'd come straight from the airport to the apartment, only to find it empty, and the attempt to distract himself by catching up on the work he'd fallen behind on had clearly failed because other than burning out his old man eyes, he hadn't gotten much done.

He picked up his phone for the hundredth time, thumbing to her contact, and checked messages. Nothing. Four years ago, she would have texted regularly, but apparently the Lucy of today did not. His fingers hovered over the message icon. The Joel of four years ago would have sent her a message by now asking when she'd be home or if she needed a ride or...

Quickly he tapped out a brief message.

> I'm home. Let me know if you need to be
> picked up from anywhere.

The car fob was gone, so he knew she took the car. But he wanted her to know she could call on him if she was stranded somewhere for any reason. Because if she was stuck somewhere in a city she was unfamiliar with, alone while it was getting dark... His chest tightened with anxiety. He knew all too well the harm that could come to women, his experience with Ivy had taught him that, and the thought of any harm coming to Lucy made him want to put a bodyguard on her twenty-four-seven. Better yet, she could never leave his side, that would work too. He glared at his phone willing those three dots to start blinking. Nothing.

By eight forty-five he was considering driving around the city until he found her, when his phone buzzed. His hand flew out so quickly he nearly knocked his glass of water over.

> The guys are at the bar if you want to come
> down for a drink.

Gabe. Not who he was hoping to hear from. Digging his fingers through his hair, he stared at his phone. It was either sit here and wait for God knows how long or go down to the bar and try to distract himself with friends. With a heavy sigh, he shut his laptop and set his glasses on the table. He could use a Scotch.

A few minutes later, he walked through the side door that separated Bowie's from the apartments and headed toward the front. Gabe was drawing beers behind the bar while Sean and his brother Jordan sat on the other side, sipping their drinks. Joel plopped down on a bar stool beside them.

"Sometimes it's nice living a flight of stairs away from a drink, huh?" Sean slid a bowl of pretzels Joel's way. "Beats sulking alone in your apartment."

"Who says I was sulking?" Joel tossed a pretzel in his mouth.

"The frown that's burned into your forehead kind of gives you away, my friend," Gabe said.

Two fingers of Scotch slid under his nose, and he tipped his head in gratitude toward his brother-in-law, who knew his taste well by now. He took a swallow, savoring the warm burn of liquid.

"What do you do when you get a note in the morning

saying, 'be home by dinner' and then nothing else all day?" He caught the look that passed between Gabe and Sean. "What?"

Sean's lower lip stuck out as he shook his head. "Nothing."

"Bullshit. Explain that look?" Joel waggled his finger between the two men. "You guys know something. Spill it."

Gabe busied himself wiping down the bar while Sean took a long sip of beer and became fascinated with a piece of art on the other side of the wall.

Joel leaned forward and caught Jordan's eye. Sean's brother was a massive motherfucker, built like a beast, and scary as hell when you first looked at him. But as it turned out, Jordan was a quiet introvert. He tended to mind his own business and keep a low profile. Like right now, as he sat hunched over his soda.

"Jordan, what are these losers not telling me?"

Jordan shrugged. "Why should I know? The only reason I'm sitting here is because this guy"—he jerked his thumb at his brother—"made me come out tonight."

Gabe's jaw dropped. "It is freaking scary how well you can lie."

Joel whipped his head to glare at his brother-in-law.

"Come on man!" Sean leaned over the bar and gave Gabe a shove. "You just gave us away. I knew you would."

"Shit, sorry. It's scary though, right? Like he didn't even flinch." Gabe gestured to Jordan, who still stared into his soft drink. "You should play poker."

"No thanks," Jordan mumbled.

"Okay, that's it, someone tell me what's up or I will buy this place and turn it into a Garden Center."

"Jesus, no need to get nasty," Gabe chided. "Nothing's up. The girls are out, that's all."

"What girls? Out where? Is Lucy with them?" His questions tumbled out in a wave of relief.

"Well, Ivy is with them. I think her hairdresser too, and Lucy's sister, maybe," Sean told him.

"Vanessa," Joel supplied.

"That's the one," Sean said. "Ivy was excited to get to know your fiancée better, and apparently her sister is a famous model or something, so she wanted to meet her. Anyway, they went to Silk."

"Silk?" Joel leaned forward. "That nightclub across the river." Techno music and strobe lights didn't sound like Lucy's style. At least not the Lucy from four years ago. Then again, a drunken Vegas wedding hadn't sounded like her either.

"They're fine. Jordan is a bouncer there twice a week. He put a guy on it. Anything off happens and we'll know," Sean reassured.

Jordan grunted in assent.

A guy on it? What the hell did that mean? What guy? He gulped down the rest of his Scotch. He didn't like the idea of some random bouncer in charge of his wife's safety.

"Trust me, my friend. You do not want to go over there and interrupt their night," Gabe said, reading his mind.

"Don't I?"

"You absolutely do not," Sean agreed. "I get it, I do. I, myself, have been there and done that. They don't like it. Don't mess with girls' night unless they allow it."

Joel didn't like it.

"They're usually home before midnight," Gabe reassured him as he filled his Scotch glass again. "Just distract yourself in the meantime."

Right, easy. He'd been distracting himself for four years. What was a few more hours?

CHAPTER TWENTY-TWO

At 12:03 a.m. Joel heard his front door click unlocked. He'd stayed at Bowie's for an hour, had two drinks, brooded the entire time, then headed back upstairs. Work had always been his best distraction, so he opened his laptop, put his glasses back on, and made a few more million.

And that was where he was when Lucy sauntered into the living room.

"Fuck me." The words flew from his mouth as he took her in over the frame of his glasses.

She halted abruptly, the surprise on her face mirroring the shock exploding through his chest. Maybe it was the late hour, or the tension headache building behind his eyes, or the sheer relief of finally seeing her again, but the way she looked—cheeks glowing, hair a wild mass around her shoulders, plump lips parted enticingly and painted a glossy red to match her dress—had his heart caving inward.

The red satin hugged her curves like a second skin, swooping low at her breasts, and riding high on her thighs. The only thing that appeared to be keeping it on her fucking stunning body were two thin straps over the shoulders.

"Oh," she said breathily, as she came toward him. The wobble in her strut told him she'd either had a bit too much to drink or hadn't walked in heels in a while. Knowing Lucy, it was probably both. "I didn't expect you to wait up."

"I wanted to make sure you got home safely."

"Well, the car you sent to pick us up made sure of that." Her purse strap slipped off her shoulder, and she teetered again when she moved to set it on the corner of his desk. "Thank you for that. Vanessa didn't want to take an Uber."

When she wobbled again, he jumped up and caught her elbow before she toppled. Her body swayed against his, and her scent hit him like a two-by-four traveling directly to his dick. He clenched his jaw as he struggled to regain some dominion over himself and the situation. Everything about this woman threatened the one thing he'd always counted on—his control. He'd lost it with her time and time again. He couldn't afford to do it now.

"Oh no, no, no, no, no. Not fair. I'm supposed to be mad at you." She tugged her arm out of his hold. "You can't use your sexy professor glasses and jaw clench on me like that. I've no armor against them, and you know it, especially not after a few martinis."

The bitterness in her tone ignited his own memories of Vegas and everything after. It all passed silently between them like ammunition.

He bent to bring his gaze level with hers, and pinned her with a stare, daring her to read his recollection of past events in his eyes. "From where I'm standing, Luciana. You're not the one who needs a defense."

To his surprise, her expression softened, and she let out a long sigh. It brushed his lips like a curse. "See, Joel, it's even the way you say things. You can't help it; it's the way you are. Everything about you screams *Have sex with me. I promise it'll be the best you've ever had.*"

She swayed toward him and slapped her hand on his chest, the softness morphing into an instant irritation. But he could keep up with her vacillating temperament. He felt the same at the moment. Everything all at once, all the time.

"And then it freaking is! It's the best sex. *And* I remember it all too well. Every touch, every sensation. It's like an ache I can't ease, an itch I can't reach." She inhaled a breath and gazed up at him, eyes widening, pupils dilating.

He watched the idea bloom in her mind. *Oh fuck.*

"Can you reach it, Joel?" She leaned toward him, tipping her chin up. Her lips brushed his ear as she whispered, "Or are you a better man these days? Too noble to have a little temporary fling." She drew back sharply, gasping like she couldn't believe she'd just used her outside voice.

But he could. Pain lanced his chest and he welcomed it, because finally, finally, she was admitting what he always knew she believed about him—that he'd abandoned her when she'd needed him most. And she'd never forgiven him.

"I'm sor—" Her cheeks flushed and her glossy lips quivered as she tried to step out of his reach.

He grabbed her wrist, preventing her retreat. "You're angry." He waited until her gaze shifted away from his, her sign of acquiescence. Then he jerked her wrist up, so her ring finger sat front and center between them, the diamond he'd given her blinding. "But you're still wearing this."

Her eyes flashed with resentment, the previous regret evaporating.

"And as long as you're wearing it, Luciana, I will send cars to pick you up. I will wait until you get home. I will make sure your coffee is hot every morning. I will move heaven and earth," he growled, his own misery manifesting. "But I won't fuck you. Not until you're not angry anymore. And not until you understand."

Lucy forcefully yanked her hand out of his and took a step back. This time, he let her go. He'd said what he needed to say.

"There are a lot of reasons we shouldn't have sex, Joel."

"There are."

"We've barely spoken in four years."

"For one thing."

"And we haven't talked about..." She glanced away. "Anything."

"We will," he promised.

"And this is all a sham." She fluttered her hand between them.

"For now." If she caught his mumbled words, she didn't show it.

"But I wasn't expecting to come home to you and your stupid sexy glasses, because you've been gone for three days straight."

That's what this really was about. She was angry at him for leaving—because he'd left before, and their world had upended. He should tell her why, tell her where he'd been and what he'd been doing. But that might also make it worse.

"You know," she said, eyeing him suggestively. "Angry sex is the best sex."

Christ, his fingertips were tingling. He was so ready to rip the red excuse for a dress off her body. He'd take her up against the wall, and make it so good for her. His body was at full attention, his cock screaming at him to do as she was asking. "We've never had angry sex, Luciana."

When the anger came, there'd been no sex at all. Only silence.

Lucy leaned in, red lips pouting. "There's always a first time."

There was absolutely no way he could continue this conversation, not when she was eating him alive. A one-eighty was required. "How about a shower?"

"Together?"

"No, Lucy. Just you. Alone."

Laughter rolled out of her completely without humor, and when she advanced, every muscle in his body tensed. "You want me to take a shower all by myself, Joel?" she purred as she edged closer, brushing her body to his, leaning in as her lips touched his jawline. "Will you be out here thinking of me under the steaming water? Naked and wet."

If she was trying to prove a point, she'd made it when she'd first entered the apartment. He wanted her. He'd never stopped.

"Luciana," he groaned. She was so close the scent of her made his mouth water.

"Mmm," she moaned. "I love when you say my name like that. Like I'm a sin that you want to commit." She looked up at him, her eyes suddenly shiny and vulnerable, the mask falling off. "Do you remember how it was, Joel? Between us?"

He caught her by the shoulders and dragged himself away. His control had been frayed since she walked back into his life, and now it was snapping. "You know I do. I remember every fucking second in vivid detail. The minute I left, I wanted to come back. But it's not about me, it's you. It's always been you, Lucy." He held her gaze prisoner until he was sure the words had absorbed into every brain cell.

"And that's why you're going to go take a long shower before you tuck yourself into bed."

Of all the reactions he expected from her, the livid anger flashing through her eyes was not one of them.

"Fine, Joel Morgan. You sit out here like a good boy and suffer your blue balls for the sake of your pride. I'll be in my room."

With a decisive twirl away from him, she sashayed down the hall toward her bedroom like she was on a mission.

CHAPTER TWENTY-THREE

What was it about honorable men that made her blood boil? On paper, Joel was perfect. Rich, powerful, competent, among many other things. He held a silent gravity that everyone respected and was drawn to.

But there'd been a cost. Perfection was his biggest flaw, and he'd created a lonely world for himself. He was always thinking of what was best for others, living his life making sure everyone else was happy.

Once upon a time she'd cracked that veneer, seen him take what he wanted and needed. Then it vanished almost as quickly as it came, and he'd gone back to being the immaculate version of himself. The version that couldn't hurt anybody.

The fool was too honorable for his own good. He'd totally killed her buzz. Why did he have to send a car for her, or wait up, wearing those stupid sexy glasses, no less? How dare he turn her on when she was mad at him. It was infuriating.

Damn his moral compass. If he could only see her now rummaging through her suitcase for the vibrator she'd packed. Fricking glasses. Fricking jaw flex. Fricking gorgeous, reasonable man.

The silicone vibrator was tucked discreetly in an inside pocket, a trusted travel companion. Using it didn't usually result in anything dramatic, but the way her lust raced through her now, like a firecracker ready to go off, she wondered if she should find a way to gag herself to keep from screaming.

She moved to the mirrored dresser. Maybe there was a tie or something she could use. But when she caught sight of herself in the mirror, she faltered. Hours later, the magic Brit, Nat, Vanessa, and the crew at the salon had worked was still breathtaking—even to her self-critical eyes. The dress her sister let her borrow, the hair, the make-up, the desire heightening the color on her cheekbones.

She ran her fingers across her breasts, enjoying the contrast of her soft flesh and firm nipples that pebbled under her touch. Her sister was several sizes smaller than her, so this dress was tight in all the right places. She wasn't without body image issues, but overall, she loved the way she looked. Her curves, the olive-colored skin that conveyed her heritage, even the ample curve of her behind. For years society had been telling her that she should lose at least ten pounds, but she learned from her sister that meeting those expectations came at a high cost and few of the rewards it promised. So she took her ten extra pounds and enjoyed them.

She slipped her finger under her dress's thin shoulder strap. The lingering warmth of alcohol and unsated lust made her bold. With zero shame, she let the strap fall off her shoulder, so the neckline lowered, exposing her areola. Her over-sensitized skin ached with need. She'd had enough of suffering. If Joel wouldn't give her what she wanted, she'd give it to herself.

Flicking on the vibrator, she rolled her nipple through the fabric of her dress with her left hand, while slipping the vibrator under the hem with her right. When the humming silicone met her wet flesh, she inhaled sharply. God, it felt so good to be touched, even by her own hand.

She was so wired she knew she wouldn't last long, especially as she took in the sight of herself. Masturbating in front of a mirror when you looked like a goddess was sexy as fuck. Ten out of ten recommended.

"Ahh!" Her moan rang long and loudly through the empty room. Her pulsing need built to a fever pitch, electric waves of pleasure coursing down her legs. She wished it was Joel touching her, pinching her nipples just short of discomfort like he'd used to do, bringing her to the edge of agony but never quite over it.

Closing her eyes, she imagined it was his body giving her pleasure, his demanding, dominant sex-god persona taking over both of them in the bedroom. Oh, the bliss he'd shown her. The heights he'd taken her too. What she wouldn't give to have him doing that to her now. Who cared if she was mad at him? She still wanted him to fuck her into oblivion.

As her breath caught in the telltale mark of her crescendo rising to its peak, a thump on the door broke her concentration.

"Lucy!" The voice on the other side was gruff and strained. "Dammit. I know what you're fucking doing. I can hear you."

With a wicked smile curling her lips, she pressed the vibrator deeper between her legs, her inner demon coming out to play. Maybe he wasn't so honorable, and she wasn't the good girl everyone wanted her to be.

Pouting, she watched herself in the mirror. "Go away, Joel," she whined. "I'm not in the mood to play games, not when I'm this close."

Another hard thump hit the door, a single fist banging the frame. Or maybe it was his head. Who knew?

"Dammit, Lucy. What are you doing to me?"

Tasting victory in his defeat, she couldn't help but smile. "Come in and find out. No one is stopping you."

Silence. She knew he was running every possible scenario through his head. The pros and cons of each. What he should do, what he wanted to do, and what he was going to do. The consequences of everything. That was how Joel's mind worked. Nothing he did was without endless reasoning. Which was why it hurt so much when he'd left, because for whatever reason, he'd considered being away from her the best course of action.

The silence stretched so long, and the throb between her legs increased with every passing beat. God, she was close. But she needed more.

Open the door and come to me, she silently begged. She couldn't hold off much longer, and she whimpered loudly as the ache grew.

The door flew open. Her gaze snapped to his, and if she could have freeze-framed the look on his face as he took her in, she would have. The tick in his tight jaw, the burn in his eyes, the heat she could almost see radiating off his body. What a picture he made. His powerful body tensed with need.

His chest expanded as he inhaled deeply. "Did you think I was going to chill on the couch and scroll Netflix to the sounds of you fucking yourself in the bedroom?"

When she smiled, his frown deepened.

"You did this on purpose."

"I didn't do anything on purpose except try to take the edge off of this...lingering energy I have. If my husband can't satisfy my needs, what else am I supposed to do?"

He stalked over to her, his long legs easily eating the distance, and even though she could never fear him, a thrill shivered through her. His intensity filled the room. His fists clenched at his sides, his silver gaze fixed and determined. He was hungry, after all.

He stopped behind her, his body close enough that his heat surrounded her, but not so close that they were touching. The vibrator continued to make a low buzzing sound. She met his gaze in the mirror. After a moment of scrutiny, he shoved his hands in his pockets and cocked his head to the side, calculating. The boss was back in control.

What was he going to do? His casual perusal of her body, like she was a piece of artwork that he was considering investing in, was turning her on to a breaking point.

When his gaze had ravished her body multiple times over, he met her eyes in the reflection. "Take the other strap off."

She remembered that tone from years ago when they'd been together this way. The gears had shifted, and Joel was in control now, but the satisfaction was all hers.

Slowly, like a languid lioness, she trailed her finger up her arm, enjoying the tickle as she took her time making her way to the strap. When she got there, she kept her eyes fixed on his, as she dragged the thin ribbon down her shoulder. It fell to her elbow, pulling the material down with it. Her breasts were decent-sized, big and swollen enough to keep the material from falling all the way down. She was exposed, but not naked, her nipples peeking out of the thin fabric, desperate to make an appearance.

"Touch them. They're aching for it. I can see it from here."

That was absolutely accurate. They were aching, but not for her touch.

"You touch them," she whispered, her voice so thick and raspy she wasn't sure he'd understand her.

"Luciana." The single word, a warning that carried a threat and a promise.

She'd challenged him in the bedroom before, and he'd punished her for it, but never in a way that truly hurt. Joel Morgan's brand of punishment was one she'd take any day of the week. But she knew the pleasure would be greater tonight if she played it his way, so she clamped her fingers around the swollen peak of her nipple. Her inhale was sharp as the bite of ecstasy shot to her throbbing core.

"Run the vibrator over your other nipple," he commanded, and she complied.

The vibrator buzzed along her skin, flicking the material entirely off her breast. She let the bullet purr over the distended bud, massaging her breast as it moved. Any second now, she'd start panting.

"You're beautiful. You see it, don't you?" Stepping closer so his chest brushed her back, Joel lifted half of her hair over her shoulder. "See it and tell me."

She stared at her reflection. She hardly recognized this wanton version of herself, uninhibited, in killer heels, loosely curled hair, and smoking lipstick, with a vibrator massaging her breast—she felt fan-fucking-tastic.

"I see it," she panted. "I'm beautiful." All flushed skin, swollen lips, eyes glazed over with desire, breasts full and heavy.

"Fucking gorgeous," he murmured against her ear, and he might as well have licked her clit for all the pleasure his voice sent there. "Move the vibrator under your dress, Lucy. Let it touch where you need it."

"I need you!" she cried, her voice thick with desperation. She wanted to chuck the damned vibrator out the window and replace it with his hands, his body. The need to feel the weight of him on her, in her, was so great she was ready to do anything for it.

"Put the vibrator on your clit," he told her, his voice rasping against her ear. "Rub it there until you come. I won't touch you until you do." His voice had taken on the sharp edge of demand and she knew he meant what he said.

So she did as instructed. The second the vibrator hit her most sensitive aching flesh, her knees gave.

"Joel!" She gasped as the intensity of sensation rolled over her. Her legs buckled, and she started to fall, but Joel caught her under her breasts, easing them both down to the floor on their knees, his straddling hers, his chest pressed firmly against her back. Deftly, he moved his hand over hers, then lower, sinking two fingers into her and pumping them in a forward motion, his palm pressing the vibrator harder against her flesh.

She orgasmed on a scream of relief so loud the patrons at Bowie's probably heard it, but she didn't care. In ecstasy, her head fell back onto his shoulder, her body clenching and convulsing. Her sweet relief was so acute it was nearly painful. Her shout melted into moans, and she sagged against him, gasping. One strong arm was still banded around her torso, while the hand that had just been inside her, skimmed up her chest before looping loosely around her neck.

He gently tilted her head to the side so his mouth

brushed her ear. "Your husband satisfies your needs every time. Remember that."

Nothing and no one had ever made her feel this limp and relaxed. She was certain the tension emanating from Joel's body was the only thing holding her upright. The entire muscled wall of his chest flexed against her back with every hard breath he took. She shifted slightly, taking some pressure off her knees and when she did, there was no mistaking the iron hard length of him poking her back.

Joel's raging erection was climbing her spine, and as her own world cleared, a smile found its way to her lips. Because now it was her turn to play.

CHAPTER TWENTY-FOUR

His decision was made. He wasn't losing Lucy. Whatever it took, whatever it cost, he wasn't letting her slip through his fingers again. Having her fall apart so violently and beautifully in his arms had sealed the deal.

When this started thirteen days ago, she'd wanted her father's company and he'd wanted to atone for failing her four years ago. Those things were still true, but now his mindset had shifted and locked in. He wanted to make up for what he'd done, *and* he wanted to keep her. Forever.

Nothing could have prepared him for the detonation that occurred when Lucy gave in to her pleasure. How had he lived so long without this? Having her lax and limp against him as if she was content to fall asleep right there in his arms. If it weren't for his raging hard on, he might have let her, but he needed to move, relieve some of the tension, or this evening would end on a very messy, low note. Gently, he lifted her from him, and she moaned in protest.

"Come on gorgeous, time to tuck you in." He set her on her feet, intent on getting her to bed without looking below her eyes.

Her dress was a mangled mess around her waist, her panties twisted at her hips and thighs, so her unbelievably stunning breasts had to be on full display.

So...it was eye contact only, as he ushered her to her bed and sat her on the edge. Only when her eyes zeroed in on his crotch did he realize her face was now perfectly level with the part of him that was threatening to explode if he didn't leave her room soon.

"You need help getting into your pajamas or are you good?" he croaked.

Without taking her eyes off the bulge in his jeans, Lucy slowly shook her head, then lifted her fingers to the button above his zipper.

Oh no. His hand shot out and wrapped around her wrist before she could flick the button. "You don't want to do that," he warned.

Lucy's wide eyes looked up at him. Clarity had returned, and her red lips curled into a wicked smile—the kind that was designed to cut a man off at the knees. "Oh yes I do." Her fingers ran the length of him, and his cock twitched behind the constricting fabric. "I want you in my mouth. Watching you while I swallowed you down my throat is one of my go-to memories."

Jesus. He'd never had a lover talk dirty the way Lucy did. And as she intended, it was turning him on to no fucking end. If he didn't move away soon, he'd let her do exactly what she promised and likely a lot more. Gritting his teeth, he forced himself to pluck her delectable fingers away from his pants, then he turned to the drawers.

"I think you've had more than your fill tonight," he said, managing to sound surprisingly normal considering he was now so hard it hurt. Pulling a comfortable looking t-shirt out of the drawer, he walked back to her. She hadn't moved, still sitting bare chested on the edge of her bed, her gaze unashamedly following his cock around the room.

Unfolding the t-shirt, Joel held it above her head. "Arms up, wife."

A small smile played across her lips as she obeyed without a word, and her trust in his command tugged something inside him that was deeper than the tug in his dick.

He dropped the shirt over her head, relaxing a little when her gorgeous breasts were finally out of view. "Stand up for me," he urged, holding up his hand.

Again she came to him, rising on her feet, but this time she pressed herself against his chest, and set her mouth to his ear. "Let me touch you...husband."

Husband. His jaw immediately clenched. There was no room for his dick to even twitch in his pants. She'd made sure of that with one word alone.

Did she mean it? Or was she fucking with him? Playing a game. He honestly didn't know, but he was desperate for relief. Gripping her face between his palms, he crashed his mouth down on hers and kissed her desperately.

And she met him there, her passion as unchecked as his, her hunger matching every stroke, every dive of his tongue. His hands tangled in her hair as he angled her head the way he needed. Her fingers clawed at his back, hauling him closer. They devoured. And it went on like that until Lucy moaned into his mouth and Joel had to call upon every last drop of his evaporating control to drag himself away.

When they pulled apart, they were both breathless. With unsteady fingers, he stroked her hair out of her face and swiped his thumb along her swollen bottom lip. God, he wanted her so badly. It did not help matters that he knew she'd let him have her anyway he wanted, all night long.

"We're doing this differently this time, Lucy," he whispered.

There was a line of confusion that creased between her eyes, so he pressed a kiss into the spot on her forehead. He eased her down onto the bed before she could say anything. Pulling the covers up her body, he tucked the material in on her sides.

"Sleep tight, Luciana," he murmured, and because he simply needed one last taste of her, he brushed another kiss across her temple.

Flicking off the light and leaving her alone in her room twisted his gut into knots, even though he knew it was the right thing to do. One way or another their time would come, but it wasn't now.

Good thing he was a patient man. That virtue had served him well in life. The one time he'd rushed into something had been with Lucy, and although those had been some of the best days of his life, they'd been followed by some of his darkest. If that experience had taught him anything, it was that the rush was never worth the pain of the fall. So he attacked life with patience and control, and that cocktail did not often let him down.

Though it did leave him with one pent-up emotion he currently had no viable outlet for. Lust. For Lucy.

Closing himself into his room at the opposite end of the hallway, he considered using his own hand to slake the need, but after what happened in Lucy's room, it seemed empty somehow. What he needed was a hard run, a cold shower and a few hours of decent sleep.

After changing into athletic pants and a shirt, he tugged on his trainers and tiptoed out of the apartment. Fifty minutes later, he returned from his run and took a shower on the coldest setting. He stood under the spray, letting the water beat down the back of his neck until he couldn't take anymore. Finally, after toweling off, he laid down in bed.

But sleep, the bastard, antagonized him. When he was under, he only saw Lucy, naked and needy, panting his name like he was the new Messiah. His dreams tortured him, leaving him hot and breathless. A beautiful kind of nightmare. But when he was awake, he longed for the unconscious, so he could feel the blissful torture again. And so it went—restless, fitful, lustful spurts of sleep until he eventually gave up and staggered out of bed at five-thirty in the morning.

As always, work was his most reliable companion, and he lost himself in the rhythm of the process for a couple of hours. Two offers on new plots of industrial land on the east coast, one meeting with the contractor of his current Portland build, and a lot of tedious paperwork—and his personal problems or distractions, melted away. Without Morgan Construction, he wasn't sure how he'd have survived the last four years.

He loved his work. There was something hugely satisfying about buying land and building something on it that made it more valuable, not only financially, but for people. There was something hugely satisfying about creating homes with designs that made sense for the practical lives people led, and not simply trying to fit as many humans as possible into tiny boxes for the sake of profit.

Two years ago, he'd partnered with the city of San Francisco and a local non-profit to build a housing complex to support those without homes. As his home city exploded in population and poverty rates, affordable housing had become his passion project. And while Morgan Construction was known for their elite high rises—featuring luxury penthouses that Barone & Sons finished with exquisite interior—he enjoyed building safe and affordable housing for those who needed it most.

There wasn't much return on mixed income housing, but he'd never stop being involved in them.

By 9 a.m., he heard the bedroom door down the hall open and close, followed a minute later by the sound of the shower running. A smile curved his lips as he pictured a groggy Lucy getting under the steaming water. Or would she need a cold one, like he had?

He got up from the table that served as his desk and poured water into his espresso maker. By the time the bathroom door squeaked open, the smell of rich Italian espresso filled the kitchen.

Lucy emerged in the dining room wearing leggings, a loose t-shirt, and her damp hair tied up in a messy bun. Fucking irresistible.

"Coffee?" he asked, pouring some into a cup, because he knew the answer was yes.

Sure enough, she nodded, her gaze dipping before popping up again. Her tell that she had something uncomfortable to say. He took a fortifying inhale.

"About last night..." She slid onto a chair by the table and downed half the espresso in one gulp. "You should know I remember everything."

"Alright." He took a sip of his own coffee as he assessed her. He wouldn't have touched her if he had a single doubt about her memory.

"I wanted you to know, so you didn't, you know, feel like you'd taken advantage of me or anything. I remember it all, and I enjoyed it so—" She shrugged like none of it mattered, her eyes flitting to the side. "Thank you."

Joel studied her while trying to contain the annoyance that shot through him. The eye contact was gone, her cheeks were several shades brighter, and she continued to sip espresso even though he was pretty sure the cup was empty.

She was going to brush it off as nothing. He considered challenging her, then opted against it. He wouldn't play it safe forever, but this morning wasn't the time to dive into the deep end.

"You're welcome," he settled with as he brought the coffee pot to where she was now sitting cross-legged on a dining chair. "Would you like more?"

"Coffee, or...?" She let the innuendo hang there.

He cast her a warning look. She'd already pushed the limits of his restraint last night. If she chose to play with fire, he could make it burn.

"You're too easy." She giggled then nodded in the direction of the coffee, and he poured.

When he was done, he shoved a plate of fresh croissants he'd picked up earlier in front of her. "Breakfast of champions."

She immediately grabbed one and bit into it.

Damn, she was cute. Fresh faced and relaxed. The opposite of the stunning showstopper she'd been last night. He loved both versions. All versions. There wasn't a single version of Luciana Barone that he wouldn't marry over and over again.

The ring on her finger sparkled as she lifted her cup up to her lips. When she caught him staring, she quickly put her cup down and sat on her hand. "Now that I'm wearing it, it does feel a bit ostentatious. Vanessa said I needed a bodyguard for it. I can return it for a different one if you want."

"Do you like the ring, Lucy?" he asked as he strolled over to her.

She nodded slowly. "Of course I do. I mean, who wouldn't?"

He gently tugged her hand out from under her butt. "Then we're not returning it. And I expect you to wear it everywhere you go."

"Right, so the whole world knows I'm yours." Then she had the gall to roll her eyes when there was a fifty-thousand-dollar ring sitting on her finger.

He had to wander back into the kitchen to hide his smile. "Yes. That's right." He opened the fridge and pulled out the tomato juice he'd bought. "Want some of this?"

When he set the glass of thick red juice in front of her, she blinked at it, then back at him. "Tomato juice."

He nodded as he sat down beside her. "Yes, the best hangover cure, right?"

"You remembered."

The morning after they'd woken in Vegas, they'd shared the mother of all hangovers. Probably a thousand times worse than what she was feeling right now. Neither of them had many memories of exactly what happened the night before. Only a highlight reel of an Elvis impersonator, a Chippendale witness, and a trip to a souvenir shop for a cheap silver ring. The sex that had followed, yeah, not even being dead could have killed that memory. But save those snippets, most of it had been hazy.

Lucy had Googled *how to cure a hangover in less than a day.* The search had brought up a tomato juice hack that promised to instantly relieve even the worst hangovers. So Joel had dragged his half-deceased body out of the hotel room and found the nearest kiosk that sold it. They'd spent the morning chugging bottles, showering together, and making love again.

"I told you. I remember everything." The entire four months of bliss with her were a core memory.

Her eyes narrowed, but never left his as she took the glass. "I wouldn't really call this a hangover, but thanks." She swallowed some of the juice and winced. "Ugh. I forgot how bad that tastes. Promise me that no matter how bad our engagement party on Saturday gets, you will not let me get drunk."

"Of course," he said smoothly. "I'll have your back."

Lucy choked on the croissant she'd been chewing, making Joel wonder if she'd been remembering how well he'd had her back last night. Literally holding her as they sunk to their knees, her back pressed against his chest, his fingers buried inside her, finishing her off.

He cleared his throat. "I thought I would take you to the construction site this morning." Strangely, he was nervous about inviting her to see his Portland project. He'd taken her to worksites before because he'd always valued her opinion about business.

Lucy had fantastic ideas, a keen eye for detail, and was far better at seeing outside the box than he was. Which was why he was apprehensive about bringing her today. He was trying something far outside the Morgan Construction box and what she thought about it mattered to him. Unless, of course, she didn't want to go...and judging by the blank look on her face, he couldn't exactly tell.

"Look, you—"

"I'd love to," she interrupted, and his heart started a happy dance. "Let me put something on other than pajamas, and I'll be ready to go."

Before he could say another word, she stood and walked back to her bedroom, leaving him sitting at the table with only his sheer relief and a tomato juice as company.

CHAPTER TWENTY-FIVE

The new Morgan Construction build was located on the other side of town. As they drove there, Lucy took in the surrounding neighborhood from the passenger window. The eclectic mix of high-rises and businesses hugging the periphery of downtown created a perfect place to put up an apartment building. The area was a good location, on transit routes, walkable, but not quite in the dense part of the urban core. Location was everything, and Joel knew how to pick it.

"As soon as we realized Hope was going to settle down in Portland, Dad and I figured it made sense to expand the business here," Joel explained as they drove. "We saw this strip of land for sale and snapped it up."

Lucy laughed out loud, and Joel took his eyes off the road for a second to give her a perplexed look. "What?"

Lucy deepened her voice to mimic his. "I just snapped it up for a cool hundred million." She snapped her fingers, then dropped her hand with a breathy laugh. "I love how the ultra-rich talk."

Joel frowned. "It was 102 million, actually."

She bit the inside of her cheek. She'd annoyed the billionaire by teasing him about his riches. "How many stories?"

"Twenty-five," he grumbled.

They pulled up to the site. Joel got out of the car, stopping to get something out of the trunk before he met her on the sidewalk. He held out a bright yellow construction hard hat.

"Is this necessary?"

"We're going behind the gate, so yes." He plopped the hard hat on her head before putting on his own.

"A real tour then," Lucy mused as she faced one of the site's entrances. "Too bad I forgot my steel-toed boots."

"I have some for you." Joel went back to the trunk and pulled out a box.

"Seriously?" Lucy opened the box, sure enough a very nice feminine looking pair of black steel-toed boots sat inside.

"Safety first." Was all she got from moneybags.

She'd been around construction enough in her life to know that going into an active site without the hardware was ill advised, she'd assumed they'd be lingering on the sidewalks outside of the site. Her mistake.

Several minutes later, a security guard opened the main gate of the construction site fencing surrounding the property. The foundation was already laid, with concrete poured and the skeleton was starting to go up.

"Who did the design?" she asked as they walked a safe distance around where the crew was working.

"We used a local architect. We felt it was important to get someone who knew the city and had their hand in other developments here. They were fantastic. It's going to look incredible." Joel turned into a different person when he talked about business.

And Lucy lapped it up. He spoke with utter confidence about property development and construction, and she thought again how lucky Walter was to have a child who was so deeply invested in the family business. And how lucky Joel was that his father considered him worthy enough to entrust his empire too.

Pushing her envy aside, she followed him around the extremely organized site while she listened to him describe the differences between Oregon and California when it came to permits and building restrictions.

He slowed his pace when they reached the far end of the site. "We also decided that half would be subsidized housing and half rentals."

This stopped her. "What?"

"It's new for us, but there's a need in this city, and we can make it happen. It's not something I've ever done before but we've connected with the right people and have been working closely with city planners."

He wasn't making any eye contact, and the confidence she'd been admiring had diminished. Was he...nervous?

"Joel." She stopped him with her hand on his arm. "That's a very worthwhile project." Did he honestly think she wouldn't think so?

His posture relaxed as he released a long breath. "Yeah, it really has been. I've loved it."

Lucy couldn't stop her smile. His passion was so evident it was contagious.

"Tell me everything about it. How many subsidized units? What's the square footage? How is the community responding? Can Barone & Sons do the interior? I want to know everything." But more than that she wanted to hear him talk about it in the exact way he just had, full of passion and drive.

For the next hour, he did exactly that, and his enthusiasm spurred on her own. At one point, she stumbled over some uneven ground, and he caught her around the waist. The way he'd leaned down, there was a moment she thought he might kiss her, and maybe he would have, but a loud horn from a truck backing up interrupted their intimacy, and Joel had pulled back. Regret flooded her on the tail end of her need. The only consolation was that he held her hand for the rest of the tour.

"What are you calling it?" she asked when they finally headed back to his car.

Joel pointed to the banner attached to the wired fencing, one she'd missed when they first entered. It read *Per Sempre by Morgan Construction*.

"*Per sempre*," she murmured, her heart picking up speed. That was Italian for...

"Forever," Joel said, finishing her thought. "I want it to be a place people feel they can stay in long-term. Without fear that rising rents and an unstable economy will force them out. I want to build them something that lasts."

Well...just, well. How on earth was she supposed to leave this man after a year? And why had she ever let it end in the first place?

"Lu, I love you but you're crazy."

Hours later Lucy was standing with Vanessa in Zia Ella's spare bedroom that she'd vacated to move in with Joel. The room she had left spotless was now covered in clothing options for the weekend's engagement party. So far

Lucy had vetoed half the options. This was a fake engagement gathering at Bowie's. Not the Met Gala afterparty.

"Lasering your bikini line is an absolute must with our coarse Italian hair. You'll thank me when you don't have to wax down there anymore."

Lucy rolled a skintight white dress down her thighs. Yeah, that one wasn't going to work either. "I hardly wax anymore. I hate waiting for it to grow out long enough to wax."

Vanessa dropped the stilettos she was holding on the floor with a clatter, her mouth following as her jaw fell open. "Luciana Barone, please don't tell me that you sh-*shave*." Vanessa whispered the last word like it was dirty.

Lucy couldn't help but laugh. She'd missed her sister. "Look, Ness, not all of us have an army of beauticians at our beck and call, ready at the drop of a hat to make us look like supermodels. Shaving works for me."

"But, Lu, you're getting married to one of the Forbes Top 100. He's probably the most eligible bachelor in the state, in the country! You can't tell me you're going to go on your honeymoon with razor burn up your thighs. For God's sake, have I taught you nothing?"

"Of course not!" Lucy admonished. "I was going to go full bush."

Vanessa broke out in a fit of giggles and threw a very expensive-looking purse at Lucy. "You're gross."

"So how come you never told me about that, by the way?"

"About lasering? Lu, I've been telling you for years!"

"No, about the Forbes Top 100 thing. I didn't know until Natalie told me." Lucy was still embarrassed that she hadn't known her own husband's state of wealth, or when exactly he'd gone from millionaire to billionaire status.

"I thought you knew. I thought everyone knew. He's given, like, TED talks and shit about entrepreneurship. There are pictures of him all over social media and he doesn't have his own account. Only the Morgan business ones run by his PR people exist, but he's interesting enough that people post about him any chance they get. I assumed... you'd see it at some point." Vanessa glanced at her oddly. "Also, I didn't think you'd care, since, you know, you couldn't be bothered to tell me you were dating."

Lucy busied herself by pulling on a beautiful red gown that managed to just fit over her hips. "Yeah," she said evasively. "It happened very fast."

"No kidding."

Lying to her parents was one thing. That was more like a means to an end, a way of getting them to look at her in a different way. She was able to rationalize that away during the countless conversations she'd had out loud with herself in the shower.

But lying to her sister—that was a harder sell. Even though a five-year age gap separated them, they'd always been close. Maybe that was the byproduct of sharing the bond of having the same overbearing immigrant parents, even though they'd been affected by that in different ways. The truth was, Lucy had spent most of her childhood interceding on her wild sister's behalf.

By modern standards the Barones were very traditional parents. She and Vanessa had had strict curfews and weird social rules that punctuated their childhood. No sleepovers unless with family, no away camps, no cool school trips that took them out of town. No makeup until they were sixteen. Definitely no discussion of dating.

Going to university was not optional, so good grades in secondary school were expected, which meant no reward for getting them either. A career had to be respectable and appropriate but not artistic. And no one was to move out until they could afford to buy their own place or got married.

Long story short, Luciano and Maria Barone had made it clear they had immigrated to America for a better life and more opportunity for their children and that sacrifice was not to be wasted.

While Lucy had spent her entire life trying to live up to that impossible standard, Vanessa had doubled down and done her level best to be the exact opposite.

It wasn't so much that Vanessa was disobedient. She simply lived as she wanted to. Always the life of the party, she made breaking curfews a sport. With her naturally stunning good looks and bubbly personality, she was always easily the most popular person in the room, bringing home her first boyfriend at age fourteen—the poor guy hadn't had a chance against Luciano's third degree, and they'd never seen him again. But the only thing Vanessa had learned from that encounter was that she had to become better at hiding things like her sexy clothes, make-up, shenanigans and boyfriends.

Eventually she became so skilled at hiding her noncompliance she got away with almost everything. And if she ever got close to being caught, Lucy covered for her. Every time.

The Barone sisters stuck together, always had and always would. Which was why Lucy had to tell Vanessa the truth. Besides, it was highly likely she'd needed her sister to cover for her at some point in this charade.

"Ness, I need to tell you something."

Maria chose that moment to throw open the bedroom door with no regard to privacy, because, you know, who needed to knock?

"What are you girls do—?" Maria gave a low gasp. "Luciana, what are you wearing?? You look like a salami!"

Lucy glanced at herself in the mirror on the closet door. The red dress was pretty, and it was tight because it was her model sister's...but a salami?

"She's wearing it to the engagement party, Ma."

Maria looked between them with a slack jaw. Then burst into a loud litany of Italian that sounded like she was half crying, half laughing hysterically.

"You are getting married to a very well-established man," she cried. "You must look respectable. You cannot wear your sister's clothes." Maria thrust a hand in Vanessa's direction. "She gets paid to walk around half-naked. She's too skinny. Why would you embarrass me this way? You're a good girl."

When the hand flutterings started, Lucy began removing the dress straps. "I'm obviously not wearing this one, Mom. I was just trying it on. It's pretty."

"It shows too much skin!" The flutterings graduated to brisk hand gestures. "Do I have to take you shopping?"

"Oh please no." Vanessa helped Lucy out of the dress. "I'll take her. I promise not to let her buy anything that would offend the Barone name." She said this so sarcastically that Lucy winced, but Maria did not seem to notice.

"That is right! Your father worked hard in this country to make a name for himself. To give you the life you have. He earned his respect. Now we show our respect to him by behaving in a way that will not waste the sacrifices he has made."

She and her sister stayed silent under their mother's admonishment, knowing they were always in the biggest trouble when she spoke to them in Italian only. As if making them work to understand her was a part of the punishment.

Or maybe because she could only express herself most fully in her native tongue.

"I won't wear the dress," Lucy repeated, placatingly.

"It was a joke," Vanessa added sullenly.

Maria's eyes filled with a kind of sadness that Lucy was unsure how to interpret. "It was not a funny one, Vanessa." She moved around the room collecting an armful of laundry. "Come eat something. I have soup on the stove." Then, she was gone.

"How do you stand it?" Vanessa asked, flopping down on the bed with a bounce.

Lucy didn't have to ask what she meant. It was no secret Vanessa and their mother always butted heads.

"I got used to it a long time ago, Ness. I kind of tune it out."

"Ugh, gross. I couldn't do it. The constant nagging. Nothing is ever good enough. I always felt so suffocated, like there was no room to breathe."

Lucy shrugged. "It was different for you. You were younger, prettier."

Vanessa grabbed the brush beside her and smacked Lucy's arm.

"You were and you *are*," Lucy insisted. "You have that classic Italian glamor that I never had. Combined with your bubbly free-spirited personality, they were always harder on you. It was protective. They wanted to keep you from getting hurt or rushing into things. But I'm not like that."

"Oh please, Lu, you make it sound like you're some dried up spinster who's good for nothing but taking care of the old people and keeping Dad's books in the black. You'd think the fact that having a guy like Joel ask you to *marry him* would have given you a little boost to the ole confidence."

Lucy sighed. Vanessa had been gone so long she didn't

know how hard Lucy had tried to get their father to see her as an asset to Barone & Sons. She wouldn't have understood either.

Vanessa had never wanted any part in it, content instead to chase glamor and fame. Unlike Lucy who quite enjoyed taking care of the old people and keeping the books in the black, that brought meaning to her life. But she also wanted more.

She had the confidence she needed; she knew her worth. It was her parents' confidence she lacked, and she needed Joel to help her to get it. Her mother's outbursts proved that. Maria respected Joel, more than her own daughter. If Joel thought she was good enough to lead Barone & Sons, and her parents saw that, then maybe they'd believe it too.

CHAPTER TWENTY-SIX

Joel's apartment door clicked open before the knocking stopped, and he knew without having to look that it was his sister. Hope had always entered his room that way. To be fair, around the time he became a teenager, their mother had spoken to her about the importance of knocking and privacy, because up until that point, she barged right in without knocking at all. After the talk, Hope had simply assumed that knocking while barging in was sufficient and stuck with that.

The only way he'd kept her out had been to lock his door. Which he had unfortunately failed to do this afternoon.

Sure enough, her cheery voice rang through the living room, and he could no longer pretend to focus on his laptop. Sometimes he really did miss his office on the eighteenth floor, with the floor to ceiling glass walls that fully tinted with the flick of a remote.

"Hey you, long time no see." She wandered in carrying what looked like a massive cake box with two coffee cups balanced precariously on top.

"What's this?" Joel asked as he got up to take the load from her. "Did I miss the memo that I was hosting a birthday party?" The box was heavier than expected. "And why on earth are you carrying this? I thought women who were about to give birth were supposed to rest."

Hope laughed loudly. "That's funny. You're funny." She did, however, proceed directly to his couch and sank down onto it with a heavy sigh, leaving him holding the cake box and cups. He set them on the table, picked up one of the cups, and inhaled.

Peppermint. Gross. He handed the tea to his sister, then lifted the next cup. Americano. That was more like it.

"You're not hosting a party. But it is a cake." Hope took a sip of her tea.

"My birthday is in February."

Hope stretched her leg out and barely missed kicking his shin. "It's an engagement cake, doofus. For you and Lucy to sample and approve before your engagement party."

"Right." The engagement party. He sank down to the couch next to his sister.

"So," Hope drawled. "You and Lucy, huh?"

Weary but braced, he regarded Hope over the rim of his cup. He knew this time was coming. In fact, he'd been surprised she'd stayed away this long. "Yep." Best keep things monosyllabic.

"How come we didn't know about her?"

"You've known her for years," he countered.

"Okay, Mr. Evasive. So how come you never told anyone you were dating someone you were considering getting married to? Kind of important, no?" Hope kicked off one shoe and lifted that foot onto his coffee table.

He allowed it because she was about to give birth to his new niece.

"You have to admit it's suspicious. Her popping up out of nowhere."

"She's been around. Just not where you could stalk her." It wasn't a total lie, and also part of the reason they'd kept their impromptu wedding secret all those years ago.

The Morgans and Barones had one very important thing in common. They loved to meddle in their families' lives. And Hope would have been on him and Lucy like a dog after a bone if she had a single whiff of their wedding. One hundred percent.

"Are you in trouble?"

"What? No!"

"Is she?"

He felt Hope's intuitive eyes burning into his temple, so he took a long sip of his coffee before turning purposefully to face her.

"Of course not." Not exactly.

"Joel," Hope said with a sigh. "I'm not trying to pry."

"Yes, you are."

She ignored him. "I like her, I do. Growing up, she was always like a big sister to me, or at least a close cousin. Going out the other night was fun, even though I didn't make it past 7 p.m." She rubbed her big belly. "Lucy's easy to talk to and doesn't take herself too seriously, but—" She chewed her lip as if contemplating what to say next. "It's not like you, to be impulsive like this, and I want to make sure everything is above board, you know. Like, you're not doing something that will come back to haunt you later."

There was a lot of history between him and Hope. They'd been through a lot. Hope had been through a lot. She'd learned the hard way that if something didn't add up, it was probably because something wasn't right.

And in this case, he couldn't even tell her she was wrong.

She was also too smart not to pick up on a lie or embell-ishment.

So he told her what he knew with absolute certainty. "I will never regret marrying Lucy."

Hope surveyed him, stripping him down with her sisterly scrutiny. "So, how long have you been dating then?"

Joel set his empty cup on the coffee table next to her foot. "Does it matter?"

"It matters to me." Hope placed a hand to her heart. "Look, four years ago you dropped everything and came to help when Ivy and I needed you. Then you did it again when I found out about my adoption. You kept our family together, Joel. You kept me together. You've always been a tether to everyone, keeping them sane and safe. You don't ask any questions, you simply arrive and save the day and move on."

Why was she making it sound like a problem? Of course he would do whatever it took to help the people he loved. He couldn't imagine any other way.

"But you've never truly seemed happy," Hope went on. "Like deep down, happy. You've always been too busy taking care of everyone else. And I want you to be happy, because you deserve it. And if Lucy is that for you, then I'm all in. It's just..." She lifted a hand, then let it flutter back to her belly. "I want to be sure you're not dropping everything again to rescue somebody instead of focusing on what could bring you joy. I want to be sure that this is your happy, you know?"

Warmth flooded his heart. This was why he had no trouble loving her from the day she arrived in his life. The reason he stopped locking his door after the first time she couldn't get in. Hope had one of the biggest hearts he knew, and she only ever wanted what was best for him.

"Lucy and I have a history. We've been together a long

time, and we chose not to tell anyone because we liked our little bubble. Our lives are both so busy and chaotic that having this space where only we existed was peaceful, we didn't want to interrupt it."

At least that had been the truth before they'd had the biggest interruption of all. There was no way he could tell her that the night Ivy had called to tell him that Hope needed him immediately, he'd been with Lucy in that blissful little bubble. Or that when he was away helping Ivy and Hope, Lucy had lost their baby, and he'd left her alone during the most horrible moment of their lives.

He knew his sister well. She'd blame herself and feel guilty when there was nothing to be guilty for. It had happened. It was done. The only regret he had now was how he'd handled the situation with Lucy afterward.

"We've let our little secret go on too long, and now everyone thinks this is a big shock and surprise, when really, all along it's only ever been Lucy for me."

This seemed to appease Hope because she let out a heartfelt sigh, reached for his hand, and squeezed. "Okay, that was romantic enough that I believe you," she said with a small smile and shiny eyes. "Well, shucks." A tear rolled down her cheek. "That was kind of beautiful, big brother. I think you should use it in the groom's speech."

He chuckled and shook his head. He could not imagine the kind of wedding that was currently being planned for him and Lucy. The little chapel in Vegas seemed more enticing than ever.

"Whelp," Hope said, patting her belly. "I'd say I'll be on my way, but I'm pretty sure I'm permanently molded to this couch now, so you might be stuck with me for a while."

"Fat chance, sis," Joel said, getting to his feet and sticking out his hand. He was hitting the gym before Lucy got home, and then he planned to take his fiancée out for dinner. "Let me give you a hand. If that doesn't work, I'll get the crane from the building site to swing over and give you a—"

Hope's foot found his gut before he could finish the sentence.

A few hours later when Joel arrived home after a hard session at the gym, the first thing he smelled was onions, and he knew immediately something was wrong. Dropping his gym bag, he b-lined it to the kitchen where he found Lucy, back turned to him, as she chopped onions at the counter.

"What happened? What's wrong?" The panic flaring in his chest made his voice sound more demanding than he meant to be.

Lucy stopped chopping, her shoulders slumping in defeat. Without thinking, he took her shoulders and gently turned her to face him. His heart seized when he saw her wet lashes and shining eyes. *Please let that be the onions.* But he knew better.

If Lucy was cooking, she was upset.

"What happened?"

She snorted a small laugh. "Me. I happened. I'm such an idiot."

"Never. Not possible. Not in a million years could you ever be that."

Her head dropped against his chest, any animosity between them from the night before forgotten, and he ran his hand down her back.

As sick as he was over her being upset for any reason, the fact that she was leaning on him for comfort filled his soul with something that had been missing for a long time. "You want to tell me, or should we cook first?"

Depending on what was bothering her, she'd either want to decompress by cooking in silence, or she'd want to get it off her chest first then debrief every detail while cooking together. At least that's how he remembered it.

"I told Vanessa everything." Her voice was muffled against his shirt.

Okay, talk first, it was.

"Told her what?"

"Everything, Joel. Well, almost everything. Not about—" Her hands swirled in front of her open mouth, but no more words came out.

He knew the words she was choking on. She might have told her sister about their marriage, but even though she'd said *everything,* she hadn't told Vanessa about their baby.

Her fist thumped his pec, then she clutched his t-shirt. "One minute we're bitching about how unfair our mother can be, and the next I'm telling her every detail of our Vegas whirlwind like I'm catching her up on a soap opera."

"I see." He contemplated his next words carefully as he kept the steady rhythm of his hand rubbing her back. "Did it feel good? Telling her?"

"Yes. Until I remembered that it's Vanessa and these days, she comes with over one million social media followers who eat up every detail of her life like its life or death. Nothing in her life is a secret."

His hand halted halfway back down. "I don't know about that. Everyone has secrets."

Lucy drew back, her gaze meeting his and narrowing. "You think she has secrets?"

"I think," he said, cupping her face as he swiped the wetness off her cheeks with his thumbs. "That Vanessa has been in the public eye for enough years that she under-stands what to feed her followers and what to hold back. She loves you, and she wouldn't betray your trust by disclosing your private life to everyone."

"She said almost the same thing."

"But you don't believe her."

"It's not that. She's still only twenty-four. She doesn't always think things through before she acts. She gets caught up in the lights and cameras. But also...it's the first time I've shared any of that with anyone, and now that it's out there, it feels like I've lost control of it. Does that make sense?"

"It does." Which was part of the reason why he hadn't confided in his sister. Their secret had been a secret for so long, letting go of it caused more anxiety than continuing to hold it. At the same time, he'd always wondered... "But did it also feel freeing? Being able to talk about it with someone."

Lucy released a big sigh. "Yes. And after she finished yelling at me for not telling her sooner, she had some pretty thoughtful words of wisdom. Sometimes I swear she's lived a thousand lives."

"Maybe she has. Fame can throw a lot at you."

Leaning back on the counter, Lucy crossed her arms and assessed him. "Is that why you keep such a low profile? You don't want your billionaire status to change you."

"It doesn't change me." Not where it counted.

"You could buy a private island, Joel."

"I could," he replied as his finger traced the delicate line of her jaw. "And yet, there isn't enough money in the world that could buy me back what I really want."

Their eyes locked as the weight of his words settled between them. No amount of money could buy back what they'd lost, and they both knew it. Lucy frowned, so he changed course.

"Vanessa won't tell anyone, and if she does, I'll wipe whatever she shares off every corner of the internet. That is something my money can do. I promise."

He turned to the cutting board and picked up the knife. "I'll finish chopping these. Are we making lasagna?"

"How did you know?" Lucy asked as she pulled a pan out of the cupboard.

"You always made lasagna when you were stressed."

"Huh, you really do remember everything." She grabbed her phone from the counter. "I hope you also remember to dice the onions into tiny pieces so they don't show up in the sauce later."

Joel laughed. "I do."

Lucy held her phone up as he chopped.

"What are you doing?"

"You're wearing gray sweatpants and cooking. I want photographic evidence for future reference."

He stopped mid-chop. "Future reference for what?"

Lucy shrugged. "Stuff."

A low growl rumbled out of him. "You'll be the death of me, wife."

Lucy snorted. "Just make sure you chop the onions properly before you kick the bucket, moneybags."

CHAPTER TWENTY-SEVEN

This was supposed to be her de-stress lasagna, but Joel standing there in his athletic tee and gray sweatpants stirring sauce while drinking wine, had somehow turned it into an erotic experience. Everything suddenly had sexual undertones.

"Taste this," he said, turning to her with the sauce ladle, his hand underneath ready to catch any drips. "Watch out, it's hot." He blew gently on the sauce.

No shit, she'd thought, watching his forearm flex as he brought the spoon to her lips.

"Good?" he asked.

Yes. More, please.

By the time they were layering the alternating strips of pasta, sauce, béchamel and cheese, she was so turned on she was ready to strip those damn sweatpants off and ride him on the kitchen floor. Judging by the way his dimple popped every time he caught her ogling him, the jerk knew it too.

Joel put on some music, and the soft lyrics played

through the apartment as they cooked, assembled the dish, then tidied up while the lasagna baked. This was why she called it her de-stress dish because every step required so much attention that it distracted her from whatever she'd been worrying about. Well, she was certainly distracted.

They dried off the last pot when there were still fifteen minutes of bake time left. The apartment smelled like an Italian restaurant, and she inhaled deeply. Her lasagna was the best, better even than her mother's—not that she'd ever tell Maria that. Her secret was simple. She used homemade béchamel sauce instead of spinach and ricotta, and she never skimped on the Bolognese sauce, always laying it on thick between noodles, so they'd become saturated with the flavor while baking. It wasn't calorie-wise, but not a soul had ever complained.

Joel slung the dishcloth over his shoulder as a new song started up. The melody filled the kitchen, slow and seductive, and memory flickered across her mind just as he said, "Dance with me."

Three simple words, but Lucy knew they were game changers. How many times had they danced in their kitchen in San Francisco? How many times had he said those words before scooping her up in his arms? Each time they'd ended up naked somewhere in the penthouse, either burning dinner or working up an appetite for it.

Dancing with him now wouldn't be a little spin around the kitchen because a good song was playing. It would be a surrender. An acceptance that this thing between them, this agreement, this farce, wasn't that anymore.

She wasn't sure she was ready to shift into the new version of what they could be. There was still so much they hadn't spoken about. So much she wasn't ready to speak about.

"Luciana," he said as he held out his hand. "Please dance with me."

The truth hit her hard as she stared at his outstretched hand. It didn't matter whether they talked about the past or not. It didn't matter if Vanessa knew their engagement started as a sham. It didn't even matter if they went ahead with their fake wedding or didn't. She would never not dance with this man.

Molding herself into his arms, he lifted her until she was on tiptoes, hugging her like he'd just found her after years apart. Which maybe wasn't so far from the truth.

They didn't dance so much as Joel crushed her to him and swayed while she buried her face against his shoulder. The sting of her tears were absorbed into the fabric of his shirt. And when the song ended, and another one started, he didn't let go, not until the oven timer went off, and even then it was a gradual release, a peeling apart, as they realized it was either that or deal with the fire alarm going off.

They didn't speak as Joel pulled the hot dish out of the oven and set it on the stove to cool. They didn't speak as they laid the table, Joel filling their glasses with more wine, as Lucy carried out the salad and warmed bread. They didn't speak when he pulled out a chair for her to sit.

The tension only broke when Joel took his seat across from her and lifted his glass. "Cheers." His eyes sparkled like silver in the low lights overhead. "To celebrity sisters keeping their mouths shut."

Lucy laughed, picking up her wine. "I'll definitely cheers to that."

They clinked glasses, then dug in.

"Fuck, this is so good," Joel said through his first bite. "The best I've ever had."

"I know." She didn't brag about much, but when it came

to her lasagna, there was no point in denying the truth. "I should open a restaurant and serve only this. I'd make millions."

"Say the word, and I'll make it happen." The way he was devouring his first slice and reaching for another, she believed he might actually be serious.

"Okay, moneybags. I'll start scoping out possible locations. We should probably open a chain. We'll call it Gluttony, and the slogan can be *'Come for a slice, stay for a pan.'*"

They spent the next hour laughing, eating, drinking, and talking about everything from quack businesses they'd open to the custom dream homes they'd love to build for each of their relatives. A comfortable familiarity tugged on her muscle memory. The remembrance of the quiet months when it was just the two of them. Three if you counted the baby. And for the duration of dinner, everything between then and now was tucked out of her mind.

Finally, the need to move was greater than her desire for another bite of saucy, creamy deliciousness, and Lucy pushed away her plate with a groan. "That's it. I tap out. Not another bite until leftovers tomorrow."

Across from her, Joel stood, chuckling in that low way of his that sent fissures of pleasure directly to her core. It was a sound more delectable than the food she'd eaten. He moved with ease, as if he hadn't devoured a quarter pan of lasagna, picking up their dishes as he went.

Begrudgingly, because she knew the fragile moment of peace between them was coming to an end, Lucy also got up, gathering napkins and the parmesan shaker.

From the speaker, a new song floated through the air. The lyrics haunting, painting a picture of a couple that separated and the longing that lasted long afterward.

Over the mess on the table, their gazes collided, and she

froze under his assessment. The melody rolled between them, Joel's eyes never releasing her from the prison of his intensity.

"Don't," he whispered.

"Don't what?" It was all she could breathe in return.

Was he talking about the way she was staring at him or the parmesan shaker she'd picked up? She'd never been hypnotized before, but she imagined this would be what it felt like. A magnetizing pull, outside of your own control, to do whatever was being asked of you.

"Don't—"

She could practically see his mind racing. A silent movie played across his eyes.

Then he blinked, mumbled, "Fuck it," and she was in his arms.

They kissed like it was their last chance, a tangle of tongues, bodies angling for best possible access. Joel made a low growling sound in the back of his throat as he devoured her in a way she hadn't experienced before, his whole body enveloping her in the embrace. Fingers combing through her hair, skimming down her back, squeezing her ass while pressing her closer. Mouth on her jaw and neck, tracing her collarbone before working up to her swollen lips.

Heat flooded every corner of her until she trembled with need. When he wrenched himself away from her, she cried out in protest and then launched herself onto him for more. And again, they consumed each other, like the four years starvation was insatiable now and they were ravenous.

"Lucy," Joel gasped between kisses. His palm skimmed up her shirt, around her rib cage, along her breast. "This isn't supposed to go like this."

"Yes, it is," she gasped. "It's supposed to be exactly like this." Her hand dove to the front of his sweatpants and she groaned when she felt his imprint there, a hard ridge under soft material. She felt the phantom sensation of his cock buried inside her. The ache between her legs was pounding for it.

A groan rose between them, but she was too far gone to place who it came from.

"No!" Joel wrenched himself away, leaving her bereft and throbbing. His breath was heaving as he glared at her. "Not like this. Not before we've talked about things."

Her brain rallied to catch up with his damn reasoning, but then lagged in a shockingly uncharacteristic betrayal. Where was her sanity? "We don't need to talk."

"We do," he insisted, hauling her back, cocooning against his chest. "We do."

"Do we?" She wasn't sure she could. Some things were impossible to talk about. Too painful. Too gut-wrenching.

"I have to, Lucy." He sounded desperate. Pleading. "*I have to.*"

Tears flooded her eyes, because she knew she would talk for him. She'd dig through the rubble of her greatest heartache and discuss it with him. For him. Because she loved him. And it was achingly clear that wasn't going away anytime soon.

"Okay," she whispered, eyes downcast, heart reeling with the cacophony of emotions splitting her chest in two. She needed time to prepare, to organize the chaotic grief she'd been carrying all these years. "Can I just have a little more time."

"For what?" He leaned back, his brow furrowed, the gray in his eyes gathering like a storm.

"I know, I know." She saw his meticulous patience waning. And she couldn't exactly blame him. "But I don't want to dump four years' worth of emotion on you. I want to be thoughtful."

For a long moment, Joel said nothing. Then he dragged her back toward him, his lips pressing her forehead, his heart thundering under her palm. "Tomorrow then. Think about what you want to say, Luciana, and we'll talk."

CHAPTER TWENTY-EIGHT

Sleep was going to be impossible. Lucy knew it. Post-it notes were strewn on the bed around her. Each one with different things she wanted to say to Joel. Tightness pulled at her lower belly. God, she felt sick.

The sexual attraction between her and Joel was a given. They'd started their relationship on a night of Vegas fueled sexcapades, and that tension had never ended for her. Joel was the only one she fantasized about. There'd never been anyone else. She'd stayed faithful to him like she'd never taken his ring off her finger.

But it was their connection underneath the chemistry that had returned over the last two weeks, like air blown on the embers of a dying fire. The time between them in a new city, under different circumstances, had coaxed old feelings back into life.

And if they had any chance at all, he was right, they had to talk.

She pulled one of the notes off her comforter, staring at the word until her vision blurred. *I miss Luca.*

The baby. A little boy. When Joel finally arrived at the

hospital, after she'd lost their son, she insisted they name him before she was discharged. She couldn't stomach the thought of leaving without doing so, as if naming him would secure his place in the universe, a tangible someone to remember and talk about. So they did. *Luca*. But it turned out they didn't talk about him. She could never speak his name without feeling like she was dying inside.

She'd carried him for sixteen weeks. The same amount of time they'd been happily married. The most perfect sixteen weeks of her entire existence. When she lost him, the despair had consumed her, and she pushed everything away, including and especially Joel. At the time, it had seemed easier to go back to how life was before. Before Vegas, before their wedding, before her pregnancy and their perfect dream world in the penthouse on the hill. The secret they'd kept made it easier to slip back into her old routine, so she had. As though none of it had existed. As if the sixteen weeks had all been a hallucination.

Except it hadn't been. Those weeks of quietly laying the groundwork to build their family had halted when Joel left. It had been ignored and neglected, but it still stood. And maybe now was the time to start building again.

Setting down the note, she got up and wandered her room, wondering if they could rebuild something on top of that abandoned foundation that was stronger than a house of cards this time? What if they could try again, but better, stronger? Fewer secrets, more faith.

She stopped at the bedroom door. Was Joel awake right now? Was his mind racing between the past and present like hers? Or did he already know exactly what he needed to say? Probably. He wasn't exactly the cue card kind of guy.

With a frustrated sigh, she glared at the post-its stuck to her bed. Who was she even kidding? There was no way to prepare for something like this. She was putting it off. Again.

No wonder he was growing impatient with her. Well, sue her for trying to protect the scar on her heart a little bit longer. She'd been completely shattered when she lost Luca. For months she felt like a porcelain doll that had been glued back together after cracking. Why would she want to go through that again? The fear was paralyzing.

But if not now, when? And at what cost?

She opened her door a crack and didn't hear anything but it didn't matter. He was still awake; she could sense it.

Too bad there wasn't a way to heal without hurting. Too bad that working through pain sometimes hurt more than the initial injury. Taking a bracing breath, she stepped into the hall. She'd never get Luca back, but maybe there was a chance for her and Joel.

Ignoring the ache in her heart she padded down the hallway.

Time to find Joel and insist they talk now. After four long years of inaction, the urgency that propelled her forward was startling. Or maybe it was her heart finally giving her brain a kick in the butt.

She hadn't realized she was holding her breath until she turned the corner into the dark living room. The couch was empty, and the light was off in the kitchen too. Turning back to the hall, she looked the opposite way from where she'd come. Joel's door was shut tight. No light glowed from under it.

Disappointment had Lucy's resolve slipping. She could waltz into his room, curl up next to him in bed and draw some of the comfort she so desperately needed from him. The thought of tucking herself in against his warm solid body, and resting until morning, was deeply enticing. They could talk in the morning, and until then, she could quiet her mind in the security of his proximity.

But two steps toward his door, she stopped. They might still be married, but they hadn't lived a married life in years. Slipping in between his sheets wasn't a privilege that was hers anymore.

On that very demoralizing thought, Lucy escaped back to her own bedroom, and flopped face down on her bed, crushing the sticky notes. She groaned into the mattress; the noise vibrating through her body. When she vibrated again, without her groan, she realized her phone was trapped under her stomach. Digging it out, her heart stopped dead in her chest when she saw a message from Joel.

> Why are you wandering around the house in
> the middle of the night?

"Ohmigod, omigod, omigod!" she whisper-squealed as she pressed the back of her phone to her mouth. Her heart thundered so violently behind her rib cage it rattled her eardrums. Her anxiety made her text back.

> Wasn't me. Maybe an intruder?

Reply bubbles popped up immediately.

> An intruder lurking outside my bedroom
> door?

Oh Lord. He'd heard her! So much for a dainty footfall.

> How did you know it was me?

> I could smell you through the door. Like
> cinnamon and vanilla.

And just like that, certain parts of her melted like honey as well.

Did you need something from me, Lucy?

She stared at the words. The simple message—that could have been interpreted so many ways—did nothing to slow her heartbeat.

What was she doing? What *was* she doing? And where the fuck was the staunch resolve she'd had moments ago when she was wandering the apartment looking for him? Fuckity, fuck, fuck.

Her fingers hovered over the screen. Brief. Hesitant. She took the leap.

I wanted to talk.

Her heart thudded when she didn't immediately see text bubbles emerge. *Don't follow up with a panic text. Don't follow up with a panic text.*

Her damn fingers moved on their own accord.

And I was looking for a midnight snack.

When in doubt, behave like a teenager. She threw her phone onto the mattress and buried her head in the comforter. Immaturity was such a simple thing. When her phone buzzed a moment later, she faltered picking it up. What game was she playing? Did she want this or not? With her fear hammering in her pulse, she flipped her phone over again.

Why didn't you just come in?

Ha, well, that was easy.

> Same reason you're texting me instead of
> coming down the hall and asking me
> yourself.

Writing bubbles appeared immediately this time, then disappeared, re-appeared, and vanished. For a full minute, silence reigned. She almost thought the conversation was done, and then a soft knock rapped her door.

She flew out of bed like she'd just found a spider on her sheets, or knew one of the most important moments of her life was waiting for her on the other side of the door. She reached for the doorknob.

"Don't open the door," he said in a firm tone.

Her hand froze. "Why? Are you not wearing your make-up?" Shit, she was nervous joking. This was not the time, and yet, this heaviness between them called for something to lighten it. "I think it's okay with me, Joel. I've seen it all before."

His muffled chuckle reverberated through the barrier, then silence. After a few seconds, she tentatively twisted the doorknob. And the pulse that had been hammering in her throat spread everywhere. Her entire body, mind, and soul ached to be closer to him. She wanted the door open.

"Lucy." He sounded pained. His hand slapped the door, as if he could keep it closed if she decided to pull it open. "I'm trying to do the right thing here."

She imagined him standing on the other side, palms against the door, forehead against the hardwood, and her heart cracked under the sweetness of his admission. Yes, she wanted sex. Of course she did. Their desire was a Mack truck, impossible to ignore as it constantly barreled toward them. But more than anything, she wanted to talk. Was he afraid that they couldn't talk face to face without the Mack truck plowing them over?

"I fucked up so badly with us before. I was gone when you needed me most, then left when we were at our lowest. I've spent every day since regretting it. I need to do things right by you this time."

With so much to unpack in his monologue she didn't know where to start, so she simply replied, "There was no way you could have known what would happen." Nobody could.

"That girl who called that day that I left was…"

Lucy's mind reeled back four years. They'd been sitting on the couch watching a movie, her feet on his lap as he pressed his thumb into her arch. His phone rang, and he answered before it could ring a second time. Then he'd jumped up and raced into the bedroom.

She'd assumed it was business, but when he came out, he told her he had to go immediately. That his sister was in trouble and needed him. It never occurred to her to stop him, or to go with him, or to consider what might happen while they were parted.

"That was Ivy."

"What?" Her hand dropped from the doorknob as his words sank through her memory.

"The girl who called me that day to tell me Hope was in trouble was Ivy."

"Okay, that makes sense. They were college roommates."

Where was he going with this? She knew very little of what happened when he'd flown to Hope's college. By the time he'd returned to San Francisco, the loss of the baby overshadowed everything. They'd barely spoken about his time away or why he'd been gone. It hadn't mattered. Nothing had mattered.

"We never talked about why I left. And I know, it didn't seem important after what happened while I was gone, but it has haunted me day and night. You alone and that shit happening to you all the while wondering why I didn't drop everything to come back immediately."

It was true. That night, after he'd left, she'd started spotting. She'd called him and left messages, and he hadn't replied at first. Then, when he did, all he'd said was that he'd get home as soon as he could.

He'd arrived at the hospital before noon the next day, but it had already been too late.

"I couldn't drop everything and leave. I wanted to, believe me I wanted to get to you more than anything. But things at USC were a mess. Hope was a mess. Ivy was... I never said anything because it wasn't mine to tell. But today I asked her if I could share with you because it's important to me that you know the truth about what was going on and why I didn't come home in time. And she said okay, so—" For a long beat, the silence was thick between the wall that separated them. "Ivy was raped at a college party by one of Hope's business-school peers, though a couple of them were in on it. Hope"—his voice hardened, syllables clipped— "interrupted things in process."

Her stomach clenched imagining the scenario. "Oh my God."

On the other side of the door, Joel cleared his throat. "Ivy didn't want to tell anyone. She was adamant about that. So Hope kept her secret. But then, not long after, those assholes were caught cheating on exams, and they accused Hope of providing them with the cheating material. They held Ivy over her head. It was a fucking disaster, and Hope didn't call me because she didn't want to betray Ivy. Ultimately, Ivy called me, told me the bare minimum of details, and asked me to come help Hope."

As he spoke, Lucy struggled to piece together the web of horror he'd been dragged into while simultaneously knowing his wife was at home, very likely having a miscarriage.

"Joel, I had no idea." She wanted to open the door so badly, wanted to tug him to her and make the pain in his voice disappear, but the door was his boundary, and she needed to respect it.

"I got your first call while I was in a meeting with the college officials. Then you texted immediately after and all I could do was sit there and read it while these assholes in sweater vests told me my sister was going to be expelled." A soft thud bumped the door, as if he'd knocked his head against it.

She pressed her forehead to her side of the wood, imagining they were touching.

"I knew the worst was happening to you, to us, and I couldn't walk out of the room and go home like I wanted to. I've never felt so helpless in my life." His voice broke.

The sound unleashed the tears that had been building behind her eyes.

"Hope was being quiet. She wouldn't tell me anything. I didn't understand why she wasn't defending herself. I was going crazy trying to help her and knowing you needed me at home. Then Ivy told me what happened to her, begged me not to say anything. She wanted me to help Hope and keep her out of it. It was such a fucking mess, and all I wanted to do was get to you."

"You did get to me. You were home the next day."

"It was too late!" Another thud on the hardwood rattled against her forehead. "I worked through the night to get my sister cleared of the false charges and make sure those motherfuckers never hurt another woman again, and I still got home too late."

She pressed her hand to the door, hoping his was meeting hers on the other side. That he could feel her the way she felt him. "Joel, even if you'd been there—there was nothing—" She choked on the lump in her throat. "There was nothing anyone could do to stop it."

"Lucy," his voice was nothing but a rasp against air. "You had to drive yourself to the fucking hospital. You told me you had to sit in a fucking garbage bag while you did it. You had no one to call. And I wasn't there." Thump. Thump. "I wasn't there."

No amount of muscle mass could have kept her upright in that moment. She slid down the wall beside the door and hugged her knees to her chest. Thick tears streamed down her cheeks as she remembered that night. How terrified and alone she'd been.

"They'd kept you overnight because you'd lost so much blood, and you were sleeping when I arrived. You woke up when I touched your hand, but you wouldn't look at me. Then, when it was time to leave, you told me to take you to your apartment. Yours not ours. And I knew. I knew it was over. That I'd lost you." His voice was farther down the door, and she was sure he'd slid down as well. "I thought of all the ways I wanted to fight for you. But the harder I tried, the more distant you got. And eventually I knew the only way for you to be okay was for me to leave."

"So you did," she whispered against her knees.

"So I did." And that had been the end.

She tried her best to get on with life, to work, to be normal, like nothing happened, because no one had known it had.

She'd taken some sick days, but evading her mother while she was "sick" had proven harder than hiding her entire marriage. Lucy had embraced the *fake it till you make it* mentality with a whole new state of mind: survival.

The only thing that threatened her emotional fragility had been Joel. She'd moved back to her apartment, but he'd continued checking in, making sure she ate, wanting to talk, sitting with her in silence, asking if she would rather talk to someone else. She didn't.

All she wanted was to pretend none of it had happened.

"I kept waiting for divorce papers to arrive," he said. "Thought about sending them to you myself, if only to end the misery I seemed to cause you. Four years of that limbo, you were the only unfinished business I've ever had. But then I saw you at that wedding, and even though I know our engagement is fake, and it's supposed to be your chance to finally achieve your dreams for your father's company— nothing feels fake to me anymore."

The great, self-assured Joel Morgan had never sounded more unsure. His voice was a mixture of hesitant apprehension and desperation, so unlike she'd ever heard him. He was The Fixer, the dragon slayer, the one everyone depended on, but now he sounded so helpless, and Lucy knew the ball had landed in her court.

God, this man. Only he had the power to undo her so completely that she was ready to claw out her heart and slide it under the door to give it to him.

No way could she have this conversation and not touch him, not look at him. "Joel, let me open the door."

Before she could scramble to her feet, the door clicked open. Joel's hand appeared around the doorframe, and Lucy realized they had been sitting back-to-back, the wall between them, this whole time.

She stared at his hand, palm down on the floor, sliding back toward her. Instinctively, she placed her hand over his. The warmth of his skin traveling up her arm went straight to her chest.

The words *I love you* tumbled around inside her, chomping at the bit to break free. But she held them back. Hadn't he been explaining where they had gone wrong? They needed more than emotionally charged declarations of love and wild sex. They needed to rebuild from the ground up.

"I'm sorry I left," he said, his voice a gravelly rumble that cut her heart in two.

The knot in her throat was painful, almost choking the words she needed to get out. "I was angry at you for years." Anger was a strong word, but that's what she'd been full of. She'd been nothing but a vessel of loathing and blame with nowhere to place it but at Joel. "You weren't there, and I hated you for it. And I know—" She stared at their entwined hands and turned hers over in his, locking her fingers around his, holding on. "Now I know," she corrected, "why. I wish I'd known sooner, but I understand why you couldn't say anything."

She hadn't truly realized how much resentment she still carried with her until she'd seen him at the wedding. Turned out avoidance and separation hadn't corrected anything, it had only masked it. Time had been nothing but a Band-Aid.

"I don't hate you, Joel." She needed to say it out loud, to put it out in the universe as a starting point. "I never did. I hated losing him. I hated how empty I felt afterward, how raw. Like something had been torn from my body against my will. Not something. My son. Our son. And I *hated* it." A sob ripped out of her as her mind raced back in time. A familiar agony filled her heart, her eyes. For a few moments, all she could do was cry.

On the other side of the wall, Joel stayed silent, but his palm was warm in hers. Here. With her.

"And the first thing I saw when I woke up was you." She remembered the touch of his hand, opening bleary eyes, facing reality. "I couldn't imagine going back to how we were, playing house, being happy. Would we try to make another baby? Could we? Did I want to? What if I miscarried again? I didn't want to replace him. I wanted *him*." She scrubbed her cheeks with her free hand. "Every thought I had about the future, even the next hour, was terrifying. So I turned it on you, because it was easier to be angry with you than to think about anything else."

"You had every right to be angry," he countered, his voice gritty. "You needed me, my son needed me, and I wasn't there."

Lucy squeezed his hand. They still couldn't see each other, but somehow this connection was so much stronger, like how sensations were heightened when you put on a blindfold. There was a safety net in the blindness to express themselves freely. If she looked at him right now, if she saw the pain she heard in his voice, it would break her wide open. "You needed me as well, but I wasn't there for you. I'm sorry I didn't see it in time."

Silence stretched between them. Would they spend the rest of the night sitting there like this? With the wall and the ghost of their son between them.

"I miss him," Joel said, the last word lost in a crack of emotion.

"I know." Her words were choked.

He squeezed her hand.

She hadn't talked about him in years. No one had known

about Luca, there'd been no one to talk about him to. "I miss him too. I think about what he'd look like, sound like."

"You. I always imagined he'd be all you." Joel's gruff tone scraped the edges of her heart, making the ache deeper. "If I ever have another, I want it to be with you."

Maybe he hadn't meant to say that out loud because she heard his immediate sharp intake of breath, like he was shocked by his own declaration. Could he hear her heartbeat vibrating through the wall? Then his thumb stroked her skin, and she turned her head to stare at their joined hands, letting the tears slide down her face. A baseball sized knot clogged her throat so she couldn't talk, but she nodded, hoping he'd feel the motion in her hand.

The thought of having another child was terrifying. The fear that a miscarriage would happen again was immobilizing. But more surprising was the anxiety of having a successful pregnancy. Guilt clawed her chest every time she imagined having another baby, like that would dishonor the one she'd lost. She couldn't stomach the idea of a little soul out there, feeling like he'd been replaced. Forgotten. Like she'd simply moved on. Even the thought made her ill. And yet...the hope, the longing to one day take that leap again... If she ever did, it would only be with him.

Part of her wanted that so badly. What would it take for them to get past this? They had marriage vows and a child between them. Both had died, but maybe there was the possibility of bringing one back to life.

"So, where do we go from here?" She asked.

Joel's thumb found the rock on her finger. He outlined it, moved it back and forth while she waited for him to say something. To guide them into the next phase. A long silence passed.

"I should go back to my room and let you get some sleep." He made no move to get up or release her hand.

"Or you could stay," she offered, because the last thing she wanted was to be left alone again. The yearning to be with him, close to him, was all-consuming.

Joel laughed softly, without humor. "Lucy, you know what I'll do to you if I stay in your bed tonight. And I just finished telling you why I want us to go slow this time. No more rookie mistakes."

This time...as if another chance waited for them on the other end of the mess they'd created. In her brain she knew he might be right, but in her vital feminine organs the need had built to a fever pitch, and she couldn't bring herself to let him walk away from her tonight. Her emotions were too raw, her desire too greedy. "What would you do if you stayed in my room tonight?"

"Luciana," he groaned.

"Tell me," she whispered. She wasn't backing down. If he left her alone right now, empty and aching, it would hurt so much more than she was ready to admit.

"I'd do whatever you wanted me to do. Whatever you asked me to do."

Closing her eyes, she imagined what she'd want him to do first.

"Like kiss me?"

"Yes," came his strangled reply.

"Where?"

"Anywhere. Everywhere."

Her eyes drifted closed, the weight of the previous topic draining out of her, and she pictured where she'd want him to kiss her first. The image of his head bending to her aching nipples conjuring first.

"I remember how you taste in my mouth. Smooth and

sweet. When I'm alone in my bed, I remember those nights that you let me have every part of your body. I remember the taste and the smell, how your skin felt under my hands and tongue. Those memories have kept me alive for four years, Lucy."

Her lips parted as a new image formed, him in his bed, alone, thinking of her. She dragged in a desperate breath of air. "Tell me how you remember it," she pleaded.

His low groan rumbled through the open door. "I remember how you liked it when I sucked on your breast a little too hard until it hurt just enough that you'd almost need me to stop. Then I'd blow on them to soothe the ache, and watch them get stiff in front of my eyes. I jacked off to that memory a thousand times."

Her heart slammed in her chest as he recalled his intimate details and revealed his dirty little secret to her. Her nipples responded under her robe as the memory unfolded in her own mind. "They're stiff right now."

"*Fuck.*" He huffed out another humorless laugh. "I'm trying to be chivalrous here."

Didn't sound like it to her, but she wasn't complaining.

"Joel, you have no idea how my body feels right now, with you on the other side of the wall within touching distance. Everything we just talked about. Everything you just said. I *ache.*" A soft moan finished her sentence.

He cursed again. His hand twitched in hers. "Where does it ache? Where would you want me to touch you if I was right in front of you?"

"Everywhere."

"Be specific." His tone had taken on that dominance she craved so much in her loneliest hours.

This was the voice she heard in her head when she touched herself, thinking of him.

"Bet-tween my legs." She barely got the words out, her hand already drifting down her stomach. "I want you to touch me between my legs."

"I know how you like it too, rough little strokes of my thumb, while my tongue plays with your pretty nipples. But my hand wouldn't be enough would it, Lucy?" His voice was nothing more than a rasp of grit against the quiet air around them.

Lucy breathed out a quiet "no" before she could even think through what was happening. If there was a problem with them going from heartfelt confessions to erotic sex talk, she couldn't drum up any remorse.

"You'd want my mouth too; you'd need it so badly you'd beg for it. Do you remember how you used to beg me for it?"

Lucy moaned into the silence of her room.

"I'd lick my way down your chest first, savoring the taste. You taste so fucking good. And it's been a long time since I've tasted you. So, I'd take my time, making sure to stop at your hips and belly button to dip my tongue into the hollow. I'd use one finger to test how wet you were, check in and ask if you really wanted me to keep going."

"I would, I do." Her fingers brushed her core. "God, I'm so wet, Joel." Her head thunked back against the wall, her eyes closing as she imagined his head moving lower between her legs. In reality, her hand clenched spasmodically against his.

"You know how I like to draw it out though, how I'd make it last. I'd sink my fingers in slowly and start with a stroke, they'd dip and press just how you like it. My fingers a little rough and deep. I remember—" His breathing turned ragged, cutting his words. "How you'd scream for me when I dipped two in and twist them up toward your belly."

Her fingers mimicked his words, like he was giving her

instructions, and she moaned as she let her legs fall open. Her robe slipped off her shoulder and the cool air rushed over her skin.

"Fuck, are you doing it, Lucy? Are you touching yourself the way I touch you?"

"Yes!" she sobbed. "I want your mouth on me, Joel. I need more." Through the roaring of her blood rushing in her ears, she heard him curse loudly, then the scratching sound of a zipper being pulled down roughly.

His hand slammed down over hers, pressing it to the floor with weight. Was he undressing? She had no idea. The blindness drove her wild with lust.

"My mouth is right there, sweetheart. I've been starving for you." His voice was hoarse, desperate.

And then, Lucy stopped thinking because her thumb found her clit. She cried out loudly, the promise of relief so sharp and palpable it scorched her.

"Oh God, oh Joel!" she whined. "I'd need to feel you. Please, please."

"I'm with you, baby. I'm right fucking here with you. Like every other time."

And with those words she did fall, her hand twisting to find his, gripping so tightly she was sure it had to hurt, but it matched the intensity of the exquisite relief that consumed her. White hot flashes shot behind her closed eyes like fireworks, pleasure exploding through her body, making her shake against her hand and the wall.

Joel's own gruff grunts of relief filled the air, and she knew he'd come with her. The idea of him spilling himself into his hand or onto his abdomen only prolonging her release.

Eventually her breathing returned to baseline, even if

her heart continued to thunder. Her hand went slack against his as she released her death grip.

"Jesus Christ." Joel's voice sounded like he'd been a smoker since the day he was born. "Lucy, I—that's not—"

"Shh, don't ruin it," she murmured, knowing the wheels of honor and integrity were cranking back into motion in his mind. "That was good. Therapeutic. Satisfying." She patted his hand placatingly, letting him know there was no reason to think too hard. "We shared feelings and an orgasm. That's good progress. Don't ruin it for me by thinking too loud." She gently pushed his hand to his side of the doorway. "Good night, I'll see you in the morning."

He mumbled something incoherent in return, before she shut the door between them.

CHAPTER TWENTY-NINE

The next day was a flurry of activity. With her mother, aunt, and sister in town, there was no escaping engagement and wedding talk, and for all the awkward silence her sister had given her while she was away filming in Vancouver, she was full in on the wedding planning now. After a day of being dragged to every wedding dress shop in Portland, the four of them met Natalie, Hope, and Ivy at one of the local upscale restaurants for lunch and to finalize details for the engagement party at Bowie's the next evening.

Lucy avoided making eye contact with Ivy, who glared at her with an unnerving combination of suspicion and distrust. After Joel's revelations last night, Lucy would be lying if she said she hadn't been intrigued by what had happened. It was pure curiosity, and one hundred percent not her business. Joel didn't have to tell her any of it, but she was grateful he had, because she now understood why it'd taken him so long to get home while her world was imploding. What would Hope and Ivy think if they knew Joel had told her what had happened to them?

"Are we sure having an engagement party at a bar isn't

tacky?" Maria asked the group, cutting into Lucy's thoughts. At least Maria had the grace to cast Hope an apologetic glance. "No offence, *cara*, I am sure your husband has a nice bar, but back home we would usually rent a nice hall. Is there an Italian Cultural Center close by? Or maybe one of Joel's properties. Doesn't he have a nice one on the coast?"

"Mom, Ivy and Hope have already organized everything and booked Bowie's," Vanessa chided. "I've been to the bar. Trust me, it's nice. Classy. Plus, the media will be there. I've invited influencers. It'll put Bowie's on the map. "

Maria sniffed. "Is it an engagement party or a Hollywood affair, Vanessa? Why do we need the people from the media ? This isn't one of your red carpet events or a trashy party. It is your sister's engagement party!"

"Mom, please." Vanessa rolled her eyes, then glanced at Lucy and mouthed the word *see?*

This was why her sister had left as soon as she could. She and Maria were like oil and water. Maria was old school and her expectations were high. For Maria, success was a family affair. You did something for the betterment and the success of your family. But Vanessa had chased her own dreams, built her success on her own, and enjoyed it. For Vanessa, the pressure to be tied to family was stifling and annoying.

Lucy didn't share the sentiment. The way she saw it, her family had done a lot for her, and it was her obligation to do everything she could to support them in return.

There were times where she felt stifled, many times when she was annoyed, especially when most of her family didn't take her seriously or listen to what she said. But she was beginning to realize that had more to do with her own inability to give herself a voice than anything wrong in her family.

"Zia, the bar is perfect. Trust me, it's not some run down, side of the road biker bar you're imagining. Bowie's is popular. It's the place to be. You should feel lucky that Gabe and Hope will be part of the family soon," Natalie said, running interference while sipping her mimosa. "Isn't it cool to think of it like that? Once Lucy and Joel marry, the Barones, Morgans and Walshes all become one big family. I can give Hope a free balayage in exchange for drinks at Bowie's. It'll be great!"

Lucy glanced around the table. Except for Ivy, who was still scowling at her, everyone looked happy and excited, discussing this big event like it was real.

After last night, it was starting to feel real for Lucy. Joel had said things that made her think he'd felt the shift too. But what if they were feelings of nostalgia?

Staying married was a big commitment involving sacrifices for both of them. Would he leave after their year of marriage like they'd agreed, or would he stay and try?

The thought was too big, especially with her mother and sister arguing about what wine to serve (Italian or Californian) and Ivy still eyeing her over the rim of her glass. Needing a moment to focus, Lucy excused herself to the ladies' room.

Last night had been such a breakthrough, and the last few days together had reminded her that she and Joel were more than their combustible sexual chemistry. They shared a real bond.

But four years had passed since they separated. Joel had set up a new life for himself in Portland. Even if it was temporary, it was long-term temporary. They had their sights set on different things.

After eight minutes of sitting on the closed toilet seat, her heart still beat unsteadily. She needed a plan if she was going to sort through her messy emotions. Talking had worked for them. If they had only talked four years ago the way they had last night, maybe they wouldn't be here now. Then again, at that time in her grief, she would have never been ready to dig this deep. Timing was everything. And this was theirs.

Resolved to talk more tonight, Lucy got up, opened the stall door, and came face to face with Ivy, who leaned against the sink, arms crossed. They appeared to be the only ones in the bathroom, which, judging by Ivy's steely expression was a good thing or...maybe a bad? This girl looked like she knew how to fight.

"He told you, didn't he?" Ivy said, her eyes not wavering from Lucy's.

"Um." That was all she could say as her brain scrambled to come up with a game plan.

Ivy didn't know Lucy and Joel were married. She didn't know they'd lost a baby when he'd been away helping her and his sister. She had no reason to know or understand why Joel would have any excuse to break a confidence.

"It's okay. I told him he could if he ever needed to. I don't want people keeping secrets for me anymore. I'm in a different place now. Joel knows that. It's just, I'm wondering why it came up, is all." When Lucy didn't reply, Ivy shook her head. "It doesn't matter. I'm sorry, totally none of my business. If Joel believed it was important to tell you, then he had a good reason. He doesn't make a single decision thoughtlessly, and he never betrayed my trust, not once."

"No, he doesn't." But Lucy knew a hard, intimate truth about Ivy, and she deserved an explanation as to why. "We were talking about the complicated things that happened in our past. He told me about going to help his sister in college, in a very vague, limited way."

"Ah, the past. It has such a hold on us, huh?" She turned to the mirror and pulled out a lip balm from her bag. "Funny how the bad shit can haunt us like a motherfucker. But when the good stuff happens, we don't even blink. As if we deserve it somehow. Truth is, we don't deserve the good or the bad. Both happen to everyone. And they both affect you. But have you ever thought about what life would be like if we invested more energy in the good than the bad?" She caught Lucy's gaze in the mirror as she applied a coat.

Had she? Not in those terms. The realization of how much time she'd lost holding onto the negative was unsettling.

"Well," Ivy went as she rubbed her lips together. "I'm still trying to figure out how to give the good stuff more power than the bad, but I'm getting there." She turned toward the door, then stopped. "Joel's had his fair share of shit to deal with. He's always fixing everything for everyone else. Me, his sister, patching his family back together after Hope's adoption bomb. Joel is always picking up pieces because he's a natural born leader. He walks into a room and people have a compulsion to do what he says. His authority is hypnotic, but I can never hate him for it because he's so...good, you know?"

Lucy did know, and yet she'd, nonetheless, spent four years being angry with him. No, not him, the situation. Only yesterday had she started to truly understand that.

"I've wondered if he'd ever have anything for himself. He's always holding things together. It's reassuring to know that he might finally have someone to hold him together." She cast a long, meaningful look at Lucy. "You'll take care of his heart, right?"

Guilt slammed into her. When he'd needed someone to hold him together, she'd been too broken to even recognize it. Whether she could now was something she wasn't entirely sure of, but she wanted to try, so she replied, "Yes."

"Good, 'cause he's a catch and a half. And for once, he needs someone to make sure he gets as good as he gives." Ivy clapped her hands. "Okay, no more moping in the bathroom. Let's go finish eating. Joel's footing the bill, so we might as well order dessert and a bottle of champagne to go."

Joel was supposed to be in meetings all day.

"How do you know he foot the bill?"

"Oh, because when Maria asked for the bill, the server told her it was already taken care of by a gentleman who phoned earlier. We knew it was Joel because that's the kind of stuff Joel does." She shot Lucy another look. "That good and bad stuff in life I was talking about, well, Joel's the good stuff. And he's yours, so don't hurt him, okay?"

Ivy was out the door before Lucy could do any more than nod.

CHAPTER THIRTY

After lunch, her mother and Zia Ella insisted on inspecting Bowie's, so they all headed to the bar where Lucy had the joy of meeting Carter, one of the head bartenders, who shamelessly flirted Maria and Ella into a puddle of coy adoration until they honestly believed the idea of hosting the engagement party in a bar had been their idea all along.

"Did he just do that?" Lucy asked Hope as she tasted a specialty cocktail Carter had made for her and declared it be called the "Barone ball buster."

Ella and Maria were already on their second.

Hope laughed, sipping at her own virgin ball buster as she regarded the bartender affectionately. "Carter has the unique ability to charm the pants off a snake. Gabe sees difficult clients coming and shoves Carter in front of them. He can make anyone walk away thinking they're best friends and Bowie's is the best establishment they've ever been to."

Lucy appreciated Carter's boyish good looks. He was tall and slim. A sleeve of beautifully designed tattoos ran up his arm in a way that would have made most men look tougher, but it only made Carter seem like a piece of nouveau art.

"We compensate him well enough so hopefully he never thinks of leaving," Hope told her. "He's an asset for sure."

"Will he be bartending tomorrow night?" Lucy was quite enjoying her ball buster.

"Oh yes. Besides, I don't think your mother and aunt would have it any other way now. They're positively smitten."

It was true. Both middle-aged women were fawning over their new friend, watching raptly as he told them Bowie's history, and how lucky they were to host a party here.

"I should go see if the kitchen needs any extra help for tomorrow," Hope told Lucy. "Let me know if you need anything, okay?" She moved off toward the back, giving Carter a thumbs up as she passed behind Maria and Ella.

Seconds later, an arm slung around Lucy's shoulder, and she looked up to find her sister. "Imagine how different life would have been if he'd been around to distract Mom while we were growing up. The son she never had," Vanessa mused, watching the scene. "They would have had the boy they always wanted to take over the family business and propagate the family genes, and we wouldn't have had to endure their constant nagging."

"But then you and I wouldn't have bonded as we conspired for hours on ways to break free from under the thumb of their tyranny."

Vanessa threw back her head and laughed in that musical way of hers. "Yes, except you never broke free. You stayed where you were. I never did figure out how you did it without going crazy."

Duty. Their parents had made so many sacrifices for her.

The least she could do was make them proud. Even though that was proving harder than anticipated.

Then there was Joel. His constant friendship, emails, phone calls, and looks of solidarity during odd business events. They'd had similar goals and drives and having him in her life had always been a reassurance.

And of course, there was the company. Barone & Sons meant so much to her. Her dream that she'd one day see their family legacy into a new generation of success was a big reason she'd stayed around. All of that and, unlike her sister, she'd never felt the urgent need to leave. She loved her crazy family, even when the relentless chaos grated on her every nerve. She'd never disapproved of her sister leaving to pursue modeling when she was only sixteen, but she wondered if Vanessa had found the happiness she was looking for out there.

The sound of their mother's high-pitched laughter made them look over.

One of Vanessa's perfectly microblade eyebrows shot up her forehead. "She never laughs like that for us," she said. "Do you think we can adopt him?"

Lucy looped her arm around her sister's shoulders and led her to a bar table off to the side. "Look on the bright side. After tomorrow, you get to jet-set back to Vancouver for your next film shoot."

Vanessa shrugged. "Actually, I'm thinking of taking a break from acting."

"What?" Lucy tried to school the shock from her voice.

Acting had always been her sister's dream. After a couple of years modeling, Vanessa had gotten a commercial gig for a high-end clothing brand where she had a few speaking lines, and she pursued that dream ever since. Transitioning from modeling to acting hadn't been easy. The world of the latter never quite taking the former seriously. The grind had been uphill, but then she earned a permanent spot on an up-and-coming paranormal drama series, and Lucy had assumed Vanessa was well on her way up the hill.

But maybe she wasn't? Was that why she'd gone radio silent for the last several weeks? The way her sister had looked when she'd walked into Natalie's salon had poked her sixth sense that all was not right. "Is everything okay, Vanessa?"

Another shrug of her sister's shoulders was her only answer.

"You'd tell me if it wasn't, right? If something was wrong?"

A shadow of a smile ghosted Vanessa's lips. "Of course. Don't worry about me. I just need a break."

"Will they let you take one?" It didn't seem like an industry that let you spontaneously take a mental-health break.

"You better believe it. Especially after Joel barged onto the set and—oh shit." Vanessa clamped her hand over her mouth, but it was too late.

Lucy's heart rate picked up. "What do you mean, barged onto set? What are you talking about?"

"Nothing. Don't listen to me. I'm overwhelmed, not thinking. My imagination has a tendency to go wild. It's very vivid, you know..."

"Vanessa Barone, tell me right now. When was Joel on your film set?" Something uncomfortable tightened in her chest.

"Really, it wasn't what you think." Vanessa started inspecting her nails.

"I don't know what to think, because up until this second I didn't know about this development."

"Ohmigod, Lu, it's not a development! It's not like I called him over." Her sister's face twisted. "I barely know Joel. You two were way closer than I ever was. I'm like a baby sister to him. Not even. A baby cousin maybe. An annoying baby cousin who can't take care of herself." Vanessa flipped her long ponytail over her shoulder in a frustrated gesture. "Argh, fine. He came to get me from Vancouver a few days ago, okay?"

Silence slid between them and numbed everything. The noise in the bar faded. A few days ago? When he left abruptly, with nothing but a sticky note and pastries in his wake. "Why would he go get you?"

Vanessa sighed loudly. "Because of you. You were trying to get a hold of me for days. You'd texted me about your engagement, but so did everyone else. Jesus, that night of Mariana's wedding, I think I got messages from every female in our family. And two from Zio Gambo. Apparently, there was an epic bathroom scene where Joel walked in and declared undying love for you."

"Exaggeration," Lucy said. "But go on." She gestured with her hand impatiently.

"Anyway." Vanessa averted her gaze. "Things in Vancouver have been complicated. We have this producer, he's—used to getting his way. And I didn't think I could leave, but being away when all this juicy stuff was going on for you, it made me sadder than I already was, and so I didn't respond because I didn't want to drag you down. But I guess I underestimated how much you really wanted me here."

"I did. I do." Lucy reached across the bar table to clasped

Vanessa's hand. "You're my sister. Plus, I need your help deflecting Mom."

A sad, half-smile cracked Vanessa's lips. "I thought I wouldn't be much by way of company, and Kurt, the producer, was making things…" She twirled the stem of her glass between her fingers for a few seconds. "Difficult for me."

There was more there. Much more, and if they had been anywhere but the middle of a bar surrounded by family, she might have pried.

"And, geez, you should have seen Joel take him on. Kurt's such a fucking bully and no one ever challenges him. But Joel was so smooth, so quietly kickass and intense, Kurt didn't stand a chance. Anyway, the next thing I know, I'm sitting in a private jet with the Morgan name written on the side, coming home for my big sister's fake," she whispered this word, "engagement party." She leaned over and gave Lucy a side hug. "He told me not to say anything to you, by the way, so you cannot tell him I told you. He'd never trust me again. Lu, you're so lucky. But also, you deserve it, and I'm happy for you."

Lucy's mind was a tornado of thoughts, everything her sister had said made her dizzy. He'd disappeared to go play hero and hadn't told her why. *Again.* And he told Vanessa to keep it a secret from her. Frustration tightened her chest. She'd thought they'd shared all their truths last night, but he'd left this one out.

"Why?" she asked aloud. "Why didn't he tell me?"

Vanessa shrugged her elegant shoulders. "Maybe he wanted to surprise you? Or maybe he wanted to shield you? The paparazzi make a big deal out of everything in his life, and mine. There was no reason to draw your attention to it. He was doing a good deed. That's all. Let him."

"Shield me from what?" How deeply had Joel's life changed in four years?

Vanessa's eyes narrowed. "Do you really not scroll the socials, sissy? Like, not even a single Google search on your guy, or what?"

Lucy frowned. "More and more I'm thinking it's a good idea not to."

"And you would be absolutely right." Vanessa nodded. "The pap took pictures when they saw us together at the airport and I don't know how those losers do it, but they make everything look compromising. He didn't touch me even once, but somehow there's a pic on TMZ of us boarding a plane with his hand on my back. Like how?"

Lucy choked on her drink.

Her beloved sister simply offered another casual shrug. "*Billionaire and his model mistress.* Makes good press, even if it's a load of shit." She tossed her hand in the air. "And what the fuck is with that anyway? I might not be a billionaire, but I've got enough cash in the bank to retire if I wanted right now. Models have such a bad rep, like all we're good for is looking pretty and sex." Her gaze lowered. "Actresses aren't much better, apparently."

Too much information was coming at her at once. Lucy swallowed the rest of her drink and leveled her sister with a glare, her mind fixated on one thing. "There are photos of you and my fiancé floating around with the title *Billionaire and His Model Mistress* attached to it?"

Vanessa smirked. "Welcome to my life, Lu. And his." Her expression softened, and this time she reached across the bar table to take Lucy's hand. "And you wonder why he doesn't tell you stuff? He doesn't want to stress you out. Besides, I don't think the drama lasted long. His money carries power. He makes things go away pretty quickly."

"It's the internet, Ness!" Lucy barked. "Nothing ever goes away!" Since when was her sister this naïve?

But maybe she wasn't, because Vanessa's whole body immediately tensed, shifting away from Lucy. "No shit, Lu. Tell me about it." She sighed loudly. "Okay, maybe he can't make things go all the way away, but he does better at it than most of us. And in this case, I think he moved pretty quickly."

Lucy's mind raced. The thought of rumors circulating about Joel and her sister was nauseating. Paparazzi had never followed him around before, not to her knowledge. But then again, he was a different caliber now. Apparently.

"I'm not surprised he's head over heels for you," Vanessa went on. "Because, hello, you're a total catch. Smart, beautiful, patient. But a life as Joel Morgan's wife? That's not going to be basic. Are you sure that's what you want? Paparazzi and the kind of power that can bend even the will of men like Kurt Robertson?" She regarded Lucy with an arched brow. "I know you two had a spontaneously wild Vegas wedding, and things were probably fantastic when you lived in a private bubble that no one knew about. But what happens when the bubble pops, Lu?"

The bubble *had* popped, and they'd fallen apart. What would the difference be this time?

"Speak of the devil," Vanessa muttered under her breath. "Here comes Mr. Not Basic in the flesh, looking like a million bucks. Or shall I say, a billion?"

Lucy whipped her head to the entrance. Joel entered, all athletic grace and innate power decked out in his corporate gear. He moved like the leader of a pack of lions, with an air of authority both dangerous and magnetic. Today's custom gray suit hugged his body like it had been designed for him alone, the dark fabric highlighting every impressive cut of his anatomy to perfection. Everything about him made it impossible not to stare. No wonder the press loved him.

"And he's all yours, sis," Vanessa mused, with a light pat on Lucy's hand.

He scanned the room until he found her, and the smile that landed on his mouth when he did unlatched the butter-flies caged in her stomach. They erupted in her abdomen with a force that should have been concerning, if she could have thought of anything beyond the conversation she'd just had.

As per usual, everyone vied for his attention the moment he entered the bar. Immediately, he was waylaid by a group of party planners, his sister gripping his arm to keep him in place as she pointed to the tables and chairs, outlining her plan for the set up. When he finally broke free from Hope, Gabe called to him from behind the bar, shouting something about beverage options for the next day. Even her mother stopped him, patting his cheek and laughing as she spoke. He responded with a kind smile and murmured something that had her blushing.

He's all yours, her sister had said. But was he? Or would he always be everyone's? The hero who everyone shared and needed?

Her thoughts spiraled even as Joel found her gaze again. This time he held it, a faint crease appearing between his eyebrows.

Despite her frustration and apprehension, one look from him was all it took for her body to respond. Heat bloomed low in her belly, working its way up to her heart and throat, and she caught her lip between her teeth as she watched him watch her.

This relentless desire, the heat and the need, hadn't been enough before, and it wouldn't be enough this time.

Was it selfish that she didn't want to spend a lifetime competing with whoever needed Joel Morgan most? Or the paparazzi making her second guess herself, making her wonder if she was just another project to him.

Her frown was making her brain hurt, and Joel must have noticed, because he disentangled himself from Maria's grip and turned toward Lucy with intent in his eyes. Removing his suit jacket as he stalked toward her, he dropped it on a nearby chair at an empty table, loosened his tie and started rolling up his shirt sleeves. She didn't realize she hadn't taken a breath until he was standing in front of her, and then his scent slammed into her, the intoxicating intensity of it sending a fog over every thought ricocheting in her head.

"You're overthinking," he whispered so only she could hear, dipping his head until his lips brushed against hers. When he straightened, he addressed her sister. "Vanessa," he acknowledged with a nod.

"BIL," she replied.

"Pardon me?" His voice was a rumble of confusion.

"B. I. L. Brother-in-law. It's what I'm calling you from now on. Since, you know, you are. And you're my favorite one, too." Her smirk matched the twinkle in her eye. She was loving this. Scooting off the bar stool, she adjusted the skirt that had climbed its way up her thighs when she sat. "I'm going to let you love birds"—she waved her hand between them— "do whatever it is you need to do. I'm going to convince Mom and Zia it's time to go home and make me pasta. *Ciao*." She air kissed their cheeks and sashayed off.

"She's trouble," Joel said, as they watched Vanessa strut over to the older women.

"Since the day she was born, I'm afraid," Lucy agreed, trying to ignore the kaleidoscopic of emotions churning in her chest. "Some days I wonder whose heart she's going to eventually lock down."

"Hopefully someone who knows that her kind of trouble is worth it, then sticks around to fight for her instead of with her."

Lucy swiveled her head toward him. What a typical Joel thing to say. Both elusive and insightful. Like he knew things no one else knew, except this was her sister, and she wanted to know. But before she could interrogate him, he turned and braced a palm against either side of her on the table, sheltering her in the circle of his arms. "So, what were you overthinking about? Your mother?"

"For once, no." His intoxicating closeness made the truth fall right from her lips, all thought of Vanessa, or anyone else for that matter, completely evaporating from her mind. "I was thinking about you. About us."

"And..." His breath fanned her face as he leaned in, tracing his nose along her cheek. "What conclusion did you come to?"

Her heart hammered in her chest, and she was sure if he focused on her neck, he'd see the beat pounding under her skin. Had she come to any other conclusion than he smelled fantastic? She couldn't remember.

"I can't think when you do that," she admitted hoarsely, turning her cheek toward his, until the corners of their mouths brushed.

"I can't help it. I've missed you," he whispered, his lips now directly over hers. "All day I've been thinking about this exact moment. With you, I'm like a fucking moth to a flame. I can't stay away, even when I know I'm going to get burned. And I'll take the pain every time, because being burned by you is a thousand times less agonizing than being apart from you."

There was no time to ask him what he meant, no time to even fully digest his words, because he kissed her, and not soft or gently, not inconspicuous, or appropriate for the public setting they were in, but passionate and ravenous. As if he truly could not wait another second for this kiss. His mouth devoured hers, but even through the heated embrace he still exercised his control, his arms braced against the table, keeping a distance. If she wanted, she could have pulled away and ducked out of his hold. She considered it.

What had he meant when he'd said he couldn't stay away even if he knew he'd be burned? Did he expect her to hurt him? Did he honestly think she had that power? Half the time, she was at his mercy. If anyone was going to be hurt here, surely it would be her. The sharp edge of pain traced around the frayed edges of her heart, reminding her that she already was.

She pressed the palm of her hand into the firm wall of muscle protecting his heart.

"Joel." She pulled away, breathless. "We need to talk." So much to talk about, so little ability to concentrate when his face was suctioned to hers.

"Talk, yes. We should, shouldn't we?" He drew back enough so she could focus in on his eyes.

She tried to read what was in them, but they were immediately guarded. Somewhere between their kiss and her palm on his chest, he'd reassembled himself.

"You kiss like that tomorrow and you'll set the fire alarms off," Carter said, sidling up behind them. He leaned forward, propping his elbows on the tabletop, chin resting in his palms, watching them casually. "I'm thinking of creating a cocktail to name after the two of you, *Jucy*, you know, for Joel and Lucy." He looked back and forth between them. "Too tacky? I thought of merging the two last names, but *Morone* just sounded—no."

Lucy turned her head to the side to look at Carter. Even though she meant what she said to Joel, and she did want to talk, she had to defend her culture. "I'll have you know Morone is a very respectable Italian surname."

"Really?" Carter narrowed his eyes, considering. "Nah, Jucy is way better."

"Do whatever you want. Lucy and I have to go." Joel held out his hand, which Lucy took in an automatic response she had when it came to him.

"Wait, are you giving me carte blanche on your engagement cocktail? Like, you don't even want to offer flavor suggestions. I can go wild?"

"Go as wild as you want," Joel told him, already leading her toward the door down the back hallway. But before they were out of ear shot, he shouted back, "In fact, if you keep everyone out of our hair tomorrow night, you have dibs on the wedding cocktail too."

The last thing she heard before she was pulled into the hallway was Carter's cry of delight.

CHAPTER THIRTY-ONE

Joel held Lucy's hand all the way up the narrow stairs that led to the apartments, the sounds from the bar fading into the dull white noise he'd grown accustomed to. He continued to hold her hand as he fumbled with the key and opened the door. When they were safely ensconced, he led her to the couch, but she resisted, and that was when the first tendrils of panic jabbed his insides. She didn't move. She simply stared at him with the million thoughts that were circling in her brain that he wasn't privy to.

"Is this the part where we fight, then?" he asked, resignation leaking into his tone.

When she still didn't speak, he stepped forward, fingers threading through her hair as he gripped her skull and tilted her face up to meet his. No hiding.

"Is this the part, Lucy, where you tell me we have to break off the engagement and I tell you there's no chance in hell?" Heart thundering in his chest, he moved even closer, until their foreheads nearly touched. "I don't have it in me to be apart from you again. Please don't make me," he whispered.

Lucy's eyes fluttered shut, and she sighed, then pulled back from him. "Where did you go earlier this week, when you left for three days?"

With those words, his heart sank. He should have known. This time he didn't speak.

She broke free of him completely. "Where did you go, Joel?" She stood rigid, watching him carefully.

He sighed deeply. "I didn't want to tell you in case it didn't work out." He didn't bother spelling it out. She obviously knew where he'd been.

"But it did work out."

"Yes. It did."

"Argh!" She whirled away from him. "Why are you so annoyingly calm all the time? It's infuriating." She turned again and glared at him hotly before pacing back and forth. "She told me you told her not to say anything."

"I did."

"Why!?" She threw up her hands in exasperation, stopping abruptly. "Why wouldn't you tell me? Why would you think leaving me here alone for three days, to go get *my sister*, after you asked me to move in and not telling me where you were was a good idea?" Her voice escalated to a shout, and he caved to it.

"Because you wanted her here," he shouted back. "And I wanted you to have something important that you didn't feel you owed me for."

"Well, maybe I do owe you! Like everybody else does." She swirled her arm to the side as if *everyone else* was in the room with them. "Because it sounds like you saved her from a major creep."

He took a purposeful, measured step toward her. "You do not, and never will, owe me anything," he stated firmly.

After a pause, a bleak sadness bled into her eyes. "We need to break off our engagement."

Only his years of practice in the boardroom made it possible for his face to remain expressionless. He couldn't allow his expression to reflect the way his stomach had just bottomed out. "No. Fucking. Way."

She broke eye contact, focusing on her hand as she fiddled with the ring he'd given her.

"I get it. You have a deep desire to fix things. I don't blame you. You're good at it. But this is too far. You saw them down there. They're planning an extravaganza, a colossal party where our families will drink too much together, and your mother and my mother will name their future grandchildren. I barely know Carter, and he's making us engagement and wedding cocktails named after us. It's out of hand. You came here to grow your business, not get wrapped up in this. It can't possibly be what you want."

"I need you to stop fucking telling me what I want." His intonation must have been sharper than he intended because her eyes flew to his, and in return, he burned his gaze into hers. "How do you know what I want?" His voice grew harsh, even to his own ears, but he couldn't help it.

For four years he'd carefully avoided her, given her the space she seemed to need, watched her from afar as she meticulously picked up the pieces of her life and moved on without him. He'd endured it because he thought it was what she wanted, what she'd needed, *what would make her happy*. But after last night, he'd realized how wrong he'd been, and how much time they'd fucking wasted. That made him angry, especially since she was trying to backpedal now, looking at him with tears in her eyes, after she told him to break off their engagement. Fuck no, he wasn't taking that.

"I knew that if I told you I was getting your sister, you would feel indebted, or you'd want to come with me, and I wanted to avoid both of those inevitabilities. I should have known she'd tell you."

"Fairly short-sighted of you considering she's my sister. The very reason we were making de-stressing lasagna only yesterday." Her half-smile gave him a glimmer of hope.

"You wanted her here," he repeated quietly. "And with me, you will always get what you want. Simple as that."

"But you can't keep me in the dark all the time." Her voice was lower, but not completely without frustration. "You just take off, under the cover of darkness, to go Batman a situation, and leave me to wake up alone. I can't—I can't do that the rest of my life."

The rest of my life...it was more than a glimmer and he reached out and grabbed it. Taking a calculated risk, he hooked his finger under her chin and tipped it upward.

"Is that what this is about, Lucy? Are you afraid that I'll leave again one day and I won't be there when you need me?"

She shifted her face away from him, like she couldn't face the truth, but the tears that spilled over her cheeks were loud enough. She wiped them away with the back of her hand. "I'm afraid you'll only be there because you think I'm another person who needs you."

His soul shattered at the hushed acquiescence in her voice. She truly believed she hadn't been first in his heart this entire time. He nudged her chin back his way. When exactly had the trust between them been broken?

He couldn't totally blame her line of thinking. Somewhere along the way he became the one everyone called when they were in crisis. He'd left her before to go help someone else. What was stopping her from believing it could happen again?

"Is she okay? My sister," she whispered, switching gears.

Joel sat back, his thoughts jumbled. So much he wanted to say and no idea where to begin. Might as well start by telling her the truth about her sister.

Vanessa was the opposite of Lucy in every way. And honestly, he had no clue if she was okay, but he knew that, temporarily at least, she was safe.

"The producer she worked for is a dick of massive proportions. I can't believe he still has a job, though when I'm finished with him, he won't."

Lucy's eyes widened at his vehement proclamation.

One of the things he despised most was men who used their positions of power to hurt women. "Anyway, let's just say he didn't want to let her go, and he was holding something over her head so she couldn't."

"What was it?" Her tears were gone, replaced with a concern that only came when you loved someone the way Lucy loved her sister.

The way he loved Lucy, protectively. Instinctively. Territorially.

"There was a video." He left that sentence hanging until he saw the realization dawn in her eyes.

"No."

"Yes." Raking his hand through his hair, he contemplated his next words carefully. "It was from a few years back. She was just breaking into the modeling scene. I haven't seen it, but I think it's—not something Vanessa would want leaked."

"Oh my God."

"Don't worry, I got rid of every copy we could find. I put

my best tech team on it. And with nothing left to hold over her head, she could go. I would have gotten her out regardless. Ball-less fucker." It had been an ugly few days. When he'd left Lucy sleeping in the apartment, he hadn't anticipated having to erase his sister-in-law's sex tape off the face of the planet, or some sick asshole who thought he could use a young woman's mistake to manipulate her entire career. "I could've stopped him from firing her, but Lucy, she's better off away from him. I think her character is going to be mysteriously killed off mid-season."

"Oh no." Lucy shook her head. "I had no idea. She told me about the pictures of the two of you, but nothing about a video."

His blood chilled. "Lucy, those pictures of her and I—"

She lifted her hand, stopping him. "I know. They're nothing. Just paparazzi doing what paparazzi do best. Ruining lives, and not giving a single fuck." A small smile lifted on the corner of her lips. "Another reminder to stay off the internet."

"I promise you," he said zealously. "I will do everything in my power so you never have to see anything like that."

Lucy eased his worry with a sigh. "Joel, you're a great many things, but you're not an asshole. I don't worry about any of that. Not seriously, anyway." Still, she frowned. "I'm worried about Vanessa though. She never told me any of this."

"I think there are a lot of things about your sister's life under the lights that we know nothing about." He couldn't resist reaching out to brush a loose strand of hair off her cheek where it had gotten stuck by earlier tears. "But at least we've solved one of her problems."

Lucy's eyes shot to his. "*You* solved one of her problems. And it sounds like it was a pretty damn big one." She rubbed her cheeks. "I'll have to talk with Vanessa about this. Maybe a break is what she needs."

"Is that what you want with us?" he asked, circling the conversation back to them, where he needed it to be. "A break?"

A long pause ensued as she studied the fingers of her left hand. Somewhere in the last few minutes, her right hand had become tightly locked in his, and he held on for fear of losing his mind if he let go. When she lifted her gaze and revealed to him all her turmoil, her indecision, he lost it anyway. He let go of her hand so he could cradle her face.

"Lucy, *what do you want*?" His whisper fanned across the fresh wave of tears falling down her cheeks. He used his thumbs to brush them away.

"I want you to be free."

Her words were so unexpected he jerked back from her, and she followed for a millisecond, like she hadn't been ready to disconnect.

Joel shook his head. It was laughable. Unbelievable. "Free," he repeated, incredulous. And then he laughed completely without humor. Did she really think he'd find any kind of freedom away from her? Unable to stay sitting, he got to his feet and moved aimlessly around the living room.

"Joel?" Her voice was wobbly, her eyes wet and confused.

He turned his back on her and pushed his hands through his hair, inhaling deeply, searching for control, for the right words.

"Four years," he said finally.

"What?" Lucy murmured behind him.

He turned and regarded her on the couch, sitting there, looking a little stunned and breathtakingly beautiful.

"Four years, Lucy. I haven't felt free in four God awful

years. Not since the day I left you. It's like I've been sleep-walking through my whole fucking life, wanting nothing more than to turn back time." He moved forward, dropping to his knees in front of her. "There is no freedom without you. All of this"—he gestured around them, referring to their whole charade—"was for you."

She steeled herself, like a curtain being drawn. Had he unlocked something in her?

"Exactly. For me, not for you. I don't want you to live your life to fix mine. You've done that for everyone. Nearly your entire adult life you've lived to ensure everyone else's happiness and security. Your family, the whole situation with Hope, even just now," she exclaimed, pointing down-stairs. "You walked into that bar, and everyone needed you for something."

Of course they did. They always did. What did that have to do with anything? He'd never not help the people he loved if he could.

Lucy looked resolute, like she hadn't finished making her point. "And you do it. You always have, and you always will. It's who you are, Joel. You have lived the entirety of your life for others, and I can't—" She made a sound, half choke, half hiccup as the tears flooded again. "I can't be another person that's some kind of duty for you, while you deny yourself all the things that might make you happy."

How could she still be so clueless when he thought he'd been so obvious with his feelings these last two weeks?

"You are—" He inhaled, trying to rein in the desperation coursing through him. And the fear. Losing her was not an option. "My. Wife." He let the words hang between them. "The only freedom I have ever known has been with you."

There. The truth. His heart, soul, and pride laid out for her to demolish or protect.

"Joel." It was no more than a breath off her lips. Indecision and understanding warred in her eyes.

"I want us to get re-married. I want you to have Barone & Sons. I want a lifetime of us. That's what I want. We see this through." His voice must have carried the weight of finality he'd hoped, because after a moment she nodded. "Say it."

"Okay," she whispered. "We'll see it through."

He only meant to kiss her as a punctuation to their conversation, but he should have known better, because the moment his lips brushed hers, his world exploded.

Lucy's mouth opened under his. A deep moan filled the air. Unsure whose it was, he angled his mouth and swallowed the sound. Her hands weaved into his hair and grabbed hold, anchoring herself and her lips to his.

The curve of her waist molded under his fingertips, the rigidness of her ribs expanding as he ran his hands upward. He relished how her breath caught when he touched her there and below her breast. One firm tug and he would have her on his lap. A careful pull of her skirt, a firm jerk of her panties and she'd be naked over him. He'd be no more than a slide of his zipper away from sinking into her.

She wanted him to feel freedom. This was where he found it most. Bared to her, body and soul, stripped of all his calculated confidence and strength. The only time he could be his truest self was here, and that was his freedom.

"I don't want to hear you say ever again that you are my duty," he said against her lips, between kisses. "You aren't an obligation, or a burden, or even a goddamn commitment. You're an honor, Lucy. I made a promise to you that night in Vegas and I never turned back from it, even when you told me to leave. There's been no one else for me but you, and I'll choose you every time. Do you hear me?" He gripped her hair as he lay his forehead against hers. "I need you to believe me."

"Okay," she said breathlessly. "Okay, I believe you, Joel. I believe you."

Music to his fucking ears. Her faith in him was all he required. If she trusted him to be there when she needed, he was a complete and happy man.

His fingers dug into her hips as he tugged her forward against his raging hard on. He hadn't lied the other night when he told her they should go slow. Their sexual frustrations could not overshadow the trust that was more essential. But God help him when she bucked upward, rubbing her center against him, he wanted nothing more than to dive into her.

"Lucy," he gasped. "We should—"

Her fingers popped the top button of his pants.

"Oh fuck!" Why did he want to go slow? Why was he waiting? His brain cells reeled as they scrambled to line up in his head, trying to remember the reason. "Wait, we should wait." Hell, he couldn't even breathe without wanting her.

Lucy dipped her head, her lips finding his neck as she undid a few buttons on his shirt. "You know, I'm getting really tired of hearing you say that." Her tongue swiped the underside of his jaw, where it met his ear, and she moaned softly.

"*Fuck*. Lucy." He wrapped his arm around her waist and stood from the couch, taking her with him.

"Yes," she moaned. "Please fuck Lucy."

His control unraveled like a string being pulled, and he turned them in the direction of his bedroom. If he was giving in to his ultimate temptation, they were going to be in a bed. "Be sure, *wife*," he rasped against her ear.

She nipped his earlobe into her mouth and pulled on it gently. "I was sure two nights ago when you finger fucked me in your spare bedroom—*husband*."

Her crudeness ripped a loud groan from him, and with one swift movement, he lifted her all the way up, until her legs looped around his waist like a vise, and her mouth obliterated him with a kiss. Every thought of honor, decency, and integrity disappeared from his mind like he hadn't spent his entire life building them into the foundation of his character.

The only thought he had now was Lucy.

CHAPTER THIRTY-TWO

It's funny how the things that should feel like mistakes almost never do. At least that was the thought that went through Lucy's head as Joel carried her down the hall to his bedroom.

How many times had he told her that he'd wanted to go slow? And yet, she'd watched him war with himself over wanting her for days, while she would have gladly given herself over to the lust that night after clubbing with her sister and friends. This closeness she craved with him; it had never felt wrong to her.

Mine. That's what he'd called her. And maybe things were still fragile between them, and maybe it could still go to hell. But as much as she was his, he was hers too, and as his lips traveled down her neck, words whispering against her skin that she couldn't quite make out, she knew this would be worth it. If it only ever remained a memory, it would be worth it—like all the other memories they'd made.

In his bedroom, he set her down and stepped back

inhaling deeply as he took her in, his jaw bunching tightly. She could guess what he was thinking.

"You're thinking that we should go slow," she said.

The tic in his jaw picked up.

"You want to prove to me that you meant everything you said?" She kept an eye on that betraying flinch on his cheek, the only tell in his otherwise set, unreadable features. She pulled at the knot of his tie, fully releasing it, and letting the silk slip through her fingers to the floor. "You want to be careful and gentle because of our past." She worked a few more buttons free before she brought her mouth right to that tic. "You forget that I never liked it when you were gentle."

She licked across his cheek, already rough with a day's worth of stubble, and that was what cracked him.

Poke the bear and the claws come out, was how the weight of all Joel's untethered desire came down on her. His kisses were ferocious, all-consuming, like he needed to devour her entirely if he had any hope of survival. One hand gripped her nape, while the other yanked up her skirt, his hand moving expertly to find the soft spot between her legs.

Lucy gasped, her head tipping back,

He jolted. "I can stop," he whispered harshly against her mouth. "One word from you and so help me God, I will stop, Luciana."

He meant it. She trusted that his control was too well honed for her to believe otherwise. He might push her to the edge, but he'd always be able to stop. Except stopping was the exact opposite of what she wanted. What she wanted was for the full force of Joel Morgan to be unleashed on her so she could finally end this four-year starvation. So she let a slow smile stretch across her lips, before lifting her fingers to mimic zipping her mouth closed. There would be no stopping tonight.

A grunt tore from him as he yanked her blouse over her head and flung it somewhere along with the skirt he'd shoved down her legs and the shirt and tie she wrenched from his body. If there was a tearing sound and a spray of buttons when she'd done it, neither of them batted an eye.

They were down to their underwear as she stepped backward toward the mattress. He turned her swiftly, pressing her back against his torso, his hand settling in a loose grip around her throat. With a nudge, he tipped her head sideways and sucked the spot on her neck just below her jaw, hard enough so that there would be a mark there in the morning.

"So everyone who sees you knows what we did tonight," he told her right before his fingers dipped into her panties and delved between her drenched center. "Oh fuck, Lucy, if that's how wet you are for me already, I don't think I can go slow."

"Then don't," she begged, her voice vibrating against his palm.

He spun her, his eyes burning into hers for the briefest moment, and she let him see it all, her desire, her need, her consent. Content with whatever he absorbed from her gaze, he pressed her down onto the bed, laying her back until she was fully spread out before him.

With intense focus, Joel tugged her panties down over her thighs, his gaze never leaving the apex.

"I'm hungry," he growled in a voice that brought back a wave of déjà vu, a memory of having done this before with him so many times. A memory she hadn't allowed anywhere near her head space in years. He raised his eyes to look at her intently. "Can I?"

Lucy nodded, and he pushed her thighs apart, gripping them as he lowered himself, running his nose along her seam as he inhaled, then moaned, the sound vibrating on her skin. When he licked his tongue right through her slit, from bottom to top, curling around her clit before doing it again, her back arched reflexively, mouth opening as she sucked in air.

Her thighs trembled beyond her control. She was ready to come apart right now.

His grip tightening on her flesh stopped her. "Not yet, Luciana. I'll say when."

Good God, the authority in that voice. The controlled, precise way he instructed her. It sent another flood of moisture to the place he was feasting on. After two weeks, it was hard to deny that she'd missed him, but she'd be outright lying if she said she hadn't missed *this*. The way his body awakened hers. The way he had her begging for it within minutes. His kind of witchcraft went beyond seduction. His was a domination she welcomed.

"Joel, I can't—" The pressure was already peaking. No way would she last.

"You can," he intoned against her flesh. "And you will." He slid his hand up her torso, over achingly sensitive breasts, where he found hers clawing desperately at her neck, as if she might be able to open her throat for more air.

Like a life preserver, she grasped his offered hand, clinging to it, lacing her fingers through his, as she held on for dear life, trying not to drown in the ecstasy. Holding off was taking every ounce of her concentration, sweat beading at her brow with the effort, but she did it, because he told her to and she'd learned long ago that doing what Joel asked of her in bed never failed to benefit her.

And then fingers found the inside of her, pressing

upward to her belly and stroking. "Now," he commanded, and she let the giant wave take her under.

A loud shout filled the air. Sweet relief, heat and pleasure, a sensation that boarded on the right side of pain, flooded her.

Clamping a hand over her mouth, she squeezed her eyes shut, trying to stifle the tail end of her shout. When the sensations ebbed, fingers around her wrist tugged her hand away from her lips, and she willed one eye open. Joel leaned over her, his lips glistening with what he'd just feasted on, eyes lit with lust.

"I like it when you're loud." He dipped his head to her neck and his tongue stroked the spot he'd bitten before. "I want you to be louder next time. So loud that the people in the bar downstairs will know my name. Understand?"

There were a lot of delicious things in that statement, but she focused on one. "Next time?"

Joel responded with a grunt as he shifted his body, the movement bringing his massive erection flush with her thigh. "And it might come sooner rather than later."

"Oh," she gasped, and he moved again, settling between her legs. "Oh—"

"Breathe, Luciana. If I remember correctly, it fits just fine."

Yes, she had the same memory. She had fit him like a glove, tight and snug, but warm and comfortable. Her hips wiggled in anticipation, and he dropped his head to her collarbone with a moan.

"Please," she whispered, remembering the word that drove him the wildest. When she begged for it, there was no holding him back. Wrapping her knees around either side of his hips, she locked herself in, not letting him move anywhere but into her.

The hard length of his flesh inched forward, and it was like a memory coming to life. The first time he'd done this flashed through her mind. She'd been inebriated then. They both were, but this moment was crystal clear. A homecoming, a welcoming that was ingrained in her mind forever.

"No one has been here since me," he told her, as he continued to ease his length in. "I can feel it. You're so fucking tight. There hasn't been anyone since me, has there?"

Her response was a low moan. What more could she say? Yes, he was right.

"Tell me," he growled, pausing in his movement. "Look at me and tell me."

Lucy opened her eyes, locked them on his, and was surprised when she found apprehension there. A very uncharacteristic uncertainty. The great Joel Morgan wasn't sure.

"What would have been the point, Joel? No one would ever erase the memory of you."

The force with which he slammed into her shoved her up to the headboard, her breath catching in her throat.

"Right answer. Only me for you, and no one but you for me. This is the last pussy I ever want to be inside, and the only one that matters." He moved, driving her into the mattress, rough but quiet sounds emerging from deep within his throat, his skin slick with exertion and need. Everything telling her that he was close to snapping.

Her body responded like an orchestra to its conductor, moving to the rhythm of his dictation, her world building to a final crescendo.

And then he stopped. Stopped thrusting, stopped moving, stopped breathing, just stopped.

"Joel?"

"*Fuck.*" His body vibrated with the effort to resist continuing.

"What's wrong?" She felt his hardness against her, the tip of his shaft already pulsing inside her. What happened? Panic started to list the worst-case scenarios in her mind, but when Joel raised his head, the eyes that met hers were deep with regret, and—sadness?

"I'm not wearing a condom."

The sentence hung there between them, like a ghost in the room. And maybe there was one, because her heart started beating a bit faster.

They'd never once made love with a condom on. That first night of their wedding, they were drunk, beyond thinking. The next morning, they'd gone at it again, sober but still not thinking, as if they'd never had a freaking sex ed class between them. They'd had wild, unprotected sex multiple times and never had it occurred to them to discuss contraception. After they discovered she was pregnant (surprise, surprise), there hadn't been much of a point. Then they'd lost the baby, and the sex had stopped altogether.

Until now.

And suddenly, the weight of the possible consequences fell, like a pall, around them.

Joel started to pull out.

"Wait," Lucy said, tightening her knees around him.

He looked at her, gray eyes haunted with regret, for so much more than not having a condom at present.

"I—" What? What was she going to say? She'd opened her mouth, hoping a solution would come out. It did not.

"Do you have something?" Joel asked, a flicker of hope lighting the gray.

Lucy shook her head and frowned.

He matched it with one of his own. "Are you on—are

you—?" He wasn't a man who got awkward, but she knew what he was trying to ask, and felt bad for asking.

The onus of protection shouldn't have been on her.

She shook her head again. "I'm not on the pill." A fact she'd never regretted until this very moment. "You could pull out?" God, maybe she really hadn't had a sex ed class in her life?

Joel dropped his head into her shoulder again and groaned. "Lucy, I can't take that risk right now, I'm not—" He didn't finish his sentence. Instead, he started with another. "The happiest day of my life was when I woke up married to you. And the second was when you showed me those two lines on that test." He pressed his forehead against her collarbone, his voice catching. "I told you the other day that if I ever have another, I want it to be with you, but right now —" He swallowed. "We're not ready."

Lucy shifted beneath him as tears and the truth burned her eyes. A hiss sounded against her cheek.

"Christ. Wait, don't move." He pulsed dangerously inside her. "I have to pull out."

"Joel—" She was so torn between knowing he was right and wanting him to be wrong.

When he feathered a kiss along her brow, she sighed, and he withdrew.

"Wait," she whispered, running her hands over his warm torso. Her fingers danced over his heartbeat, then she splayed her hands over his pecs and gave him a push.

No way was this night ending like this.

CHAPTER THIRTY-THREE

What the hell was she doing? Joel thought as Lucy wiggled, shimmied, and maneuvered until she was out from under him. Lucy seldom took control in the bedroom, so when she did, he let her do her thing, and apparently, she was on a mission, because she didn't stop until Joel found himself sitting on the edge of the bed with Lucy standing between his splayed knees.

"You look like a woman with a plan, Mrs. Morgan." The prefix had been a slip, and he watched her closely to gauge her reaction.

A sensual smile spread across her tantalizing lips, and he almost gripped himself to keep from coming.

"Call me that again. See what happens."

Oh fuck, she was up to play that game? Fine, tonight he could take it.

"Mrs. Morgan." He dipped his finger through her still soaking core, then brought it to his mouth to lick it clean. "Even tastes like mine."

Lucy's lips parted in a shocked gasp, and a fleeting sense of victory shot through him. But then she lowered herself to her knees until she was on the floor in front of him, glancing up at him through lowered lashes. "Choke me with it."

Before he could respond, she opened her mouth around his straining cock, circling the tip of her tongue around the head, before taking him all the way into her mouth. She moaned before popping her mouth off again. "You taste like me." She licked around his shaft once more. "I love it."

"Why?" Suddenly, he needed the answer more than he needed her to finish, and that was saying something.

Lucy considered, as she teased his cock with shallow strokes of her tongue, as if she was licking her flavor off him. "It reminds me of how connected we are." She stroked him gently. "And how safe I am with you."

The tension he hadn't even realized he was holding dissipated from his chest, and he wove his hands through her hair as she worked him down to the base of her throat.

Testing her, he pushed his hips forward. She made a gagging sound, so he reassured her by stroking his palm down her silky mass of waves. "Breath through it, Luciana," he coached. "I remember how well you can take it."

Lucy groaned, and the sound vibrated down his dick to his balls, every nerve ending electrified and fully engaged. Fucking amazing. When she swallowed, the suction hollowed out her cheeks, and put just the right pressure on his engorged length that he almost blew right there. "Oh fuck, honey, that feels so good. I'm not going to last long now. Relax your throat. Let me all the way in."

Lucy inhaled loudly through her nose, and on the exhale, he felt her throat give a little, taking more of him in, and using the pressure of his palms on the top of her head, he set a rhythm in motion that had him barreling to release.

He didn't even try to stop his grunts and moans. Instead, he used them to encourage her forward, pushing her to take more, praising her when she did. Until the pressure was so strong, he couldn't hold back any more. "Luciana," he gasped, his hips coming off the bed as he thrust into her mouth.

Fingernails dug into his thighs, and she made a choking sound, but he was too far gone.

"Ah, yes, that's so good. It's coming now, take it. All of it. That's it, fuck that's so good. You're so good."

Everything in his body contracted as he came down her throat, his cum escaping from the corners of her mouth as she looked up at him, tears streaking down her flushed cheeks. Fuck, she was looking at him like he was everything to her. Everything. When the opposite was true. There was nothing he wouldn't do for this woman, no world he wouldn't burn, no universe he wouldn't travel to, no law he wouldn't break. He'd give her anything, do anything. And she didn't even know half the power she had.

When it was finished, Lucy brought her mouth off him with one last swallow, and Joel immediately dragged her into his arms, kissing her deeply, tasting himself on her this time. He held either side of her face as he devoured, offering more praise between kisses, his words less filthy, more adoring. When he'd had his fill of her mouth, he carried her to the shower, where he washed every inch of her, carefully using the soapy sponge to caress her body, taking her weight when she leaned into him, exhausted, spent. He took his time, wetting her hair, shampooing it, massaging her scalp until she moaned with pleasure.

"You're good at that," she murmured, as he rinsed the shampoo meticulously.

"I take care of the things that are valuable to me," he replied, finding it safer to say that than to admit out loud what he was really feeling.

Shutting off the water, he sat her on the edge of the tub, drying her off from top to bottom. And when he was satisfied that he'd done a thorough job, he scooped her up once more and carried her to bed, tucking her between the sheets and crawling in behind her.

"Mmm," Lucy murmured, drowsiness slurring her speech. "This is our second last night together."

Joel tensed. "What do you mean?" He'd been making plans for forever and she was down to two nights?

"We have tonight. Then tomorrow is the engagement party, and I have to get back to work in San Francisco the next day."

Not happening. They were not sleeping apart ever again. "I'm sure your father will give you more time off if you asked him, Lucy." And if not, he'd buy the old bastard out and set Lucy's hours himself.

She turned in his arms, snuggling into his chest as she watched him. "Joel, I want to go back to work. It's what all this is for, remember? I love Barone & Sons. I want to be there."

His heart went down like the Titanic. That's what this had been for, Lucy taking her place at the head of her father's company. It was what he'd agreed to, what he wanted for her. So why did it feel like a hole had just been blown through his heart?

CHAPTER THIRTY-FOUR

Bowie's had been decked out like it was hosting something between an Oscar's afterparty and a backyard kegger, but it was the only compromise that Gabe and Vanessa had come to, so Joel had allowed it.

The damn headache those two had given him with their bickering over floral chandeliers and hanging bauble garlands only eased off after he'd put Jordan in charge of overseeing the final approvals with the vendors. At first, Jordan appeared less than thrilled with the role of mediating between Gabe and Vanessa, but alas, not even he could refuse the numbers on the offer Joel had made him.

Turned out, Joel's gut instinct was right. Jordan had the disposition of a rock, solid and unyielding, which helped with de-escalating Vanessa's exuberant ideas. He also had the intriguing side quality of being a stickler for the rules, which put Gabe at ease. One could not, after all, risk having a five-foot tall floral centerpiece breaking fire code and shutting down the bar.

Regardless, it had all ended up being worth it, if only to

see Lucy laughing with a glass of golden Dom Pérignon in her hand that matched the dress she was wearing.

Last night, Joel had allowed himself the simple pleasure of watching her sleep. She'd appeared so peaceful, so free of the grief and pain she'd endured, and he'd whispered his silent promise to her that he'd spend the rest of his life doing everything in his power to keep her that way.

Barone & Sons would be hers. He'd give her family this sham of a party and wedding. He'd pay for the over-sized centerpieces and outrageous finger food that Vanessa had flown in from New York City. The number of zeros next to a receipt he'd seen for handmade rose-shaped milk chocolate party favors had been ridiculous even to his eyes, but he'd paid it.

The money didn't matter. To him, it was a drop in the hat. Their families needed this ostentatious display of celebration for a reason he hadn't yet deciphered. This circus was for someone else's benefit.

Lucy was already his wife in his heart and on paper. He'd married her in a little chapel in Vegas. But he'd marry her in a hundred-year-old cathedral next month. He'd marry her under a bridge in San Francisco with traffic whizzing over their heads. He'd marry her in the living room of his brother-in-law's Pearl District apartment. He'd marry her anywhere, just so he could call her his wife in public.

Logistical kinks would be worked out. He'd already spent most of his night working out his schedule so he could maximize his time in Lucy's proximity. Being apart from her was not something he wanted to entertain. Four years of separation were enough to last him a lifetime.

"Well, it looks like you got what you wanted." Nico's

voice slithered over Joel's shoulder like a snake that had been defanged. Vile but harmless.

The reminder that he still needed to deal with this fuckwad cut through his joyful mood. As it turned out, ending Nico had been more complicated than he'd anticipated. The dickhead was Barone family. The son of Luciano's favorite cousin. Cutting him out of the picture by tossing him off the St. John's bridge wearing nothing but cement shoes was not going to win his father-in-law's affections.

So he'd had to be subtle in his takedown. Which, unfortunately, took longer.

"Indeed," Joel replied casually, keeping his eyes on the diamonds that glinted around Lucy's neck every time she laughed. Diamonds he'd given her this afternoon when she'd come out of his bedroom wearing her gold-colored dress. He took a long swallow of his Scotch.

Nico believed Joel was after Barone & Sons, and that it bonded them somehow, a secret rivalry between the two of them. Dipshit.

"A shame you have to leave before the wedding."

Nico bled into Joel's peripheral vision, shock lining his face. "How did you know I was leaving? My father only called me an hour ago."

"I didn't know," Joel lied. "I assumed you'd be leaving America now that there's nothing left for you here." In truth, he'd negotiated the deal himself.

Nico's father had a modest cabinet-making business back in Italy. After researching every inch of the company, Joel had found that some unfortunate financial choices had put the company in peril. Six months max and they would have had to fold. Probably the reason Nico had come sniffing over to this side of the pond. His own inheritance was in jeopardy, so he'd come after Lucy's.

Joel had called in a couple of favors to ensure that Nico's father's company would survive enough to entice the bastard home without the threat of him ever coming after Lucy again. It hadn't been difficult, but it also hadn't filled the vengeance Joel craved for this shithead.

"My father needed me home. Our company is doing well, but he needs my expertise," Nico stated smugly.

This conversation could not end soon enough. "Safe travels home." *Don't ever come back, dick face.*

"Yes. And you enjoy the spoils of your victory, in both the boardroom and the bedroom."

Joel halted mid-step, his entire body seizing, his muscles quivered with the restraint it took not to punch this motherfucker in the face in front of their combined friends and family.

Slowly, he turned to face Nico. "What did you say?"

Nico, oblivious to his arrogance, shrugged. "Luciana is a very beautiful woman." As if he had no will to live, Nico added, "And her sister even more so. As you know, since you've had them both. Victorious in all things, my friend." The leech smiled.

Heat clawed up Joel's throat. "What are you talking about?"

Satisfaction gleamed in Nico's darkened eyes. "Your rendezvous with Vanessa in Vancouver. The photographers were eager for pictures of the billionaire and his young model mistress. How could I not send the paparazzi your way?"

This ass twitch had organized that? "No one knew I was in Vancouver."

Nico's casual shrug followed his nonchalant smile. "What do you Americans like to say? *All's fair in love and war.* I've been keeping a close eye on you, and it was not difficult to find out where you'd gone once I'd caught wind that you had left poor Luciana all alone."

"Do not say her name ever again." Anger filled him with an urge of violence so great he curled his fists into tight balls instead of putting them through Nico's face. "You'll never earn the right."

"I have been calling her by that name since she was in diapers. We are second cous—"

"Finish that sentence and it will be the last one you ever speak."

Nico chuckled. "Relax, my friend. You've won. I put in my best efforts, but I know when to bow out. You can enjoy Barone & Sons and my beautiful cousin."

Disgusting ass fuck. Joel's fingers itched with the need to put this scum in his place. One call and he could destroy Nico forever. His finger twitched against the phone in his pocket.

"Ah, my two favorite boys." Luciano's loud baritone filled the space behind Joel.

On a deep exhale, he unclenched his fists and faced Lucy's father with a grim smile. If Luciano noticed any tension, he chose not to show it. Then again, he might have been beyond picking up social cues based on the pink glow on his cheeks and the near empty wineglass in his hand. Joel guessed it wasn't his first of the night, or even his third.

"You know," Luciano went on, clapping a firm hand on Joel's shoulder, then doing the same on Nico's, drawing them a step closer to each other.

Joel's molars threatened to grind into dust.

"I might never have had sons, but God blessed me with the two of you." He laughed loudly at his declaration, as though he'd bestowed the highest honor.

Joel nearly crushed his Scotch glass in his hand. His beloved father-in-law had put him on the same pedestal as this rat.

Nico, the oblivious jerk, grinned, inclining his head as a show of gratitude and respect, then murmured something in Italian that Joel's language app had not yet taught him. Fuck. Another reason to hate the dipshit. Nico and Luciano had a secret language Joel didn't understand. He made a mental note to work on his Italian before the wedding.

A laugh rumbled from deep within Luciano's chest, and he clapped Nico on the shoulder again. "Your father will be happy to have you back, but I will miss you here."

Nico glanced in Joel's direction, his smug lips lifting infinitesimally. But whatever the second cousin from hell saw in Joel's face had his expression morphing. His smile faltered and his eyes widened, like prey realizing their time was up if they didn't run. Fast.

Fuckwad might have been a first-rate sleaze, but he wasn't as dumb as Joel previously assumed, because he kissed Luciano on both cheeks and excused himself to get more wine.

Joel tracked him until he was sure that Nico was walking in the opposite direction of Lucy. When he saw him head toward Vanessa, he almost excused himself as well. No way was this jerk getting his claws into the next Barone sister, but then his gaze found Jordan, who was standing not far from Vanessa. After one exchange of looks, Jordan gave a resigned nod and went to intercept Nico. The man took instruction without words needing to be exchanged, and

Joel wondered where in his corporation he could use a mind like that.

"Ah," Luciano sighed, pulling Joel's attention back to him. "It does my old heart good, seeing this." He gestured grandly around the bar.

"You like the flower chandeliers?" Joel ventured.

Luciano laughed. "Your marriage to Lucy is a good thing, Joel."

On this, they could agree. "The best thing that has ever happened to me."

"I should have seen it long ago. You two are very similar, where it counts. You understand family and connection. Building things into bigger things."

Where was this going? Joel took his final sip of his drink and let his eyes roam over Lucy again, his gaze lingering on the round shape of her ass under her gold dress. Tonight, he was taking her to bed. He'd strip that golden silk off her body and worship what was underneath for hours. Then he'd bathe her, feed her, and do it all over again. And again, until—

"Barone & Sons will be yours."

What. The. Fuck? Every single molecule of his attention snapped back to Luciano. "Excuse me?" He must have misheard, but pride was shining so brightly in the old man's eyes, Joel was nearly blinded.

"I love my daughters. My wife. Every hour I have worked, every late night, every risk I took, it was all worth it to provide them with the best life I could. But I never had a son." He rubbed one of his gruff paws over his age-worn face, stopping to pinch between his eyes. "You have grown up around business your entire life. When you took over your father's company, it was the proudest moment of his life, and you have done well for Morgan Construction, more than well." Luciano clapped Joel on the bicep, giving it a firm and affectionate squeeze. "You will take care of my daughter and my company, and I will retire knowing both are safe and secure."

Something turned in Joel's chest, something that ached and hurt like a bruise that was so deep inside he only felt it when he breathed. He knew how much Barone & Sons meant to Luciano, and how fucking honored he should be to have him say the things he had and offer what he had. But that bruise, the ache deep in him, thudded closer to the surface because he knew that he wasn't the one who should have been given these words.

"Luciano..." He wasn't often unsure of what to say or do. In fact, he made sure he always knew what to say or do, but this was...personal. Delicate.

Across the bar, Lucy observed them, a small smile tugging at her full red lips, an elegant eyebrow arched. She was wondering what they were talking about. If only she knew.

"The papers are ready to sign. I had my lawyer draw everything up. I cannot imagine a better person to pass my life's work onto. Not even Nico. He's family, but he doesn't know Barone & Sons like you do."

Without taking his eyes off Lucy, Joel murmured, "I can."

"What?" Luciano leaned in, trying to hear over the crowd.

Joel shifted his gaze to his father-in-law. "I said I can imagine a better person to pass your life's work on to." He let his gaze trace back to Lucy, slowly this time, purposefully, so Luciano was forced to follow the movement. "In fact, I cannot understand how you do not imagine it yourself, since it has been happening for years."

They watched her together. Under their joint scrutiny, her cheeks heightened in color, like she was embarrassed to have been caught staring. Lucy gave them a little wave and a bashful toothy grin before she turned quickly back to the table where she sat with Hope, Ivy and Natalie.

"What are you talking about?" Luciano asked, sounding confused. "Lucy would not want the business."

"Wouldn't she?" Was the old man blind or obtuse? "Has she not worked alongside you every day for years? Has she not learned every aspect of cabinetry, product demand, design? Is she not in charge of all the financials? Did she, like her sister, turn away from your company? Seek other opportunities? Ever once make you think she wanted to do something else?"

Luciano stood, wide-eyed in his shock, like the dots had never connected before in his brain. "But she's—she's," he stammered. "My daughter. All that work, it's too much."

A red haze bled through the periphery of Joel's vision. "Too much? It's not enough. She deserves your company and a thousand more." Maybe he was going too far, towing the line of disrespect that he could never take back, but his rage on Lucy's behalf unhinged him, snapping his finesse and control. "Do you even listen to her when she speaks?"

Luciano jerked back, eyes widening. Yep, he'd definitely just disrespected his father-in-law. So be it.

"Because when she speaks, she's all I hear, all I see, all I care about. And that's how I know, as you should have known long before me, that she would do anything for Barone & *Sons*." He hissed the last word like a curse, and it had been for Lucy. A twenty-nine-year curse she couldn't break no matter what she'd tried.

Obviously, not even a fake engagement or strategic marriage could help her, because the man in front of him was still staring at him far too blankly for someone who had just had an epiphany.

"With all due respect, sir, and I do respect you, I would never take Barone & Sons. It doesn't belong to me, it never did. And if you listened and looked with your heart, you'd see that it doesn't belong to you anymore, either."

"Joel—" Luciano's head whipped back like he'd had a collision but couldn't believe who he'd collided with. "Luciana is not—she could not—" He was unable to get whatever he wanted to out. Years of narrowmindedness and pride had apparently rendered him speechless.

"I'll take your daughter, if she'll have me. But I won't take her company." His vision blurred under his disgust and anger.

Lucy's father had just offered him the one thing Lucy had been fighting for her entire life, and Luciano was ready to sign it over to Joel with a flick of a wrist.

Nausea churning in his gut, he almost staggered, so he turned on the old man and walked toward his wife. He'd die a thousand agonizing deaths before he betrayed her, but even knowing that couldn't shake the guilt and shame coursing through him now.

The second his hand drifted down the soft curve of Lucy's back, the tension in his chest dissolved by half.

She turned toward him, eyes sparkling with curiosity. "I saw you talking to Nico and my father. Which was worse?" The humor in her voice a complete contrast to the burning under his rib cage. "Let me guess." She tapped her index finger to her chin, casting her eyes up to the side in mock contemplation. "My dearly beloved second cousin."

After the exchange he'd had with her father, he'd take a thousand Nico's. That was an enemy he had seen coming, and one he could deal with. Her cousin was utterly meaningless. But her father—her *father*—Joel needed to get out of here.

Tugging Lucy flush against him, he brought his lips to her ear. "I need to take you home." He needed to claim her in every possible way, to be as close as he could. Needed to wash off the second-hand guilt pounding through him. Needed to prove to her that he'd never hurt her the way her father had. "I need to fuck you until I can't see straight. Until you're carbon copied into every part of my soul."

Lucy leaned back so she could catch his gaze. A worried flicker rippled across the golden flecks in her irises. "Are you alright, Joel? Did Nico say something?"

She thought this had to do with dipshit. He almost laughed. If only. "Nico is nothing. He'll be on a plane in three hours. If we are very, very lucky, we won't be seeing him again until the next family reunion."

Lucy stroked her palm down the stubble on his jaw, and he turned his cheek into her caress. "We can't leave right now. There's still the dinner and speeches, and...what happened?"

Your father wanted to give me the company. Even thinking it made him ill. The company this entire plan had been designed to bring to her had backfired and landed in his lap. If she ever knew her father wanted to give it to Joel, it would devastate her. Destroy her relationship with her father and turn her away from Joel forever.

He could never risk that, not ever again. Running his nose along her fingers one last time, he leaned forward and dropped a kiss on her forehead. "Nothing happened. Did something have to have happened for me to want to tear this dress off you?"

It wasn't his most convincing work, but a smile curved the ruby red of her lips. "Well, I'd be lying if I said I haven't been thinking about the moment you take it off. I've been thinking about it since I put it on."

One hard tug and there wasn't enough room for air between them. Joel crushed his lips to hers, the bruising kiss a claim, a stake. She was his, and he wasn't going to give her up for anything. Not ever again.

CHAPTER THIRTY-FIVE

Something was wrong. Lucy couldn't put her finger on what, but that didn't dissipate her certainty that something had happened during the evening that had caused this...desperation now consuming him.

They'd stayed until the end of the engagement party, and he'd given another heartfelt, romantic speech that left every woman in the room with wet eyes. And very likely, wet panties too. Hers sure were.

"Where the fuck did this guy come from?" Natalie had hissed in her ear as Joel spoke. "He's like Jesus, but without the celibacy clause. Seriously, I need one. He's fucking perfect."

And he was. Adored by many, respected by most. He carried an undeniable gravity that compelled people not only do everything he said, but to want to. No one wanted to be Joel Morgan's disappointment.

But when he was like this—frantic in his need, his restraint tethered only by her request that he get through the evening—it was hard not to let that kind of power go to her head.

By the time they'd climbed the stairs to the apartment at the end of the night, they were both beyond reason. Joel fumbled with the keys as he shoved them into the lock, missing his first attempt entirely. He muttered a heartfelt "fuck", made it on the second attempt and then Lucy was up against the other side of the door, pinned between hardwood and hard muscle.

"Lucy, I—" He broke off, his lips finding her neck, her jaw, the underside of her ear.

His passion would have been alarming if it didn't match her own. Her hands clawed up to his shoulders, clinging, clutching, dragging her body along his, searching for any friction she could find.

Joel hoisted her up, making her dress bunch around her waist as he guided her thighs around his hips, then ground her against the door. "So fucking pretty. So perfect." And then he was kissing her again in that all-consuming way that made her feel like he was mapping out her mouth, tracing every corner with his tongue. "Mine," he rumbled as his hands smoothed over the underside of her legs. "Mine to keep, mine to love, mine to fucking worship."

Her pulse slammed in her ears as her head tipped back against the door. His words jumbled in her mind as his lips dragged across her neck. *Mine to love.* His words echoed in her brain, but she had no time to process them because his large hands were on her ass, massaging her cheeks before slipping his fingers between, creeping them forward, closer to her apex. Everything about the way he did this, from his words to his touch, was hypnotizing, and she willingly lost herself under his spell.

"I don't think I can—" His voice was thick, raspy, a little unhinged. "I need to—"

When she raised her head enough to meet his eyes, she

understood what he was trying to tell her. There was going to be nothing gentle about tonight. Joel spent most of his life holding everything together for everyone, but when it was the two of them like this, he could truly let go. Here, like this, she was his safe space, and she reveled in it.

Threading her fingers through his hair, she stroked through the strands. "Do whatever you need to do."

His eyes darkened, a storm coming in rough and wild, and before she could register what was happening, she was being carried through the apartment, to the nearest surface, the couch. Joel peeled her off his torso, turning her so her stomach pressed the back of the couch and with the slightest pressure on the small of her back, he guided her over the top.

"I've been watching your ass in this dress all fucking night," he murmured against her ear before he took a step back from her. His fingertips grazed along her ankles, lifting the material of her dress as he worked it up her calves, over her knees, her thighs.

She sucked in a breath when he lifted the material over her hips and dragged her thong down with a jerk. A low groan, a filthy muttered curse, and then his palms, hard and biting, were spreading her cheeks apart.

Lucy gasped at the sensation, squirming under his intimate caress.

"Don't move," he rasped against the nape of her neck.

Was he going to—? He wouldn't—?

When she didn't stop wiggling, he responded with a warning slap on her backside followed by his palms sliding up her spine to her neck, gripping her as he leaned forward and growled, "Be good."

Easy for him to say. He wasn't bent over a couch, bare ass in the air.

"Look, I'm all for being good, but if you plan to just drill in there without any lu—"

His slap came harder this time, stinging.

"Luciana," he chided against her ear. "Everyone keeps telling me you're a good girl." He soothed his palm over the hot skin he'd just smacked. "So why are you being such a bad one for me?" Another slap, softer this time, sent tremors of sensation up from her belly to her throat, and the tingling made her mouth water.

She bit back her moan, swallowing it as she let her forehead drop onto the couch, giving herself over to him. He'd never disappointed her, not once, so whatever he had planned, he could bring it on.

"Lucy." He drew her name out, guttural and vibrating. The kneading of her flesh, followed by more light slaps, left her backside deliciously sensitive, and then—and then, his tongue touched her, warm and wet in the most intimate way. He licked without hesitation, full, lapping strokes that at first had her tensing in embarrassment but soon had her groaning as the repeated strokes sent lightning streaks of color bursting behind her scrunched eyelids.

She'd experienced nothing like it, and she'd experienced a lot with him.

There was no holding back. In fact, the louder she got, the more enthusiastic his movements became. There was no thinking, no breathing under the magic of what he was doing to her. Her hips jerked against the couch, her clit searching for friction. A little more and she'd explode.

Reading her mind, Joel reached around her and slid his thumb over her aching flesh, and an unhinged sound, something between a guttural moan and a scream, tore from her mouth. Stars burst behind her closed eyes like fireworks. Sensation, quaking and unadulterated bolted through her entire body like electric shocks. The orgasm left her shaking, her limbs completely useless.

And before it ebbed, he flipped her to face him. He stood with his hands pinning her hips to the back of the couch. The material of her dress dragged up along her body, over her torso. He nudged her arms, and when she didn't move, lifeless from her orgasm she'd just experienced, his eyes pinned to hers.

"Lift," he commanded. Her arms went up like he'd pressed a hidden button on her body. "I've been thinking of taking this off of you the second I saw you in it. It had to be gold, didn't it?"

A smile quirked her mouth. "In honor of my moneybags fiancé," she quipped, tipping her head forward to nuzzle his jaw. "Win gold and wear it," she purred against his cheek.

Joel whipped forward, nipping the side of her neck where her jugular was thumping wildly against her skin. "That's husband to you," he growled. "Never forget it." With a last tug, he had the dress off her body, so she was in nothing but her engagement ring. With a cocky grin, he took a full step back, his gaze lingering on her body. In that way, that made her feel he saw every part of her.

"Win gold and wear it, indeed," he murmured.

Before she could protest, he lifted her up under the knees and carried her to his bedroom.

"Is this how you treat your trophy?" she squeaked. Her question earned her a firm smack to her bare ass.

"You're not my trophy, Lucy." He chuckled as he caressed the back of her thigh. "You're just mine."

He lowered her carefully onto the bed, like she was something precious. "Mine to carry however I like," he said as he stepped back, toeing out of his shoes. "Mine to care for." He removed his tie. "Mine to protect." He removed his shirt, and crawled over her, forcing her backward onto the bed as his knee came to the mattress beside her. "Mine to fuck, just how I know you like it."

His mouth found the ultrasensitive slope of her neck, where he spent some time riling her up again before he kissed his way to her collarbone, nipping and biting in a way that stole her breath and every thought in her head at once. The rest of his clothes came off in a few frenzied tugs. There was no holding back, no gentle caresses or lingering touches. Every movement had purposeful intent, like they were claiming each other once and for all. Each taste a vow, every stroke a pledge, as if they were branding each other into their souls.

Hooking her legs over his shoulders, Joel brought his mouth down on her, his teeth grazed her clit, his tongue found her opening, and he worked her over until she was nothing but trembling sensation, so intensely brutal that she peaked quickly and violently. Her hands scratched at his scalp as she pressed him closer, trying to draw out every drop of her climax.

Loud, panting breaths ripped from her lungs as she tried to reconnect her mind to her body, but before she even caught her breath, she was being flipped, her hips dragged up as her palms sunk into the soft duvet.

A slide of a drawer, the ripping of a box, then the tear of a wrapper, and he nudged against her opening. Lucy glanced over her shoulder, taking Joel in as he loomed behind her, and she wasn't mistaken when she saw his hand tremble as he gripped his cock. His eyes trained on the spot between them, the space that was soon to be filled, and she thought she saw a look of anguish cross his face, but when he caught her staring, it disappeared.

"Yours," she murmured, because somehow she sensed

he still didn't believe it. That he couldn't trust what they had wasn't still cloaked in a façade. And she wanted him to know that she was done with pretending. After years of living his life for others, she wanted him to have something for himself. She wanted him to have her. "*Per sempre.*"

On a roar that sounded a lot like the word "mine," Joel hammered home and rocked her halfway up the bed. The force made her arms fold until her elbows pressed the mattress. His fingers gripped her hips in a way she knew would leave marks, and she relished it. Her nipples dragged across the covers, sending little shocks skittering down her chest and to the muscles in her core, causing her to tighten around him.

"Fuck," he groaned. "It's so good, Lucy. The way you take it—" His praise went to her head like a drug, and she rocked back into him, urging him deeper. "I can't believe I get to be here again," he choked out. "You're perfect. It's such a fucking perfect fit. I could live the rest of my life just like this."

His hips rammed against hers, over and over, until her muscles were clenching so tightly against him, she wasn't sure he could fully pull out anymore. "That's it baby, keep it in. Take all of it, just like that."

Lucy groaned, her throat hoarse and spent from her earlier cries. His words, his hard body, his heart, his soul. Everything about Joel was hers to keep—forever. And with that single thought in her head, she barreled over the edge, his hoarse cry of release not far behind.

CHAPTER THIRTY-SIX

Lucy could have gotten used to waking up with gentle kisses trailing up her shoulder blade and along the back of her neck. Honestly, it had been a long time since she woke up cocooned in such a huddle of safety and security.

And then she cracked an eyelid and saw the clock read 6:04 a.m. On a Sunday. After the marathon sex they'd had, she'd been hoping for a sleep in before round...five? Six? She'd lost count.

She turned to Joel with a languid roll, her arms coming up to loop around his neck. "Are you trying to kill me?"

"I had a title to earn." He kissed the tip of her nose. "What was it again?" Another kiss. "*Sir*?" This time, she felt his smile curve through his kiss, and she rolled over onto him, straddling his hips, propping her elbows on his pecs.

"Hmmm," she considered. "I'd say you're getting there, but a few more practice rounds wouldn't hurt."

When he moved, lightning quick, reversing their rolls and pinning her into the mattress, she shrieked.

"I'll try to be a faster study then," he growled against her neck before sucking hard on a spot above her collarbone, probably leaving another mark. It wasn't the first one he'd left on her and she loved that he left marks of his untamed passion all over her.

Lucy giggled as she writhed under his weight, enjoying the ease between them, the carefree banter that had always existed before. "Also, why are we up? It's the crack of dawn on a *Sunday*. That's torture, Joel."

Some of his weight lifted off her as he propped himself up on his arms. When he tipped his head to the side, his hair flopped over his forehead, making him look younger, more relaxed. Less austere and more...what a healthy and well-off thirty-two-year-old should look like. Happy, content.

"You said you had a flight back to San Francisco at nine. I thought you'd want time to get ready."

She shoved him off with the force only panic could induce. "Oh shit! I forgot." Lucy rolled out of bed searching for something that wasn't—she glanced around her—shredded golden fabric on the floor? Memories of what they'd done last night assailed her. In their desperation to be together, they'd made quite a mess.

Joel tossed something white her way, a t-shirt that was his. When she tugged it over her head, it fell down mid-thigh. "I need to be at the airport in an hour. I need to shower, and pack, and— Am I coming back here soon? Should I leave a toothbrush? Why have we not *talked* about this?" She twirled around the room, like the answer would magically appear on the walls.

They'd talked about him coming to San Francisco intermittently to keep up appearances. But that was before. Before their talk, before last night, before she had fallen head over heels for him...again.

On her third spin around the room, collecting discarded segments of clothing—her dress was toast, her thong no longer recognizable for what it was—Joel caught her by the shoulders and dipped his head so he could level her with a stare. She focused on those eyes like they were the magnet for her inner compass, pointing her due north again.

"Don't worry," he said, his voice steady and sure. "I took care of it. You don't have to worry about anything. Grab a shower if you want, put a few things in your suitcase, and come to the kitchen for breakfast before we go."

Why did everything sound easy when he said it? And what did he mean— "We?"

Letting go of her, he sauntered over to his closet, buck ass naked, pulled out a pair of gray sweatpants and tugged them on. No underwear, just him, his six-pack and his dick print, minding their own business. "I'm coming with you," he told her conversationally. "I have business meetings set up, things I need to organize back home."

"You do?" When had he planned that? Last she checked, Portland was his home base.

"Lucy, we're getting married in a couple of weeks. You're my wife." This was all said very normally, like there was no contradiction there at all. "You're stuck with me, I'm afraid."

"For a year?" She almost whispered it. Last night had been soul-changing, earth-shattering, and they'd aired important things the night before that, but they hadn't actually discussed how that changed their fake engagement situation.

The youthful, relaxed look she'd admired a moment ago in bed disappeared. The patient, quiet control returned, etched into the alluring structure of his face. "No," he said, cupping her face in his wide palms, stroking his thumbs over the skin under her eyes. "A little longer than that."

She melted against him, wrapping her arms around his torso as she hugged him. When he pulled her tight, she let the tears flood behind her closed eyes. When she was with him like this, she believed anything was possible. And she so desperately wanted to believe that they were.

After a long moment, he kissed the top of her head. "Shower, change, eat. I'll meet you in the kitchen in fifteen."

It took her twenty-five (men had no idea how long it took to blow-dry hair), and when she walked into the kitchen, pulling her suitcase, Joel was there, holding a cup of coffee toward her like he'd promised.

"I made pancakes." He beamed.

"Real ones?"

His smile fell as flat as a pancake.

She chuckled. "The 'Just Add Water' kind don't count, Joel."

"They will when they're in your stomach and you don't pass out from hunger at the airport."

Damn him and his reasoning.

He set a stack on a plate and carried it to the table for her. "A simple thank you wouldn't kill you, wife," he muttered as he shoved the maple syrup across the table.

Giggling, she wrapped her arms around his waist like she had earlier, and dropped kisses across his chest and over his heart. "I'm kidding, *Sir*." She slid that one in for bonus points.

A satisfied growl emerged from his chest.

"Thank you. I mean it."

He grunted in approval, then headed toward the hall-way. "I'm going to shower quick, then we'll go."

Twenty-five minutes later, they were in the Taycan, cruising down the highway toward the airport. But when they arrived, they didn't veer into the parkade for domestic flights. Instead, they peeled off a side ramp in the opposite direction of the main terminal.

"Aren't we supposed to be going that way?" She pointed backward at the passing building.

"Change of flight plans," Joel murmured, keeping his eyes on the road.

"Are you kidnapping me?"

A grin cracked his stupidly handsome, freshly shaven face. "Now that's an idea."

They pulled into the private parking area, and a car park attendant quickly appeared to take their cases out of the trunk. Joel was greeted with enthusiastic smiles and professional courtesy that one only acquired when they had a certain amount of zeros next to their reputation. And because she was with him, Lucy was treated in kind.

Soon they were walking down the tarmac to a jet with the Morgan logo painted on the tail. This was obviously the private jet Vanessa had been carted back from Vancouver in.

A young, friendly faced flight attendant greeted them as they climbed into the plane. "Good morning, Mr. Morgan. Good morning, Ms. Barone." She welcomed them with a beaming smile.

Lucy didn't bother speaking until she was buckled into a lush, cream-colored leather seat. "Okay, Moneybags. We're going to have to talk about this."

"Talk about what?" Joel asked, his voice neutral as he took his seat across from her.

"About the fact that we just boarded a plane with your name on it, and the entire staff knows *my* name."

"You're my wife, Lucy—"

"Fiancée," she hissed under her breath, leaning forward to catch his eye. No one knew they were married, and she didn't want to advertise it now and be left explaining their unique history to the flight staff, or worse, paparazzi.

Joel met her in the middle and grasped her jaw, pinning her with a sharp gaze. "Wife." The way he said it made it a done deal, and if they hadn't been married already, she would have ascertained that he'd secured the deed with his tone alone. "I expect them to know your name. And as for this." He gestured around them without breaking eye contact. His tone was faintly resigned when he said, "Get used to it. I had to."

In so many ways, he was an unassuming billionaire, living in an older apartment above a bar in downtown Portland. He drove a luxury sports car, sure, but the rest of him was all subtle power, and she couldn't help but feel he preferred it that way. Maybe there was more than one reason he'd opted to avoid San Francisco for the last little while. In Portland, he could be inconspicuous. Normal. Unassuming. Himself. There he definitely appeared well-off, but not obscenely wealthy. He could hide more easily, in his privacy.

But Lucy had a feeling, now that they were heading back to home turf, that was going to change.

"You can really afford anything, can't you?" she asked, narrowing her gaze at him.

He met it, head on, something almost sorrowful passing through his eyes. "Not anything," he replied.

She wanted to say so much more, but the flight attendant came over and instructed them about take-off procedures. Once they were in the air, she decided to let the topic drop. It clearly wasn't his favorite, and they'd had such a perfect morning, she didn't want to ruin it.

So instead, she toed off her shoes, propped her feet on his lap, and asked him what party favors he wanted to give their wedding reception guests. A small frown folded his lips downward as he absently took one of her feet in hand and rubbed his thumb up her arch. Lucy did her level best to swallow the moan that rose in her throat, but damn, that felt good.

"Honestly, sometimes I wish we could elope," he told her, and despite her scrutinizing his face for signs that he was trying to be funny, he came across as dead serious.

"You're joking, right? That would defeat the entire purpose of this, not to mention Maria would have a fit." Her brain could not conjure an image of her mother's reaction if they had eloped. One reason she had dreaded sharing the truth four years ago was because she knew her mother would have a conniption when she learned they had a Vegas wedding.

Joel's sigh was heavy, tired. "Yeah, you're right. Wishful thinking."

"You'll find most thoughts are wishful when my mother is involved." She eyed him cheekily. "Get used to it. I had to."

Joel snorted then leaned back, shifting his focus out the window as the plane gained speed. His thumb continued caressing up and down her arch in a slow rhythmic motion, and between that, the white noise, and a mostly sleepless night, Lucy felt her eyes droop.

CHAPTER THIRTY-SEVEN

This was Joel's idea of paradise. Sitting with Lucy's feet in his lap, watching her sleep, knowing there was nowhere he could go and nothing he could do in this moment but enjoy the peace. It eased some of the anxiety tightening his chest, but only slightly.

For her part, Lucy slept soundly, not even the slight turbulence they'd flown through woke her. He'd kept her up most of the night, and maybe he should have felt more guilty about that, but he didn't. Last night, he'd been selfish. He'd taken everything he could from her, spent her willingness thoroughly.

His back-to-back conversations with Nico and then her father had riled him up, left him agitated, a little heated, and a lot provoked.

Nico talking about Lucy like she was a trophy to be won had been disgusting, but not altogether surprising. He was a dipshit of astronomical proportions and his flight back to Italy had not come soon enough.

But it was Luciano who still had Joel's stomach twisted in knots. He'd been sick with the realization that this whole time Luciano had viewed their nuptials as an opportunity to pass Barone & Sons on to him. The thought of what that would do to Lucy if she ever found out was horrifying. It would break her fucking heart into a million pieces.

If there was a way to make Luciano see the light without outright buying his company out from under him and handing it to Lucy on a silver platter, he hadn't thought of it yet. But he'd have to think of something fast, because Lucy could never know what her father's intentions had been. It would destroy her in a way she wasn't sure he could repair.

He watched her now, on his plane, peaceful in her sleep, not a single worry or threat interrupting her slumber, and there would be no version of reality where he would not do everything in his power to provide her with more of that. No universe where she didn't get everything she wanted. Barone & Sons would be hers. He'd find a way.

Until then, he'd have to find a way to ease the anxiety clawing inside him, because apparently not even five straight hours of sex had helped.

When the slight thud and jump of the aircraft landing, just under two hours later, failed to wake Lucy, Joel unbuckled himself and leaned over to kiss her. It wasn't a gentle fairytale prince kiss either. It was a hard and wanton kiss, where he nipped her bottom lip before stroking his tongue across it. Her eyes popped open with a shuddering breath.

"Wakey, wakey." He grinned when she shoved him in the chest and grumbled something about it being his fault she was exhausted. If she'd expected him to feel guilty, she had another thing coming.

As they disembarked, Lucy halted partway down the plane's staircase so abruptly he collided with her back, almost sending her flying forward down the steps. "What is that?"

"What does it look like?" Joel asked as he sidestepped her, making sure he was in front so that if she stumbled he could catch her.

"It looks like a brand spanking new Ferrari, in cherry red."

He retrieved a fob from his pocket as they approached the Ferrari parked on the tarmac. "I figured it was the least I could do after forcing you to drive around in the Taycan these last two weeks."

Lucy stared at the fob, then at him, toggling back and forth until she finally said, "I can't take that. That's ridiculous. I mean, I know you're Sir Moneybags and all, but I don't need any of this, Joel. You don't need to shower me in luxury like this, it's not what I want, it's not—"

"Lucy," he spoke in the soothing but firm tone that worked without fail anytime he intended to win a business negotiation. "My money is meaningless if I can't spend it on the people I love."

For several long, awkward seconds she gaped at him, so much so that he wasn't sure she'd registered his words or if the reality that she was about to drive her dream car back to his penthouse was sinking in. He hadn't meant to drop the 'L' word in there so casually, it had slipped out without a second thought, but it was his truth. She was someone he loved and always would, no matter what happened between them now.

When she didn't speak or move, he took her hand and kissed her knuckles softly. She blinked, like she was coming out of a trance, and focused her eyes on his.

"How about you just drive it back to our place? If you don't like it, we can donate it."

"Fine," she said, shrugging one shoulder, and he suppressed his smile at her nonchalant tone.

Lucy drove the Ferrari like a fucking dream, making the engine purr like a well-fed kitten. The way she handled what was truly one of the most luxurious vehicles in existence—with equal parts joy and confidence—was a bigger turn-on than her ass in that gold dress last night.

No way she could ever deny that she wasn't loving every second of it. She passed the city without a single word, making no attempt to turn off toward home. Instead, she crossed the Golden Gate bridge and took the car on a tour that doubled their time back to his penthouse.

He said very little while she drove, relaxing in his seat, letting her happiness feed his. He couldn't tear his eyes off her. She was the best view in town.

When she turned back toward Nob Hill, and pulled into the underground carpark of his building, he finally spoke. "So, who should we donate it to?"

This earned him an elbow to the gut. "Jerk," she muttered as she climbed out of the Ferrari and strutted off toward the elevator.

CHAPTER THIRTY-EIGHT

Joel found it both endearing and amusing how torn Lucy was between her discomfort being spoiled by him and her delight in it. He knew how she'd been brought up. Her father had instilled a work ethic in her that made her believe she had to earn every victory.

A vacation, a car, a house, an education—those were all earned by working hard and squirreling away money. The Barones had always been well-off, but they showed it differently than most people of wealth he knew. They had a nice house, a proper vehicle, were always generous, but none of their money was ever spent frivolously. If they went on holiday, it was to Italy to visit family. If they bought a second property, they used it as a rental. Every purchase had a purpose, filled a need, added value, built a legacy.

Whereas his family had enjoyed their wealth in the more obvious ways. His father had also worked from the ground up, but his mentality had been different. Walter didn't spoil his family, but he did indulge them. A beautiful, spacious house, vacations that included private ski lessons in the Alps or chartered yachts in Croatia, a holiday home on Lake Como. Joel's mother always sported a perfect mani-cure at her country club luncheons. His sister wore the most fashionable clothes. They went to the best of schools.

Walter focused on building his business and securing investments that advanced profitability, but the way he invested in his family was also strategic. Every action had a purpose, honed an image, built an empire. Morgan Construction was a brand Walter had curated over decades of long hard work.

Even though Luciano had used the phrase "win gold and wear it," Walter had lived the motto.

So where Joel enjoyed spending the money he'd earned on his wife, he also understood that she was sometimes uncomfortable receiving it. He'd have to be mindful of how quickly he moved forward with her, but he had no intention of withholding anything from her. Everything he had was hers.

Lucy entered the elevator and punched the button to the penthouse as if four years hadn't passed since the last time she'd done this. The familiarity in her actions put him at ease. She had the same muscle memory that he had of their old life together. No time or space could erase the imprint they'd left on each other's lives.

The doors slid open, revealing a hallway with one door, and Lucy preceded him out of the elevator. Her steps slowed only slightly as she made her way to the door. "It smells the same," she said.

"Does it?" Joel unlocked the door and waited for her to describe the scent, but she didn't.

When she walked into the foyer, she halted, fully taking in the surrounding space. His penthouse was large, with floor-to-ceiling windows that exposed the entire skyline, the whitecaps of the Bay and Pacific Ocean a spectacular back-drop from the bridges and city below them.

"It—" She walked across the hardwood floors toward the living room. Her fingers trailed over the built-in custom cabinets Barone & Sons had made. "It looks the same."

When she'd left, or didn't come back, depending on how you looked at it, he'd thought about moving a thousand times. Living here without her had been a whole different kind of agony. But the truth was, their time together had been so short there hadn't been much of a footprint of her. She hadn't moved in her own furniture or artwork. They'd only put up one wedding photo, and it had been in their bedroom.

After Vegas, she'd gone back to her condo, but when she discovered she was pregnant, she'd moved into the pent-house, and they'd immediately started playing house, with his things in his space. There had been a few odds and ends she'd added. A throw for the couch because she was always cold. Scented candles that helped her nausea. Kitchen supplies she enjoyed. Nothing significant.

When she'd left, she had simply been gone, leaving nothing but a ghost behind. And the phantom of her had been so comforting to him that staying had been the path of least resistance to his heartbreak.

"I changed nothing after you left," he replied carefully, setting his keys on the table.

After another moment of taking in the main floor, she pushed open the glass doors leading to the patio. The outdoor terrace was his favorite part of the entire place. Massive and spacious, it circled the entire penthouse, offering a 360 view of the four bridges and the city's most renowned landmarks. Many Morgan buildings were also visible from this balcony. His family's footprint stamped all over the city.

Some summer evenings, when his insomnia had gotten the better of him, he'd spend the night out here, imagining a world a million miles away from the things weighing on him.

He remembered it had been Lucy's favorite place as well. Slowly, he followed her out onto the terrace, watching her keenly as she leaned against the glass balcony and stared toward the Bay Bridge. The breeze lifted her hair, sending it trailing behind her like a flag taking flight.

She didn't speak until he was right behind her. "So, do we just pretend like none of it ever happened?" Her gaze stayed on the view as she spoke. "Or do we hash it out with a marriage or grief counselor so we don't make the same mistakes again?" She turned to face him, wanting for an answer.

"We both know pretending isn't really an option, so I pick the second."

"You'd sit on a counselor's couch for me?" She appeared serious when she asked him this, so he tried to answer in kind.

Lucy was going to need a lot of repetition and reassurance this time around, and as he leaned toward her, shifting his body so that her back was against the wide ledge and he was in front of her, one hand on either side of the sill, he found himself being totally okay with that. He'd make reassuring her an Olympic sport and win gold every time.

"Lucy," he rumbled against her cheek as he feathered kisses there. "I'd do anything for you. Seeing someone who can help us navigate our hurt and make sure we communicate properly isn't exactly a hardship. It's a no brainer."

Her eyelids fluttered downward, so he nudged her forehead with his, moving in closer until their torsos touched, their heartbeats met. When she looked up at him again, he spoke with a certainty she couldn't miss. "This time is forever and forever takes work. Everything worth fighting for does. We both know that. Hours upon hours, sleepless nights, sacrifice, the things we want most don't come easy. And what I want most is you. So yes, I will do whatever it takes."

Her eyes shone and as much as he hated to see her cry, he was okay with these tears. "Would you sit on a counselor's couch for *me*?" he asked, because he could use a little reassurance from her too. She'd come to him two weeks ago because she wanted help to secure Barone & Sons, but would she stay because being with him was where she truly wanted to be?

When she nodded, relief flooded his heart.

"I've actually been looking a few up in the area," she admitted sheepishly. "I found one with a really good reputation who has an opening for new clients."

"Book them."

Lucy snort giggled in that way that he knew meant she was happy. Satisfied. Like he was.

Her palms came up over his chest, and he hoped she could feel the way his heart sped up. "I thought it would be weird," she murmured. "Being back here where I lived the best and worst days of my life."

A dozen heartbeats passed, and she didn't speak, just fiddled with the fabric of his shirt while keeping her eyes focused on his neckline.

"Please tell me there's a *but* in there," he finally said.

Her laugh wasn't more than a breath of air, but it was enough to give him hope. "*But*," she drawled, and smiled when he rumbled in satisfaction. "It doesn't."

"What does it feel like?" He edged closer, pinning her against the balcony until her hands stilled on his shirt and her gaze met his.

"It feels like coming home."

All the pressure in his chest dissipated as he crushed his mouth to hers. The way he kissed her was rough, desperate, and he meant to slow down and make love to her slowly for once, to savor every inch of her, but everything inside him was driven by an insatiable urge to claim her. He wasn't sure if it would ever subside. This urgent need, and part of it fucking scared him, but the other part relished in how she always met him in his frenzy, equally drugged by the fervor.

Lucy's hands were under his shirt in seconds, tugging the fabric, sliding her fingertips over his abdomen and around to his back. A few more frenzied tugs between them and both of their jeans were off, and his shirt might have been tossed over the ledge to fall to the street far below. He wasn't sure, his focus was on Lucy and his compulsion to satisfy her, to make her his in every way possible.

He grabbed the condom from his pants pocket right before she shoved them down over his hips, and when he heard her soft moan of disappointment, he almost tossed the damn thing over the ledge as well, but he knew it wasn't time. Not quite yet. But soon.

"One day," he growled against the soft skin of her neck. "One day very soon, I'm going to fuck you bare, and there won't be any going back. Alright Lucy?"

Her nod was feverish against his collarbone. With a firm grip around her hips, he hoisted her up until she was propped on the extra wide ledge of the balcony that over-looked the city of their childhoods. A city that had pin drops of their family legacies all over it. Buildings upon buildings that his company had built with the help of hers. And there was something incredibly erotic about fucking his wife over the skyline of their joint dynasties. Together, they'd take over the whole world, and he was so ready for it.

"I'll put another baby inside you, and we'll build a family," he panted as he positioned himself against her. "But right now it's just you and me, and I want to savor every second of it, like we never got to do before. Okay?"

"*Yes*, yes okay." She edged closer to him, her apex seeking his. Tiny, desperate mewls fell from her lips as she licked the pulse at his neck. "Please, Joel. *Please*."

When she bit down on the skin just above his collarbone, the sensation was an electric shot straight to his dick.

"*Fuck*." Joel drove himself inside her in one hard thrust, holding her firm at the base of her back so she rocked into him and not backward farther across the ledge. He wanted her as close as possible, so they were one body, not two.

Lucy groaned, her mouth coming back to his for eager, greedy kisses. They rocked together in a tempo that was both frantic and measured. Their perfect cadence bringing them to their peaks one after the other like two bolts of lightning firing up the sky. Her scream filled the surrounding skyline, her head thrown back in wild abandon, and when he came inside her, her name tearing off his lips, all he saw was Lucy's unabashed ecstasy and the city they'd built behind her.

CHAPTER THIRTY-NINE

Being back at her desk at Barone & Sons was exhilarating. At first she was afraid she'd been away so long that she'd have missed too much. Nightmares of Nico destroying all her years of work in the span of two weeks had tortured her mind. But as it turned out, he hadn't done that bad a job. He hadn't done an amazing job, but he hadn't put them in the red. Satisfaction filled her once again, knowing she could do this job so much better.

He'd said his fond farewells to her at the engagement party, and she'd had to bite her tongue as he went on and on about how his father needed him in Italy to help with the contracts that had suddenly picked up.

She wasn't born yesterday. Nico's boastful exit had Joel written all over it. She wasn't sure exactly how he'd maneuvered it, but she knew he'd somehow found a way to make her dear second cousin disappear into the ether without losing face or causing tension in her family. It was the Joel Morgan way. Tying up the nagging loose ends without causing so much as a ripple. Her father probably hadn't even thought twice about it as he drove Nico to the airport the next morning.

And all Lucy could think was, *so long cuz.*

She sat at her desk again, ignoring the hundreds of emails needing replies, and smiled. Life wasn't perfect and likely never would be, but happiness was so close she could almost taste it. Her parents had arrived back in San Francisco late last night, but her father had been at work bright and early this morning, proudly bragging about his daughter's engagement to Joel.

At their morning meeting, Luciano had let her lead, which he rarely did. He'd also signed over a few projects to her that went beyond the accounting work she normally handled. It had seemed odd, but then she remembered that this was what her original plan had been about. It was simply unfolding. Her father taking her more seriously based on the strategic alliance she'd made with Joel. And while she was happy to see the change in how her father was treating her, it wasn't a strategic alliance anymore, it was a love match. It was her life.

And she knew it was time to talk to her father again about what she wanted point blank, instead of trying to manipulate him into giving her what she wanted.

Heaving a sigh, she gathered the files that needed signing and stood from her desk. This wouldn't be the first time she'd talked to Luciano about her desire to take over Barone & Sons after his retirement, but it was the first time she was doing it with a different outlook. Joel was a partner at her side and not the bait she would use to trick her father. She was enough, she had to be.

Making her way down the hallway to her father's office, she smiled and waved at her coworkers as she passed them. Familiar, friendly faces she'd spent years with. When

Luciano hired someone, they often stayed for life. There was very little turnover. Even the tradespeople working in the shop stayed. She always admired that about her father, his ability to retain people, to give them a reason to stay.

She entered her father's office from the business side. The room was uniquely sandwiched between the cabinetry shop and the administrative cubicles, so Luciano's office had two doors. One led to the office and entrance of the building and the other led out to the workshop. This gave him easy access to the shop, which worked out well, because wood-working had always been Luciano's first love, and the closer he got to retirement, the more time he spent in the shop side of the building.

Sure enough, he wasn't in his office when she entered. The faint smell of sawdust hit her nostrils, and she inhaled the scent of her childhood. Lucy's talents were more busi-ness oriented, but she'd learned woodworking as part of her training, and was able to hold her own with a table saw. She simply preferred and excelled at the business end of things.

Walking to the windows on the other side of the office, she scanned the shop for her father. She found him at the circular saw, safety goggles and noise cancelling ear protec-tion on. He was in the zone. She'd talk to him later. Maybe she'd even swing by her parents after work. Mooch dinner off of them and have a chat together. Maybe having her mother there would help buffer the tension...or make it worse, depending.

Turning from the windows, she went to his desk to leave the files. As she placed them neatly on the corner where he'd see them, a contract with the Barone & Sons logo caught her eye.

Tugging the contract out from under the other paper-work on her father's desk, she scanned the first page. It didn't look like any of the ones she'd been working on. Something had come up while she'd been on holiday.

Then she saw Joel's name and the contents of the contract registered in her mind. And then she lost her utter shit.

The Morgan Construction Building was located downtown San Francisco. A tall, narrow building that, she remembered, boasted a perfect view of the Bay from Joel's corner office.

But Lucy was in no mood to admire the view as she barged into his space, his frantic administrative assistant hot on her heels.

"I'm sorry, Mr. Morgan, I told her you were on a conference call but she—" The poor, frazzled thing stumbled over her words, clearly still in shock that Lucy had barely spared her a glance on her rampage toward Joel's office. "She just bulldozed right in."

Joel, who sat at his mahogany desk, back to the view, glanced up at his assistant, then studied Lucy. She was sure her hair was in disarray from her race over here. Her cheeks were flushed with heat and her death glare hadn't wavered since she'd burst out of the elevator and scared the daylights out of his unsuspecting assistant.

Flicking his gaze to his assistant once more, he dismissed her with a single nod, then he fixed his gaze on Lucy again as he pressed a button on his office phone.

"Serena, my apologies. An emergency has come up."

A voice filled the room through the phone speaker. "An emergency? Right now?" The tone was demanding.

Joel met it with an irrefutable tone of his own. The one

that compelled even the most hard-headed business people to concede to his will. "Yes, right now. I'll call you back." He clicked the button again before a reply could come and rose from his chair. "Lucy?" His inflection softened now, soothed, and as always, it only ignited her rage.

"He's giving it to fucking *you*!" she shouted, throwing the contract she'd brought with her on his desk.

Joel watched the paper flutter to the surface, then raised his gaze to her again. "I—"

"My father is giving Barone & Sons to you, Joel." Try as she might, she couldn't keep her voice below a shout. Her anger was too sharp and tunnel-visioned. "I bet he thinks it's some kind of wedding present, a gift to his new, beloved, *coveted* son-in-law." Her breath caught, backed up with hurt. "You should have heard how he bragged about you today at work. I should have known. I should have *known*."

Joel took a remote from his desk and pointed it at the floor-to-ceiling glass walls behind her. Instantly the glass shuttered to a foggy white, blocking the sight of the busy office beyond because God forbid anyone should see Joel Morgan's wife losing her fucking mind in his office.

He was calm. Too calm. And he hadn't looked at the contract since his initial glance after she threw it at him.

The truth struck like a knife to her soul. "Oh my God. You knew."

"Lucy." He raised his palms. "I told him no."

Her unabated anger trapped all coherent words in her throat.

"Lucy?" Joel asked carefully, as he came slowly around his desk to stand closer to her.

He appeared so austere in his business attire, so handsome and competent. She was all the way in love with him, and pretty sure he was right there with her. This was their fresh start. Their re-do. So why—

"Why didn't you tell me?" The words spilled over her numb lips, echoing and reflecting their past as they bounced off the walls. The same mistakes, over and over and over again. "Joel?" she pressed.

"I wanted to protect you," he blurted.

"From what?" she shouted, throwing her arms in the air. "From my stubbornly, traditional father? From the generational chauvinism that has plagued me since the doctor announced my sex in the delivery room? From the fate I have been trying and failing to change for the last twenty-nine years?"

"From all of it!" Joel's rarely raised voice silenced her tirade. He took off his glasses and set them on his desk behind him, before pressing his fingers against his closed lids.

Several beats of silence passed before his eyes opened to look at her, weary and dull, like an overcast sky. "All I'm ever trying to do, Lucy, is protect you." His voice leveled back to its usual composure, but his tone had lost resolve. "Telling you would have served no purpose other than to hurt you. And I had already told your father no, so I assumed the matter was done. I didn't think the contract was already drawn up."

"Of course it was drawn up. He's a presumptuous old bastard. He had no reason to think you'd say no."

"But," Joel countered, "he had every reason not to ask me in the first place."

His cell phone started having conniptions on his desk, but he ignored it.

"Lucy, when he asked me, I was truly shocked. And then scared shitless, because I knew you and I were on tenuous ground, and I didn't want anything to shake that. Not for this." He gestured to the contract on his desk.

His phone silenced. He looked exhausted. Sympathy snagged at her heart. What he'd said made sense. This was a typical Joel Morgan attempt at protecting her feelings. But it was a failed attempt, and now the hurt that had simmered for so long had come to a boil.

"*This* is important to me! Barone & Sons is important to me." Heat pricked her eyes. "You could have told me, and I would have known what my father was thinking." She spun away from her husband's heartbreaking scrutiny.

"I'm sorry." His voice was hoarse.

"I can't believe I was so naïve," she whispered, her words muffled by her tears. "Two fucking weeks was all it took for him to give it all to you. How dumb was I to think he'd consider me?"

"I suspect he would. Maybe he just needed someone to show him what he couldn't see himself."

She whirled back to face him. "*I* showed him! For years I have been showing him. Why couldn't he see it? Why couldn't he see *me*?"

He walked toward her, non-threatening, but still carrying his typical confident power. He wore it like a mantle, and people obeyed him when they saw it. No wonder her father wanted him.

When he stopped in front of her, his eyes were wary with regret. Good.

"Lucy, you think your father didn't see you, but I believe he was blinded by you and everything you've accomplished. Have you ever considered he wanted more for you?"

"Like what? A husband with enough money to take care of me so I could stay home and raise babies like my mother did?"

His cell phone started buzzing again, and again he ignored it as he shrugged. "Maybe. Or maybe he didn't want you to waste your life on a company that had consumed all of his life. Maybe he wanted you to be free of it."

"What?" She shook her head. He was making zero sense, and she was tired of being made to feel like she was in the wrong for wanting to be the one who kept her legacy alive and in her family. "He was ready to give it to Nico. To you. He doesn't want anyone to be free of it. He just doesn't want me to have it!" Her voice rose again as a fresh wave of hurt bloomed.

This time, after his cell stopped buzzing, the phone on his desk started ringing immediately, filling the room with its shrill sound.

"You should get that, Mr. Morgan. It might be something *important*." She couldn't keep the ire out of her voice on the last word.

The phone went silent as Joel spun to face his desk, his eyes hard and dark.

He grabbed the contract and ripped it into pieces. "Does this make you feel better? There wasn't a single fucking moment when I even considered saying yes. Not a single second where I thought our plan would end this way."

"I wish you'd *considered* being honest with me. Why can't you stop thinking that the only way to protect me is by keeping things from me?" Her brain hurt, like she was running in circles and coming up against a concrete wall each time she rounded another turn.

His desk phone started ringing again. Somebody needed him, but this time it wasn't her.

"Answer it."

Glaring at her, he grabbed the receiver and slammed it back down in its cradle, silencing the ring. "I might have fucked up again. I might be making a thousand mistakes when it comes to you," he growled in a low, dangerous tone. "But understand this, nothing is more important to me than you, and I will do whatever it takes to make sure Barone & Sons is yours. Christ, Lucy, I was willing to fake marry you so *you* could have it!"

The logical side of her knew he didn't mean to strike her where it hurt the most. Their emotions were high, scattered, but his words hit her heart like a kill shot.

She couldn't stop her eyes from watering over, lower lip trembling as she said, "I'm sorry I made you fake anything with me. I'm sorry I ever asked."

Joel opened his mouth to say something, but a soft knock on his office door interrupted him.

The door swished open and Joel's assistant cautiously whispered, "Pardon the interruption, sir, but Cassidy from Luca's Wings is on the phone, and she says it can't wait."

"It will have to," Joel commanded. Something sorrowful passed through his eyes still locked on her.

Something she didn't care to decipher because she was so over this conversation.

"Mr. Morgan can take his call now. I have somewhere else I need to be." She hurried out of the door. Hurt had swallowed the bulk of her anger, and the weight had taken its toll. She was exhausted. Exhausted from fighting her father every step of the way, from constantly trying to be seen, of having the men she loved most in her life making decisions for her. Exhausted from everything.

It wasn't until she was halfway down the elevator ride that his assistant's words echoed in her head. *Cassidy from Luca's Wings is on the phone...*

CHAPTER FORTY

Her mother answered the door.

"Luciana?" She leaned out to peer beyond Lucy's shoulder. "Did you come alone? Where's Joel?"

Lucy shouldered past her mother and into her childhood home. "Hello, Mother. So nice to see you too. I know, it really does feel good to be on home turf again."

Maria closed the door behind her and planted her fists on her hips. "What's wrong with you? Why are you talking like Vanessa?"

"If you mean condescending and rude, maybe it's because I'm sick and tired of everyone thinking the sun rises and sets out of Joel Morgan's ass. Is it not enough that your daughter wanted to see you on her own?"

A look of sheer terror morphed her mother's face. "Have you called off your engagement?"

Not rolling her eyes took every ounce of her concentrated effort. "No, I did not call off the engagement."

Maria's sigh of relief could not have been louder. "Okay then, that's good." She waved her hands, shooing Lucy down the hallway. "Come to the kitchen. I just started making dinner. You can call Joel, and he can join us. There's plenty."

There was always plenty. Lucy didn't once remember her mother cooking for two, but no way was she calling Joel. She hadn't been able to sort through her emotions regarding him yet. It wasn't fair to be mad, but she was hurt...and jealous that her own father would trust him more than her.

In the kitchen, the scent of fresh dough filled her nostrils, and despite her tumultuous feelings, she smiled. "Pizza."

Her mother made the best homemade pizza, and years of trying to recreate it had never resulted in the same deliciousness.

"You can knead the dough." Her mother pointed at the big plastic bowl with a damp dishcloth laid over the top.

Lucy removed the cloth and admired the fluffy round ball of dough. So good.

"So, why are you here?" Maria asked, as she rinsed the dishes in the sink.

Lucy shrugged as she poked at the dough. "I wanted to talk to Dad."

"You saw him all day at work. Didn't you talk then?"

Lucy focused on the dough in her hands. "This requires a longer conversation. And he was busy in the shop today."

"Ah, that man. He loves building more than anything else. I don't know what I'm supposed to do with him when he retires." Maria took out a block of mozzarella and the cheese grater and set up beside Lucy. "Why do you always knead like you're afraid it's going to bite you? Have I taught you nothing? You have to massage it, like this." Her mother took over, her hands working from muscle memory, kneading and shaping the dough. "Pretend it's Joel's bum."

"Mom!" Lucy gasped, horrified.

"What? You think I don't know anything, Luciana, but I wasn't born yesterday. God gave me your sister didn't he? I know all about you young people these days."

Lucy laughed at the ridiculousness of the conversation and resumed kneading vigorously as per her mother's demonstration, trying not to imagine Joel's ass in her hands.

"So, you want to talk to your father about something important, huh?" Maria slid the block of cheese up and down the grater with practiced ease. "What is it?"

Lucy shrugged again. She didn't even know how she was going to start with her father, never mind how she'd explain it to her mother. So she considered her reply carefully, opting to answer a question with a question.

"Mom, do you regret never having had a real job?"

"What do you mean? I had a real job. It was taking care of you and Vanessa, and God knows most days that felt like having eight jobs."

"Right." She hadn't meant to sound rude or insulting. Obviously, being a mother and a homemaker required huge amounts of work. But... "Did you miss not having a career?"

Maria stopped, faced Lucy, and propped her fist on her hip. "Luciana, I had more careers than I care to list." But she did anyway, flicking each one off a finger as she went. "I was a chef, a nanny, an accountant, a counselor, a nurse—"

"Okay, okay, I get it." At a loss for how else to communicate this with her mother, Lucy sighed.

"*Patatina*, I regret nothing of how I chose to live my life. And I don't consider it a loss that I didn't go work somewhere outside of my home for someone who didn't understand my first priority was my family and that nothing else could come before them." She went back to grating the cheese. "Besides, if I had been out of the house, you and Vanessa would have had no one. Your father worked enough for everyone. He was never home, or don't you remember?"

She did remember, but differently. "I remember admiring how hard he worked. How proud I always was that he had his own company."

Beside her, Maria snorted. "Barone & Sons would not be what it is if it weren't for me. If I hadn't done the work that needed to be done at home, raised his daughters, made sure everyone had everything they needed, groceries bought, bills paid, laundry done, do you think he would have had time for that company?" She didn't let Lucy reply. "No. We built that company together, *patatina*. Him at the shop, me at home. One could not have done it without the other. You might not see it that way, but that's the way it is. Barone & Sons was my career as much as his. I just ran a different part of it. Behind the scenes."

With the cheese grated, Maria went to the cupboard to pull out a large rectangular baking sheet, which she handed to Lucy. "Make sure you stretch it all the way to the edges."

Halfway through trying to stretch the dough to fit the pan, she heard the front door open and her father holler in Italian, "Maria! Who gave you a new Ferrari? Do you have a boyfriend I don't know about?"

When he entered the kitchen, his face broke into a surprised smile. "*Patatina*! Why are you here?" His smile dropped marginally. "Did you call off your engagement?"

"My God, what is wrong with you and Mom? Why is that your first assumption?" She threw her hands in the air, abandoning the dough to flop onto one of the chairs by the kitchen island. "Can't I come visit my family without my marriage having to be in crisis?" She would not mention that she had stormed out on Joel mere hours ago.

Her father shrugged as he deposited his lunch kit on the

island and headed to the refrigerator to fill a glass with water. "I'm only asking. So, is the car yours?"

"Hm," was her response.

Luciano raised an eyebrow over the rim of his glass as he drank.

Maria came back from the window where she'd been peering out to see the vehicle in question. "That's a fancy car, Luciana. I hope you didn't ask him to buy it for you."

"Of course I didn't! He just, I don't know. It was at the airport waiting for us when we arrived yesterday, and he said it was for me. I know I can't keep it, but it was the only vehicle I had this morning."

"You can keep it," her parents said in unison.

Frustration rose in her abdomen. Who were these people and where were her parents? "It's a hundred thousand dollar car that I didn't earn in any single way. It's way too much of a gift for no reason."

"Your fiancé gave you a gift, *patatina*. It would be rude to refuse it. Besides, Joel is a very wealthy man. He can afford to shower his future wife with gifts. Let him. Win gold and—"

"Do not finish that sentence." Lucy refused to suppress her eye roll this time. "I swear, you two act like he shits homemade meatballs. I don't get it."

"Watch your tongue," Maria said in Italian. "Do not speak about your future husband in that tone in this house or any other."

"Are you sure you didn't call your engagement off?" her father asked in English.

Tears blurred her eyes. She was so freaking close to shouting, *"We're already married! We have been for four years!"* But she didn't. Instead she said, "Why did you give him Barone & Sons?" She tried to keep the sound of her tears out of her voice, but she couldn't. This heartbreak was impossible to hide.

Her father had the decency to appear ashamed. Her mother made quick work of fitting the dough into the pan and slapping on homemade sauce.

"Why can't I be the *and Son*?" God, she hated how jealous she sounded, like an insolent child on the verge of a meltdown. She hated that she couldn't accept her father's choice.

It was a solid choice. Joel was a brilliant businessman. He could likely catapult Barone & Sons to heights she'd never even considered. There was no one she trusted in business more, and she loved how his mind worked, his ethical standard, his work ethic, his uncompromising generosity, the gravity of his leadership.

If she set her emotions aside and objectively looked at who was best suited to run her father's business, it would be Joel. And she loathed how much she envied that, because he hadn't poured years of blood, sweat, and tears into Barone & Sons. It wasn't his legacy. It was hers. And she had wanted nothing more than to fill her father's work boots since she was a child.

"*Patatina*," her father hummed gently, like he used to do when she fell and had run to him in tears. "I would never want you to be a son. You and your sister are my most precious gifts."

"Just not good enough to run the company," she stated dryly.

"Too precious to run the company," he corrected. "And why would you want to, anyway?" He sounded genuinely curious, like he legitimately could not fathom why she'd be interested.

"Dad, I've been working there since I was a teenager."

"Yes, because you needed money and it's a good job."

"Yes." God, give her patience. "And because I love it. I'm good at it. I bring a lot of new ideas to the table, ideas you've implemented, and that have made the business better. I'm invested."

Her father was oddly quiet for a moment, as if letting her words sink in. Her mother said nothing, pretending to be deeply focused on assembling the pizza.

"Luciana, how many days a week did I work when you were young? Do you remember?"

"Six and a half," she answered automatically. "Monday to Saturday, and half day on Sunday."

Luciano nodded. "And do you ever remember me taking a sick day?"

"No, but you probably should have. You went to work with some nasty bugs."

He ignored her. "What about vacations? Do you remember how many we had?"

She could see where this was going, and she answered in a dull staccato. "Two weeks a year. We either went camping or to Italy and you left home early to come back to work while Mom, Vanessa, and I stayed for the summer holiday."

"Hmm," he rumbled, nodding to himself. "Did I ever take a snow day?"

"Okay, Dad, I get it, you worked hard. You were gone a lot. But why would you think I couldn't do that?"

"*Patatina*." He reached across the counter to take her hand. "It's not that I think you can't do it. It's that I don't want you to. Why would I want that for my daughter? A life-time of slavery to a company? Nothing more than brick and wood. The time I lost with my family, I can't get that back. It's gone. Why would I want that for you?" His eyes grew shiny in a way that made her panic.

If her father cried now, she'd be a mess.

"But I don't want to be a stay-at-home mom while my husband is away working day and night either, Dad. I know Nico had his fantasies, but—"

"What fantasies? What does Nico have to do with anything?" Maria finally chimed in.

"He had the wonderful idea that he would inherit Barone & Sons and marry me and I'd stay home raising his babies and cooking him spaghetti."

The kitchen filled with stunned silence.

And then her mother started yelling in Italian. "You see, Luciano?" She smacked his forearm with a spatula. "I told you that the degenerate was out for money and power. You're too good, too generous. You gave him a chance, but I said he was going to double cross you and he almost did. Marry Luciana, ha! Never."

Lucy's jaw dropped. Wow, she always assumed her mother adored Nico, the golden boy from Italy, come to save the family business from being lost.

Luciano waved Maria's spatula away. "Of course, I'd never let him marry Lucy. He can't. He's her cousin."

"Second cousin, Dad, and technically—"

"He's gone now, so it doesn't matter, but Luciana—" He turned back to her, a regretful expression on his face. "Had I truly known how much you wanted the business, I would have gladly given it to you."

Tears dripped down her cheeks. "I told you so many times, dad."

Luciano shook his head, expression full of regret. "I wouldn't believe it. It was never what I wanted— my daughters working as hard as I did. I wanted a better life for you. An easier one."

This time, Lucy reached for her father's hand. "And it is,

Dad. If I ran the company now, it would be easier for me than it was for you. You started from scratch, no customers, no money, no employees, nothing. But look at it now. We are turning people away, we're so busy. There's money and staff who know what they're doing." She patted his hand. "I could take a vacation, get married, have a—" She swallowed the word, a familiar fear stopping her. "I can have all the things you want me to have, because you worked so hard, Dad."

Luciano pressed his fist to his eye. Maria slipped the pizza into the oven. And Lucy's heart filled with love and respect. This whole time, she thought she wasn't enough. The wrong gender. The wrong child. But truthfully, her father had wanted to protect her, to save her from a life of endless grinding, like he'd done.

Running Barone & Sons would still be a grind, always hard work, but she'd meant what she said. He'd laid a foundation that would make it so much easier for her than it ever had been for him. And for that, she was forever grateful.

"Maria," her father said, his voice rough like sandpaper. "Get the grappa. Tonight, we celebrate."

"Celebrate what?" her mother asked, shuffling to the liquor cabinet.

"Our daughter, taking over our company."

CHAPTER FORTY-ONE

Opening the door to the penthouse held an extra weight, because Lucy knew what she had to do and she really, really didn't like doing it.

She found Joel on the terrace, where they'd made love against the railing just yesterday. Hours ago, when everything had seemed so clear, so easy. He sat on one of the patio chairs, still wearing his work slacks and white shirt, tie removed, sleeves rolled up, a half-finished Scotch in hand.

Was she about to make the biggest mistake of her life? Was she really about to risk everything because she had something to prove to herself?

As she walked toward him, his gaze shifted from the view to her. His brow furrowed and his lips thinned, like he knew what she'd come to tell him. His shoulders rose and fell on a deep breath.

Whatever happened, however he reacted, she knew she needed to be touching him, so she didn't stop walking until she stood between his splayed legs. Knowing what she needed in this moment, he set his drink aside and tugged her hand until she was settled on his lap. Her tears welled, making her burrow her face into the crook of his neck. His hands rubbing her back were like aloe on a burn, and her mind raced in search of all the reasons she was doing this.

"I wasn't lying when I told you this feels like home," she murmured against his neck, her lips grazing his skin.

The hand on her back faltered infinitesimally before starting again. "But?"

"Hmmm," she hummed, delaying.

"*Lucy.*" He dragged her name out like a plea.

Lifting her head, she searched for his eyes, the gray meeting hers with worry, sadness, so much regret. She traced her thumb across the soft skin under his lashes. "I have to go back to my condo."

He shook his head. "I won't let you."

"It's not forever. It's just—"

"Just what?" He straightened, not letting go, but adjusting so they faced each other.

"You said you wanted to do things differently this time. And so do I." It hurt, looking at him like this, knowing they were going to be parted. "I talked to my father, and the conversation was good. Really, really good." She nodded, and her tears spilled. "I learned so many things from my conversation with him. Barone & Sons can't be the one thing that I hinge my happiness on like I have been doing. My whole identity has been wrapped up in that company. I felt like if I didn't have that, then what did I have?"

Joel listened with his whole body, his brow creased and his focus unwavering. She loved him so much that her heart rolled painfully in her chest.

"A part of me feels like that about you too." She swiped the tears from under her eyes. "Like if I don't have you, who am I? What do I have? The last four years I've been so lost without you, like I was half of myself. And I poured whatever was left into the company." Tears fell freely, but neither of them made a move to stem the flow. "Losing the baby only made the void worse. Like everything that was missing in my life got louder somehow. Barone & Sons became... the only thing keeping me tethered to sanity."

His expression softened, like he understood that sentiment very well, and she knew he did.

"I love Barone & Sons, and I—" Her palm moved to his cheek. "I love you."

Joel inhaled like he wanted to speak, but she forged on. "I have a chance with both now, and I don't want to screw up, and I will if I don't take time to savor all this. You and me, us, working with my father a few more months before he retires. I want to slow everything down. I want to enjoy the anticipation I now feel when I'm apart from you."

He closed his eyes and she knew he was processing what she'd told him. When he looked at her again, she continued.

"I want to go on dates. We never did that. And I want us to see a therapist, so we can talk about the things we're both terrified of—like our marriage not being strong enough to withstand another blow, or having another baby, or the dozens of other things that have kept us apart for four years instead of keeping us together. We need help."

"I told you I'd do anything you needed, and I will." He sounded choked, gravelly. "But don't ask me to stay away from you."

"I'm not. I don't want that. I want us to slow down. Eventually, I want to pack up my condo, sell it, and move my things in here—all of them, not just a suitcase full. That will take time, Joel, and I deserve it. You do as well. Please understand."

He leaned his forehead against hers and breathed

deeply, eyes closing. Her heart pounded wildly between them.

Finally, he said, "As long as you aren't leaving forever."

"I'm not. I promise."

His eyes opened and held hers fervently. "And *as long as you* still promise to marry me."

"I already did, and I would again. Every time." She looped her arms around his neck. "My soul chose you. There's no coming back from that, Joel."

They stayed sealed together. He wasn't happy about her decision, she could tell, but he'd never withhold from her what she needed. That was Joel, the focused businessman who always went after what he wanted. Bargaining but also meeting her halfway. And she loved him so much for it.

Finally, he pulled back. "We'll do this your way. Even though I don't like it."

She chuckled at his predictability and hugged him hard. "I have a feeling there will be more of this in the future, you doing things for me you don't like."

He grumbled something she didn't understand against her neck and it tickled. She loved the sensation, and him, and this intimacy. This was good. In the core of her heart, she knew this was good.

And speaking of good...she leaned back a bit. "So I did some research."

Joel lifted his eyebrow. "I'm afraid to ask on what."

She would have laughed, but this was too serious. "Luca's Wings."

"Oh."

"Yeah, oh." She waited for him to say more, but he didn't. "Why didn't you tell me?"

"We weren't speaking much, and, I don't know, I— couldn't."

"I spent a lot of time on Google. Your name never once comes up. I wouldn't have known the organization had anything to do with you if I hadn't heard your assistant mention it today."

He shrugged. "Nobody knew about Luca but you, so I stayed anonymous, put the money in place, hired the right people. I just had to—" He shrugged again, gazing beyond her, into the distance. "Honor him somehow. Memorialize him."

"So you created a charity that provides free flights for sick children and their families to get to the medical care they need." The thought was enough to make her cry again.

When he met her eyes, his were damp. "Our baby died, but that doesn't mean that other people have to lose theirs just because they can't access the help they need." He swallowed, his voice thickening. "I couldn't help our son, but maybe I can help someone else's."

She shook her head. Her tears fell and her lip trembled so hard, she stumbled over her words. "Not *maybe*, Joel. Definitely. You definitely help, and it's...perfect."

He nodded, but there wasn't a complete acknowledgement in the movement, like he didn't believe he'd done enough. They'd work on that. They'd work on a lot of things.

She planted a soft kiss on his lips. A thank you for being exactly who he was. But one kiss bled easily into another, and soon they were breathless.

"This new plan of yours, us going slow, living apart—" His voice was rough, emotional as he pulled away.

"Yeah?"

"Does it exclude or allow for sleepovers?"

Lucy glanced sideways, considering. "Hmmm, I don't know. I guess the odd one couldn't hurt."

"Can we have one tonight?" he asked, almost shyly, then rushed to add, "We don't have to fuck. I just..." He exhaled. "I just need to be close to you tonight."

She knew the feeling. Snuggling back into the warmth of her husband's embrace, she whispered, "I have a feeling I'm going to soon need to be close to you forever."

CHAPTER FORTY-TWO

Five months later...

"Why I thought it would be a good idea to bring you along is anyone's guess," Vanessa grumbled as she stumbled into the MGM Grand's foyer in her stilettos, tugging her neon-pink suitcase behind her. "I must have been having a brain malfunction or something."

"Or something," Jordan replied in an equally un-thrilled tone. He grabbed the suitcase, none too gently, out of Vanessa's hands. "Will you give me that before you hurt yourself? Focus on walking in those death traps."

Vanessa gasped, the height of offended. "These are Jimmy Choos."

Jordan snorted. "Whatever, Princess. Just watch where you're going."

From several steps behind, Lucy observed the comedy, holding back her chortle. Watching those two bicker almost made her happier than knowing she was renewing her vows tomorrow morning. Almost.

Joel's hand found the small of her back as he came up

beside her. "Before this trip is over, they're either going to kill each other or fuck," he whispered in her ear, his breath tickling the hair along her neck.

"Judging by the look on my sister's face, I'm going to say the former."

"Mmm, you're probably right. Those shoes could double as weapons. Tell me why they're here again?"

"Vanessa declared herself my maid of honor and said we needed witnesses. I think she thought Jordan was your bodyguard."

"Not a bad idea," he mused, assessing Jordan with a new glint in his eye. "For both of us."

Lucy swiveled her head to look at her husband. "I don't need a bodyguard."

"Maybe not, but I would feel a lot better knowing you had someone watching over you, especially during times I can't be around. And Jordan has that 'don't fuck with me or anything close to me' vibe that a good bodyguard gives off."

"Be careful, Joel, your domineering side is showing."

He cocked an eyebrow. "Why? Because I want to protect my wife and her family?"

"No, because you think I need protecting."

"I think we all need protecting from time to time. Especially since I don't plan on existing in a secret bubble with you forever. I live a high-profile life, and now you will too. It would be irresponsible of me not to always make sure that you're safe." A soft smile played against his lips. "Besides, someday soon you might be carrying our child, and I couldn't call myself a decent husband or father if I didn't do everything in my power to protect my family."

Outwardly, she rolled her eyes. Inwardly, her heart flopped gleefully.

They checked in, Joel asking for the thousandth time if she was sure she didn't want to share a room that night.

"It's the night before her wedding, buster. She's bunking with me for a hen night," Vanessa told him. "Besides, you get her for the rest of your life. She's with me tonight, you tomorrow night, and Zeus over there gets his own room since I wouldn't wish it on anyone to share with him."

"Zeus?" Lucy raised an eyebrow.

"Yeah, Jordan reminds me of a broody thundercloud and unfortunately he's built like a God, so Zeus seemed fitting."

"He's not that bad, you know," Lucy told her sister. "He's just…" She watched Jordan as he loaded everyone's luggage onto a trolley. "Quiet."

"Oh really? Because he seems pretty chatty when he's bossing me around."

"Trying to save you from yourself isn't bossing you around, Princess," Jordan replied evenly as he came back into hearing distance.

"Whatever." Vanessa's tone dripped with attitude. "Come on, sis, we have a spa appointment in thirty minutes. Lots to do before we go to the chapel tomorrow morning!" She skipped ahead to the elevators.

"You know, she presents like an airhead, but she's actually extraordinarily impressive," Lucy informed Joel and Jordan as they trailed behind Vanessa. "Only she could convince my parents that us eloping was their idea."

Over the last five months, the wedding planning facade had become too ridiculous to bear. Between the Portland and San Francisco crew, plans were out of control, mostly because they were completely out of Lucy and Joel's hands. And the longer it went on, the less desirable a massive Italian wedding became, not even for the sake of appeasing family. That and the lingering worry she had over her sister were the only dark spots on what had otherwise been a very lovely and healing time.

So one night, after one particularly loud blow up in the Barone family kitchen over which cathedral would be most suitable, Vanessa had somehow convinced Maria and Luciano that the stress was going to cause a breakup that Lucy would never recover from. The next thing Lucy knew, her mother was at the penthouse with a Tupperware of gnocchi and the suggestion that maybe she and Joel should just slip away for a quick wedding and have it done with.

Jordan snorted as they continued trailing after Vanessa. "Yeah, I bet she could sell sin to the devil as well." He stalked off, increasing his pace to reach Vanessa who was now at the elevator.

Joel caught Lucy's hand, stopping her. With a single tug, he drew her against his chest. "I love you," he murmured before kissing her soundly on the lips. Then passionately, his tongue sweeping inside her mouth, tasting her in that all-consuming way she loved.

Wedding planning meltdowns aside, a lot of good change had happened in the five months since she told Joel they needed space.

Over the last month, she'd spent many hours packing up her condo, gradually moving into his penthouse. The quiet evenings alone in her own space reminded her how ready she was to share her life with him, but she also savored the time, knowing that once she moved in with him and they started their life together, those long nights alone would cease to exist.

Occasionally she traveled back to Portland with him when he had meetings he needed to attend in person, and she used those days to catch up with her sister. Vanessa had remained in the city, stating she needed the space from their parents. The arrangement worked out well for Lucy, because she now got to see her sister more frequently than she had in years. They'd formed a new bond over books and had recently started buddy reading together, which kept them in touch, daily even.

And that reminded her—digging through her oversized tote, she pulled out a worn paperback and handed it to Joel.

"What is this?" he asked, scanning the cover.

"Homework," she reminded him.

"There is a cartoon drawing of a hockey player and a Disney princess on the cover."

Lucy rolled her eyes theatrically. "She's in the medical profession, Joel. Women in S.T.E.M. are a thing, you know."

He nodded raptly. "And thank God for that. But why am I reading this book as homework?"

"Because Kelsey said so, remember?"

Kelsey was the couple's counselor they'd been seeing bi-weekly for the last five months. They never left her office without a homework assignment.

"She told us to swap books." He flipped the book to read the back-cover blurb.

Heat rushed to her face because she knew what he was reading. "Yeah. Remember, she said it would help us convey important messages to each other about who we are and what we value in a partner." She swallowed nervously.

Kelsey had warned them that this would be a very personal and possibly scary exercise, but Lucy hadn't thought much about it until just now. She did feel oddly vulnerable.

Joel's gaze lifted from the book to her. "It doesn't look like what's usually on your bedside table."

"I usually read books with discreet covers, but this was

my latest buddy read with Vanessa, and she bought the copies. I just finished it, and it was excellent."

Joel continued to stare at her like he was completely unaware that he had a five-pepper rated book in his hands.

"You don't have to read it poolside, Moneybags. You just have to read it." She waggled her eyebrows. "I think you might enjoy the spicy scenes in this one." She leaned in and whispered, "It's a fast burn." She stuck her hand out expectantly. "Where's your book? I'll have time to read tonight since we won't be sharing a room and you won't be fucking me into the mattress."

His eyebrows rose microscopically over eyes that heated dangerously. Then he lowered his head until his lips brushed the shell of her ear. "Never say never, wife." He pulled back before she could do more than inhale a shocked breath.

God, the way this man turned her on instantly.

"My book is in my suitcase." The elevator pinged open, and Joel ushered her forward. "I guess you'll have to find a spare moment to come to my room to pick it up."

Damn him and his logic filled seduction tactics. Looked like she was going to get fucked into a mattress tonight after all.

CHAPTER FORTY-THREE

They renewed their vows at noon the next day.

Vanessa preceded Lucy down the aisle in a hot-pink mini dress and a cloud of expensive perfume, her high, perfectly styled ponytail swinging like a pendulum behind her.

When the cheesy tune turned into an even cheesier version of the wedding march, she walked toward her husband, and this time savored what she hadn't had the wherewithal to pay attention to the first time—the way he watched her.

His iron-gray eyes pinned her with a penetrating focus, and his lips curved into a smile that reached every place in her heart. Four long years apart stretched between them, but with every step closer to him, she imagined their past shrinking and evaporating.

She'd handed her rose bouquet to her sister and repeated after the minister's familiar vows of loyalty, fidelity, and devotion. Then got weepy when Joel did the same. When the time came, they slid their original wedding bands back onto each other's fingers. She hadn't wanted a new one.

She intended to wear her souvenir shop ring until it disintegrated off her finger or she died.

And when the ceremony was over their union felt strong and right. Deep down in her heart she knew this time would last, with clear minds, clear hearts, and clear intention.

When the minister told Joel to kiss his bride, Joel caught her around the waist and held her close for a full-contact kiss. Chest to chest, thigh to thigh. The satin of her pearl-colored dress slid irritatingly against her skin. She was so ready to take it off and be alone with her husband.

When the kiss broke, he took her in, eyes sparkling. "I finished the book you gave me."

"Already?" She laughed because she, for one, had not been thinking about books.

"It was fucking hot. I couldn't put it down." He leaned down to whisper in her ear. "I learned a lot."

"Oh, did you now? Like what?" He had more moves in bed than any book she'd ever read, some of which she was looking forward to him pulling out the second they got back to the wedding suite.

"Let's ditch the wedding party, and I'll show you." He nuzzled her cheek.

Sounded good to her.

"Oh my Gooood, that was so romantic, sissy!" Vanessa threw her arms around Lucy's neck. "You two are the cutest!" She tossed a venomous look Jordan's way.

Lucy bit the inside of her cheek to keep from smiling. Poor guy had no idea what he was dealing with.

Vanessa glared until Jordan finally rumbled, "Yeah, super cute." He clapped his hand on Joel's shoulder. "Congrats, bro." Then he offered Lucy the closest thing to a smile she'd ever seen on him. "You too. I'll admit, that was nicer than I expected."

Vanessa rolled her eyes. "Why? Why are you like that? Like, who says that to someone five seconds after their wedding? *Nicer than expected*. Were you raised in a barn?"

Jordan glowered dangerously. "Nah, baby, just prison."

Vanessa gasped, wide eyed.

Lucy cringed.

Joel cleared his throat. "Alright, post-wedding lunch is on me. Let's get out of here and toast my beautiful bride." He led their group out of the tiny, neon-lit chapel.

"Ohh, where are we going?" Vanessa asked, as she bounced along in her stilettos.

"I got them to close down STK for us." Joel told her, nodding at the chauffeur on the side of the road who'd come to pick them up.

Vanessa stopped in her tracks, mouth agape and Jordan slammed right into her from behind. Grunting in annoyance, he lifted her by the elbows and moved her aside so he could climb into the waiting car.

"You got them to *close down* STK for the *four* of us?" Vanessa squealed.

"Just for two hours," Joel said casually, giving Lucy a quick kiss before he ushered her into the car ahead of him.

When they were all settled in the spacious vehicle Joel faced Vanessa and Jordan like they were a pair of school children, and Lucy had to bite her lip hard not to laugh. "Okay look, we are going to have a civilized lunch. Then I'm taking my wife to our hotel room and locking us in there until we leave tomorrow, so you two are going to have to find a way to play nice." He used his commanding voice, the one no one could ignore.

Even her sister bowed her head in submission. Her cheeks were still pink from putting her foot in her mouth earlier.

Jordan folded his hands in his lap and stared out the window. "Sure thing, boss."

Joel nodded and tugged Lucy close to his side, whispering for her ears only. "I guess I owe Nico a favor, after all."

"Ew, why?" she asked, weaving her fingers through his.

"Because if it weren't for him, I don't think I would have gotten this second chance with you. And I'm so glad I did because I'm never letting you go again."

"Not even when shit hits the fan?"

"Especially not then."

"What about in forty years when I refuse to get Botox?"

Joel laughed and, on the hot streets of Vegas, shut her up with a kiss. "Luciana Morgan, you're not getting rid of me in any decade, in any circumstance." He kissed her fiercely, with a passion that held promise. When he finally leaned back, his stormy gray eyes burned into hers. "You're stuck with me—forever."

Thank you for reading *Finding Forever!* Keep reading to see how writing a book review can mean the world to an indie author like me!

I hope you enjoyed Joel and Luciana's story. If you did, please consider posting a review and telling all of your friends who like heartfelt, contemporary romance with plenty of steam.

Review wherever you purchased *Finding Forever* or on Goodreads, BookBub, or social media.

Leaving a positive review is a quick and easy way to support an indie author and they mean so much to us. Every time I read a positive review from a reader it fills up my whole bucket.

Don't be a stranger! Let's keep in touch. For exclusive updates and content, join my newsletter at ValentinaBurns.com

xo Valentina

ACKNOWLEDGEMENTS

As I was writing this book, I realized how grateful I am to my parents for keeping our culture and heritage alive while we were growing up. Language, food, music, traditions were so deeply ingrained in my sister, my brother and I that we carried them over to our own families in adulthood.

I grew up in a loud, chaotic, filter free home, but it was also filled with a kind of nurturing love that I felt even across the oceans that separated us from our extended family. Weekend phone calls with Nonna, birthday cards with crisp, freshly exchanged Canadian dollars enclosed. When they could afford it, there were summer visits back to Europe to see cousins, aunts, and uncles. My parents worked hard to ensure that our ties to their homeland were strong and unbreakable. And they have been. It's hard sometimes to lock down an identity when you're caught between two or more cultures, and to this day, I never quite know what soccer team to cheer for, but I wouldn't change it for anything. Thank you, mom and dad, for fostering this wild, untethered love of all things Italian/Swiss/Canadian.

Logistically, my books would never come together without the support of a whole team of people. Including one of my favorite humans in the book world, Jackie W. Thank you for reading the roughest version of all my books every single time, for leaving the most valuable feedback, and for talking me through all the hard parts. You're the best and I love you.

My editor, Jacqui, thank you for all your hours of work, your incredibly detailed mind, and all the knowledge you've shared that helped me not only with this book, but every single one I write going forward.

To Luna Day, for always swooping in and saving me with your expansive skill set and knowledge base. You are truly one of the best people I have met on this journey, and I am so grateful for you. Thank you for formatting Finding Forever, and making it look this beautiful.

Thank you, Kate, Albany, and Abigail, for beta reading Finding Forever and for your enthusiasm for Joel and Luciana from page one. Reading through your comments was the highlight of many of my days.

Thank you to Becky and Riya for reviewing this book for its sensitive content and for sharing your personal stories, thoughts, and feelings with me. I am so grateful for your input and for being a safe space for me to work through some of the tougher themes in this book.

The Book Club Beauties, The Smuttering, The Literary Poutines and the Supper Club Moms, you know I wouldn't have half as much fun doing all of this if I didn't have your feral, no filter comments championing me on. You make me laugh every day, and that means a lot.

To the best Street Team ever, Team Burners! No one lifts me up quite like you do and I appreciate each one of you. Thank you for spreading the word about The Rose City Series and the beautiful content you create: Paola A., Abigail B., April C., Natalie C., Karla E., Melissa Harris., Malin M., Brittany P., Courtney R., Abbie U.

And Matt, the Love of My Life. It hasn't always been easy, this road you and I have been on, but the best part of my day is still lying against your chest at night, counting your heartbeats. I love you forever.

Finally, thank YOU readers! You have no idea how much you've changed my life, and what an impact you have on my world. Thank you for loving my little, emotional love stories. Thank you for buying them, reading them and telling other people about them. It means the whole world to me, and I am so very grateful for your love and support.

xo Valentina